GOING DOWN ON ONE KNEE

A Mile High Matched Novel, Book 1

CHRISTINA HOVLAND

For rights information, please contact:
Prospect Agency
551 Valley Road, PMB 377
Upper Montclair, NJ 07043
(718) 788-3217

Holly Ingraham, Development Editor
Michelle Hope, Copy Editor

First Edition October 2018

This one's for Steve.
(Then again, they all are.)

Praise for Christina Hovland

Going Down on One Knee

"An utterly charming opposites-attract-story. Hovland perfectly balances simmering sexual tension with a surprising amount of emotion, and the stomach-flip-causing ending is the perfect example of why I read and love romance."

- *New York Times Bestselling Author, Lauren Layne*

The Honeymoon Trap

"*The Honeymoon Trap* is adorable, clever, funny—in short, completely charming." - Serena Bell, *USA Today* bestselling author of *Do Over*

Chapter One
THE COUNTDOWN BEGINS

Three words. Three. Little. Words. Nothing important.

Okay, so the three words were important. Massive, really.

"Congratulations, you two," Velma Johnson rehearsed aloud to the vase of a dozen yellow roses gripped in her arms. With a reaffirming gulp of Denver's crisp spring air, she hustled through the open-air parking garage to the security door of her apartment building.

Her sister, Claire, had big news. To be exact, Claire and her boyfriend, Dean, had big news. Velma had a feeling she knew exactly what their news would be—they were moving in together. The next step in their relationship. Tension in Velma's neck strung tight at the thought.

A successful career and a posh apartment she could eventually rent out as an investment were steps one and two of Velma's elaborate five-year plan. She had ticked both those boxes. Dean, three kids, and moving to a two-story house just outside of Denver had been steps three through seven.

Not anymore. Now, her sister was moving in with the man Velma had crushed on for years. The one Velma measured all others against. The one she sang Prince and Madonna songs with at the office.

Yes, they were moving in together. That's why Claire had called yesterday and asked to take her to dinner. Velma had insisted they meet at her place instead. Her invitation had nothing to do with the fact she liked having Dean visit her apartment—even if he was with her sister. She'd offered because it made sense they'd want a private location for their big reveal. And when the announcement came that they'd be embracing that next relationship milestone…well, being on her home turf sounded pretty darn appealing.

Just as she reached the security door, the sound of a motorcycle that clearly had no muffler cut through her thoughts. She turned. The bike pulled up next to her car—into the parking spot meant for her guests. A super-muscled, badass-mother-trucker of a biker swung his leg over the side of the motorcycle and stood.

Her heart stopped with a *thunk*.

Vin-Diesel-biker-dude pulled off his helmet and—sweet mother of Mary, had the temperature jumped by ten degrees? She got the picture: he rode a motorcycle, hit the gym twice a day. The type she avoided because she did not do badass. She preferred the suspenders-and-slacks kind of man. Except, at that moment, she debated how important that preference really was to her.

Focus, Velma. Head held high, she approached him. "Excuse me? Sir? You can't park there."

He frowned at the number marking the spot.

Normally she wouldn't mind sharing the space, but with Claire, Dean, and his friend Brek coming to dinner, she needed both of her parking spaces.

This man was obviously not Dean's friend. Dean's friends were all buttoned-up, suit-wearing, Wednesday-afternoon golfers. She was nearly certain.

The black leather jacket and jeans ripped at this guy's knees looked horribly out of place next to her Prius. His longish, rock-'n'-roll blond hair was nicer than hers (although his could use a trim). She didn't even mind the dragon tattoo creeping around the side of his neck or the layer of mud coating his motorcycle boots. Everything about the man screamed masculine.

Velma shifted the heavy vase in her grip. *Fudge.* Which of her neighbors was letting their guests use her spot this time?

"No, see, that's the spot for my apartment." Oh, how she wanted to rub at the headache pulsing at her forehead. She didn't have time for this. Not today. "I'm sorry, it's just that my sister and her boyfriend and his friend are coming for dinner because my sister has big news. And while I have no idea what that news is, it's important to her. So that makes it important to me. Which is why I put on a pork roast, bought roses, and got out my crystal wine goblets. That's what you do when your sister has big news, you know? Never mind she's practically living my five-year plan without even trying, and I'm over here without even a boyfriend. *That* was not part of my plan. At this point, I should be at least six months into dating my future husband."

Oh God. She was rambling. And he was staring at her with a half grin that made her skin flush. Seriously, the way the man smiled should be outlawed.

She ducked her head. "Anyway, I have company coming and I kind of need my spot."

"Five-year plan?" he asked. As though that was the important part of what she'd just spit out.

This is how one makes an absolute idiot of oneself. "You know what? It's fine. You can stay right there. Don't worry about it." She shifted the flowers again and turned on her heel.

See? People said she was inflexible, but here she was, absolutely rolling with it. She smiled at her flexibility.

"One sec," Motorcycle Dude called. "This is the number they gave me."

She paused midstride and turned around.

He ticked his head to the side. "Velvet?"

Oh dear. She could easily be swayed by the gravelly way he said her name. Well, the nickname her family called her—despite her repeated cease-and-desist requests.

"Um, yes?" She gripped the glass vase harder with her clammy hands.

"Brek." He looked at her like she should know him and pointed to his chest. "Dean's friend."

Velma stared.

Oh.

This was Brek? She'd expected him to wear khaki pants and drive a Camry. He reached into one of his saddlebags and held up a six-pack of Coors and a four-pack of Bartles & Jaymes fuzzy-navel-flavored wine coolers. "Claire asked me to bring the beer and wine, since I'm crashing your party."

Wine coolers? She stared some more. *Be flexible,* she reminded herself. *Flexible. Flexible. Flexible.*

"Great. Fuzzy navel pairs perfectly with pork roast." Cheeks burning and arms full, she managed to open the security door.

"So, you're Claire's sister?" His lazy gaze trailed over her.

"The one and only."

His deep-blue eyes rivaled the color of the razzleberry lollipops she loved. The kind that made her mouth water just thinking about them and… *Focus, Velma.*

"Can I come up, Velvet?" His deep voice held a subtle hint of roughness.

"Velma," she corrected. "You're a little early. I'm so behind. Normally, I'm much more together."

"I can come back later." Brek's eyes softened, totally contrary to his outer badassery.

"No. I am officially the queen of flexibility. It's not a problem."

He did the darn grin thing again. She silently instructed her body to ignore it.

"Queen of flexibility. That ought to be interesting," he

mumbled mostly to himself but loud enough for her to hear. He stepped next to her, balanced the beer and "wine" against the impressive muscles of one arm, and slid the vase she carried into the crook of his other arm.

"Thanks." This time it was her turn to mumble.

Without looking back, she led him up the stairs to her apartment. Another glance his way, and she'd probably trip face-first into the wall or something equally embarrassing. To prevent herself from taking another peek, she focused on sticking the key in the keyhole of her apartment door as though it took every ounce of her concentration.

There. The door swung open. He stepped through the doorframe, close enough for her to catch the scent of leather and Irish Spring soap. Close enough for her to reach out and touch the stubble running over his jawline. Close enough for her to—she shook her head to dislodge the abrupt light-headedness.

"This place is huge." With a long whistle, he set everything down on her dining room table.

Vaulted ceilings, open concept, white walls and sofa, with pops of jewel tones in her carefully selected décor; it must all appear so unnecessary to a guy like him. But these were her things, proof of everything she had worked so hard to achieve.

Brek walked into the kitchen and glanced to the slow cooker on the counter. "This smells amazing, Velvet. You a chef?"

"Velma," she corrected him again, slipping on an apron with the words *Domestic Diva* embroidered on the front. "And no, I just like to cook."

Velma took in the dinner she'd spent the afternoon planning and preparing. Vegetables had been roasted in the oven, and a chocolate cream pie was setting in the fridge. Not the pudding kind, either. A real, honest-to-goodness, made-from-whipping-cream-and-two-kinds-of-chocolate pie. She hoped she could eat those leftovers while she binge-watched Rodgers and Hammerstein musicals later.

"Then what do you do, Vel*ma*?" His emphasis on the last syllable made her wish her name wasn't so frumpy.

"For employment?" she asked.

"Yeah…or pleasure."

The expression on his face and the way he drew out the word "pleasure" made her toes curl in her sandals.

Right, employment. He'd asked about her work.

"I'm a financial planner," she replied.

Brek rubbed his hands together. "Like Dean?"

"Yup." She and Dean had worked together for years. "Our offices are across the hall from each other. That's how Dean met Claire." Claire had come to visit Velma at work and had wandered into Dean's office by accident.

That was the day Velma's dream of becoming Mrs. Dean Stuart died—all because she had waited too long to make her move and lost her chance.

Mr. Right had met her sister and they'd ended up together, making kissy faces during Thanksgiving dinner.

Actually, they never made kissy faces. The two of them were much too classy for that.

Brek leaned his hip against her granite countertop and crossed his leather-covered arms. "No idea what Dean does at his job, either, but I'm sure you're both fantastic at it."

"We help people with their financial portfolios. Annuities, estate plans, investment management, things like that. What about you?"

"I'm in the music industry." He snagged one of the crystal wine goblets she'd put out earlier and swaggered toward her.

Her stomach did a loop the loop. The swagger affected her more than expected. "You play in a band?"

"Nah. I play guitar, but not professionally. I manage a band." He popped the top off a wine cooler and poured it all the way to the tippy top of the glass. Then he edged inside her personal-space bubble and handed her the glass.

"Thanks." Normally, she didn't drink much—especially on Sundays. Monday marked the start of the week, with new chances and opportunities. She preferred to start it at her best, not hung over with a headache.

Then again, tonight was the night of change. Big-news change. My-sister's-moving-in-with-my-dream-man change. So Velma would have a wine cooler—no use in wasting it when Brek had already poured it—and ignore her attraction to Dean. Steps to a new life filled with...finding a new man who was as perfect for her as Dean was. Baby steps and all that.

Brek slipped off his jacket and tossed it over one of the island barstools. Tattoos ran from the short sleeves of his black T-shirt to his wrists. They looked tribal, mostly wild, and super-hot. If one liked tattoos. Which, she reminded herself, she did not.

"Claire says you two are twins?" Brek asked.

"Uh-huh," she muttered around a gulp of carbonated peach drink.

"You and Claire don't look like twins," Brek said.

Velma pulled a stack of small, hand-painted dessert plates from her for-company-only dish cupboard. "We're not identical."

"No kidding," he replied, serious. "It's the eyes."

Ha. Hardly just the eyes. Velma's eyes were muted gray, like a painter had finished painting for the day and just didn't feel like adding more cyan to the palette. Claire's were a rich brown. More than that, Claire was thin and Velma, well...she was Velma. All curves, like her mother. No matter how many calories she counted or steps the app on her phone registered, the curves stayed put. Velma's hair was dirty blonde. Not the attractive kind, either. In-desperate-need-of-highlights blonde was more like it. Claire's hair was a beautiful deep-chestnut color.

"Why does Claire call you Velvet?" Brek asked.

She sighed and paused, plate in hand. "Family nickname. No matter how many times I ask them to stop."

"Velma." He seemed to be testing the name, letting it melt on his tongue like warm chocolate on a vanilla sundae.

"Not a name I'd lie about." She set out the last of the plates on the table.

"I like it. It's original." The low, rumbly words made her lungs constrict in a warm way she refused to acknowledge.

"Unfortunately, it's not even original." She pulled a cutting board from the pantry. "Claire was born first, so she got the cool name. I was born three minutes later and got Velma."

"It's an interesting name."

"Velma was my grandmother's name. But there couldn't be two of us in the same family, so they all call me Velvet."

"I like Velvet," he said.

She scrunched up her nose. "I don't."

When she was a child, everyone bought her clothes with cheap velvet fabric. They itched. She hated them. As far as she was concerned, velvet was scratchy and uncomfortable.

"This news. Any idea what it is?" Velma asked.

"You don't know?" Brek replied.

"No idea." Except she was absolutely certain they were taking the next step in their relationship by moving in together, and maybe getting a puppy.

Brek popped the top on a Coors. "I figured you and Claire shared everything."

"Nope." Not this time. "Claire just said she has big news."

"Maybe she's knocked up," Brek suggested.

Velma's heart skipped five beats. She grabbed a knife and sliced into an onion with renewed energy. "No way."

"I don't know." He ran a palm over the back of his neck. "Seems reasonable to me."

"Then you don't know Claire. She's way too involved in her career to get pregnant right now." Velma set the onions aside and went to work on chopping carrots to top the salad.

Brek motioned to the cutting board. "Can I help you with anything?"

"Do you know how to julienne carrots?" Velma replied.

"Nope." He shrugged. "But I know how to cook a steak."

She laughed. "Well, tonight it's pork roast, so I'll have to take a rain check on your culinary skills."

"Absolutely. Next time I'm in town, I'll grill you up a steak." He raised his beer to her.

She stared at him. He couldn't actually be serious.

He was serious.

"Maybe they called us here because Dean needs a kidney?" he asked.

"He doesn't need a kidney." Although, Velma would probably give him one if needed. She had a remarkably hard time telling him no. "They're probably just…" *Say it out loud, Velma.* She sighed. "Just moving in together."

"Nah. They wouldn't have dragged me here for that. Maybe their big news is they're gonna try to hook us up."

"You and me?" Velma pointed the knife at Brek, then back to herself.

Of all the options, that one was the most reasonable. And, yet, totally unreasonable. No way would Claire pair the two of them together.

"You said you don't have a guy." Brek's tone turned serious.

Her body irrationally responded to his apparent interest with tingles.

"No." Of course she didn't have a guy.

She'd had lots of first dates lately.

"I get the feeling you need some help loosening up. Enjoy

some time away from your five-year-husband-seeking plan. There's a club downtown with a great band playing later. We should go." Brek's gaze raked over her.

His pointed interest was actually…nice. Still, there was no way she would go clubbing later. Brek wasn't her type. Not only because of the tattoos or the extreme need for a licensed barber or his ripped jeans. No, it was more the general sense of unease he stirred within her. Also, it was Sunday. What kind of a club was open on a Sunday night? Definitely not one she should visit.

"You stressed about the dinner?" he asked.

"No," she lied through her teeth.

"You're stressed about the dinner," he declared. "I get that, but there's nothing to worry about."

For a half second, she believed there was nothing to worry about. Truth was, there was always something to worry about. Starting with her clothes. She needed to change into something that wasn't yoga pants before her sister arrived in what would undoubtedly be a perfect sundress.

"I'm only in town for a few days anyway," he continued. "We'll get through the part where Claire and Dean do the awkward   you-two-should-get-to-know-each-other   schtick. We'll eat and then we'll send them on their way. You don't want to go to a club? That's fine. I'll stick around. What do you say, Velma?"

The way he said her name felt like silk against her skin. Silk was so much nicer than velvet.

She tried to tug off her apron, but her hair was stuck in the tie at the back of her neck. Crud. Another tug. Her hair was really stuck. "You want to go to clubbing on a Sunday night?"

"Absolutely." He nodded to where her hair was caught. "Need some help?"

"Yes, please." She pressed her eyes closed.

He looped a finger under the little bow tying the apron at

the back of her neck. His calloused fingertip traced the ribbon along her shoulder to the collar of her sweater, unraveling the knot of hair and sending little shivers along his path of exploration.

Maybe she could get away to the club for a little while. It wasn't like she had better things to do. "Where is this cl—"

"Hey, Velvet." Her sister, Claire, shoved open the front door. "Hi, Brek. You made it. Dean's so excited you're here."

"Did you lose him?" Brek squeezed Velma's shoulder.

A hit of sizzle deep in her belly echoed the motion of his touch.

"He's parking the car." Claire closed the door and sauntered to the kitchen with her svelte build and Audrey Hepburn grace. "Okay, I know I've made you wait. But…" Claire bit at the light-pink lipstick on her bottom lip. "Surprise!" She held out her fingers with a little jazz hand motion.

An *engagement* ring perched on the fourth finger of Claire's left hand.

Velma's heart skidded to her toes. She blinked hard. No, it couldn't be.

A ring.

A wedding.

Satin and lace, champagne toasts and flower girls.

This wasn't a puppy. And it was so much more than an apartment.

Velma reached for Claire's hand, her throat constricting. "Oh my gosh."

"I know, right?" Claire squeezed Velma's fingers. "I had to tell you in person."

"Oh. My. Gosh." Velma said again, this time more slowly. She looked straight into Claire's eyes and saw it—excitement and love for Dean. Happiness. Velma glued a grin onto her face. Her sister was happy. That was all that mattered. "Claire. It's perfect."

"I'm gonna go find Dean." Brek caught Velma's gaze and winked. "Now that the cat's out of the bag."

"Wait, you knew about this?" Velma asked.

"Hell yeah, I knew." Brek opened the door. "Didn't want to ruin Claire's surprise, though."

"So you asked me out instead?" Velma asked.

Claire scrunched up her forehead. "Brek asked you out? Like on a date?"

"Oh look, it's Dean." Brek feigned innocence as he held the door wide. "I'm officially saved by the groom."

"She finally told her?" Dean strode inside and glanced to where Velma stood in a swirling vortex of time.

"Uh-huh." Claire nodded, her eyes misted over.

A suit. Dean wore a tailored suit complete with shined cap-toed shoes and gold cuff links. Each black hair on his head lay precisely where it should. He was absolute perfection.

Velma swallowed the heaviness in her throat and tried to pretend it was from excitement for her sister.

"Well, then—hey, sis." Dean strutted toward Velma and wrapped her in a hug. "Claire made me keep my mouth shut for a whole week."

Velma's insides did a little flutter that was totally unacceptable. Time moved at the speed of a sloth. Like watching a car accident happen in real time, when everything went slow and then fast again all at once. "You've been engaged for a week and didn't say anything?"

They'd sat through a load of sales meetings. Two client lunches where he'd driven them both to the restaurant. He'd never given any indication he'd freaking proposed to her sister. They'd discussed retirement plans and supplemental income sources. He hadn't mentioned anything that would've even whispered of proposal news.

"Believe me, it was hard keeping my mouth shut. Can you

believe you're going to be my little sister?" His breath brushed against the top of her head.

"Uh…nope," Velma said through gritted teeth.

"It's great, isn't it?" Dean leaned back and scanned her face.

Her knees went weak, like a cheesy movie heroine.

"It is great. Totally. Great. I'm so excited." Velma stepped away from him, refusing to show anything but happiness for her sister's sake. Any feelings from now on would be purely of the appropriate sisterly kind.

Claire and Dean were engaged.

Yup, Velma's Mr. Right was going to marry her sister.

Chapter Two

COUNTDOWN TO CLAIRE & DEAN'S
WEDDING: 8 WEEKS

Those gray eyes had fucked with Brek's sanity from the parking lot all the way to the kitchen. Brek liked Velma. Aside from being stacked, she was funny. And sexy. And she smelled fruity. Strawberries. Definitely strawberries.

"Dinner's amazing," Dean announced. "Velma, you outdid yourself."

"I'm glad you like it." She glanced up from the untouched plate in front of her and flashed Dean the most plastic smile Brek had ever seen. Given his work with celebrities, he had seen some damn good fake smiles.

Velma's flinch had been nearly imperceptible when Claire had announced her engagement. No one else likely caught it. But Brek clocked her reaction, and it didn't align with Velma's insistence that she was excited for her sister. Ever since she'd escaped to her room to change, she'd gone distant. Concern stirred deep in his gut.

"She can cook, that's for sure." Brek reached for another roll.

"Thanks." She glanced from Dean to Brek.

Her cheeks turned a pretty shade of pink, and his dick responded immediately.

"Velma, how goes your house hunting?" Dean nodded to Velma.

"You're moving?" Claire asked from where she was refilling her wineglass in the kitchen. "I thought you loved this place?"

"Not moving." Velma dabbed at her lips with a cloth napkin.

Brek stared at her lips too long. She had nice lips. Full lips. Lips any man would fantasize about. He'd had to shove his hands in his pockets earlier so he wouldn't be tempted to trace his thumb along her plump bottom lip.

"I'm just looking into ways to supplement my income long term," she went on. "Real estate investments make a lot of sense. I added them to my five-year life plan."

Five-year what-a-what?

"I'm telling you." Dean was apparently oblivious to her lips and their power. "Rent out your spare room. You've got a real estate investment opportunity right here."

"She doesn't do roommates, hon. Never has. I think the whole sharing Mom's belly with me did her in." Claire returned to the table. "Brek, did you tell Dean you hit on my sister?"

"Nope." Never in his life had a button-up sweater turned him on before, but on Velma it seemed to short-circuit his brain cells. He was a moth to her flame or some shit. Times like this made him happy he wasn't sticking around Denver. A girl like Velma could easily get under his skin. He didn't need that. Didn't have time for that. He had a band to manage and a life that didn't involve five-year plans.

"He didn't hit on me, Claire. He offered to take me to a club."

"You're already moving in on Velma?" Dean's eyes turned to slits as he glared at Brek. "You're fast. Faster than that time with Chelsea. And that was freaky fast. I feel compelled to tell you she's my family now—which means, don't jerk her around."

Dean was a crack-up when he got protective, but Brek didn't particularly want to discuss his former hookups at the dinner table. His mother had instilled some manners in him, after all. He cleared his throat. "Velma, was I jerking you around?"

"Um, maybe?" She fidgeted with her fork, spearing a heap of lettuce with the tines. "With the whole bit about Claire being pregnant and Dean needing a kidney and all."

Claire dropped her spoon with a clank. "You told her I'm pregnant?"

"You told her I need a kidney?" Dean smacked Brek's shoulder. "Dude. Not cool."

In his defense, he'd been trying to distract her from being so uptight.

"How's the wedding planning coming along?" Brek made a solid attempt at changing the subject.

"I hired your sister to be our wedding planner." Claire sat taller.

Operation Change the Subject worked—for now, at least.

Dean mouthed, "Not finished with you," in his direction.

"She wasn't even taking on new clients"—Claire turned to Velma—"because she's about to have a baby. But she took us on. Isn't that great?"

"You already hired a wedding planner?" Velma's expression dropped, but she caught herself quickly. "Do Mom and Dad know you're engaged?"

"I asked your dad before I popped the question. They've known for a while." Dean looked at Claire like a man ready to hand over his dick for all eternity.

Claire glanced back at Dean like she was a woman ready to accept his dick for all eternity. "Dean swore them to secrecy. I told them we'd talk to you tonight."

"Oh. Right. Of course you talked to them first. That makes sense."

The way Velma said the words meant she didn't believe it made sense at all.

"It's all so exciting." Velma tucked a chunk of hair behind her ear, revealing a single pearl earring.

Brek didn't realize women still wore pearls. It was…retro. Different. Classy. "Aspen's the best. She'll take care of you."

His sister threw good parties. He'd give her that.

"Do you have any idea when the big day will be?" Velma asked.

"First Saturday in August. It's fast, but we don't want to wait. And Brek's sister is amazing. She says she can make it happen." Claire picked at the carrots in her salad. "Which brings me to the other reason we wanted you two here."

Shit. A quickie wedding. If Claire were really pregnant, he'd have shoved his foot firmly in his trap.

"We'd like to ask you two to stand up with us." Dean reached for Claire's hand. "It would mean a lot to us both."

Thank fuck. Not pregnant. But, shit, they wanted him in the wedding. He didn't do weddings. All that pretentiousness? No. The thought gave him the shakes. His little trip through Denver was a fast visit to see his family, say hey to his friends, and party with his buddy to celebrate his engagement. The visit was not meant to be a prelude to being forced to return and stand in front of a crowd dressed like a penguin.

"Velvet, I'd love it if you'd be my maid of honor." Claire's eyes danced with excitement. "Just like we talked about when we were kids."

Velma's lips parted. She opened her mouth and closed it. Pinched her lips together and opened them again.

Yeah, that's about how he felt about the whole thing.

"I wouldn't miss it," she finally said.

Not the answer he'd been thinking.

"But what about Heather?" Velma asked.

"I'll ask her to be a bridesmaid. You're my sister. I want you right next to me."

"Brek, you know the drill. I could ask Jase or Eli to be my best man, but they'd find a way to weasel out of it. Besides, Jase'll handle the flowers and Eli's going to have to deal with the catering." Dean leaned back against his chair and held up his beer glass. "What do you say?"

Jase, Brek, Eli, and Dean had all been buddies since high school. Dean was right, Jase and Eli would abso-fuckin'-lutely find a way to weasel out of best-man duties. Except the bachelor party. They'd be all over that.

Brek did the math in his head. Dimefront, the band he managed, would still be on break. Which meant he was about to get trapped into a wedding. "August?"

Dean nodded.

"I can probably swing that." Brek raised his beer can and touched it to Dean's glass.

"We've been thinking the theme will be 'Purple Rain.' Flowers, dresses, everything. Dean wants a beer bar. Craft beer." Claire got all animated about it. Eyes big. Talkin' with her hands. "We figured we'd embrace the insanity of a wedding theme and go all in."

"A 'Purple Rain' beer bar?" Velma gave her sister a look like she was crazy.

Again, it was like he and Velma had a mind meld.

"Well, when you put it like that..." Dean met Claire's eyes, and the two of them had a moment. "Yeah, that's exactly what we're going for."

Brek's phone buzzed in his back pocket. He checked the caller ID, expecting a call from one of his band members needing to be bailed out of jail. Not that it happened often, but often enough. He'd rather go bail out a drummer than think about putting on a tuxedo for Dean's wedding.

"Give me a sec. It's Aspen." He stood and moved to the kitchen, answering the call. "You've got Brek."

"Brek? Are you with Mom?" She sounded off.

"Nope. I'm with Dean. What's up?" He ducked his head to hear better.

"Don't freak out," she said.

Which, of course, cued his internal freak-out.

"I'm at the hospital. Lots of contractions today. It's too early, so they're trying to stop the baby from coming. Jacob's on his way. Can you bring Mom?"

"Which hospital?" he asked, already heading toward the door.

"St. Luke's." Her voice cracked a little. "Don't let Mom panic."

His mother panicked when her dog ate too much kibble. When Brek didn't check in every Sunday. When the mailman tripped over his feet on her front step. Yeah, she'd lose her ever-loving mind over this.

"I'm on my way." He snagged his jacket and shoved his phone into the pocket. "Dean, I've gotta roll. Aspen's at the hospital."

"Holy hell." Dean stood from the table. "How can I help?"

Brek was already halfway to the door. "Call Ma. Tell her I'm on the way to pick her up." His mother would pull out her own toenails before she'd get on the back of his Harley. She'd also be in no condition to drive herself once he told her the news. "Tell her to have her car ready."

BREK HAD LEFT Velma's place to pick up his slightly crazed mother and drive her across town to St. Luke's. She was now pacing the drab antepartum waiting room—that was what it said on the door, anyway. Whatever the hell that meant.

The television remained off. Cell phones silenced. The only sound came from Brek's foot as he tapped his heel against the polished tile floor. The room's fluorescent lights did nothing to calm his nerves. He and Ma didn't speak much. Not with the tension of waiting for news flowing between them like a living, breathing entity. She wasn't even trying to set him up with the pretty nurse. That said everything.

His sister and her baby had to be okay. All she'd ever wanted was to be a mother. Things hadn't panned out for her, though. Babies were a dream they'd all thought would never happen for Aspen. Until five months ago.

Jacob, her husband, finally arrived from Aspen's bedside. "She's okay," he assured them with a weak attempt at a smile. "They've been able to stop the contractions for now."

The man looked totally wiped.

"She wants to talk to you." Jacob nodded to him. "Just you."

Brek was through the door before Jacob could say more.

The lights were dim in Aspen's room. An elastic contraption covered her pregnant belly and an IV pierced her hand. Several monitors flashed colored numbers and lines. One of the machines amplified the subtle swish of what had to be the baby's heartbeat.

He pulled a chair up beside her and collapsed onto it. "Hey."

"Hey," she replied. "Thanks for being here."

"Wouldn't be anywhere else."

She gave him a look that made it clear she knew that was a lie. He'd always been anywhere else.

"I'm in a bind." She twisted to her side in the rumpled white sheets. "It's my business."

"Aspen, now's not the—"

"It's important." One of the monitors pinged. She glanced to it. Worry etched across her forehead, but the little heartbeat continued to thump. A long breath escaped her lungs, and she shut her eyes. "I jump every time it does that."

"Talk," he said softly.

She ran a hand over the elastic on her stomach. "They're putting me on hospital bed rest. I can't even get up to pee, and I've got brides—"

"Cancel." He leaned in toward her. "Nothing's more important than you and the kid."

"Dimefront is on break, right?" she asked.

The band was on hiatus for the next few months before their big tour kicked into gear. That didn't mean he'd get much of a break. Between the boys' constant threats of disbanding and their perpetual run-ins with law enforcement, Brek was always on when it came to them.

"Yeah, why?" He stretched out the last part, his intuition not liking the vibe he was getting from her.

"And you plan their concerts and stuff, right?"

He supervised them, anyway.

"Yeah, why?" Now he was really disliking the vibe in the room.

"I was thinking that maybe you might be willing…"

Shit. He knew where this was headed.

"No way. I'm not dealing with brides."

"Brek…"

"Nuh-uh. Not happening."

"It can't be worse than a concert. Everything's mostly done. All I need is someone to carry out what I've already planned."

"Ask Ma."

"Mom's got her own business to run. You're on break. You can do this. I have faith in you."

Good thing one of them did.

"Aspen…" If there was one thing worse than a celebrity rocker on a four-day bender, it was a bridezilla who wanted the perfect wedding.

"Please." The plea in her eyes nearly did him in.

He handled sound systems, parties, drunk-off-their-ass

musicians. He made good money doing it. More than that, though, he loved the thrill of his work. What he did not enjoy was an overly emotional woman in a poufy white dress.

"Business has been bad for me the last couple of seasons," Aspen said, her voice cracking at the end.

"Bad how?" The sinking feeling in his bones settled deeper.

"Competition is ridiculous right now. People are planning their own events more and more. The accounts I'm able to land just aren't spending what they used to on weddings."

He squeezed her hand. "You shoulda said something."

"I know." A tear slid from the corner of her eye.

He was a sucker for tears. Especially from his kid sister.

Working with her brides might give him cold sweats, but for her, he'd do it. "Fine. Yes. I'll help you out."

"Thank God." She relaxed into her nest of pillows. "I have a plan to turn things around."

"What's the plan? I'm good with plans." He was shit with plans. He was more of a just-go-with-it kind of guy.

"The family of one of my brides has loads of connections. Her mother's been chatting Montgomery Events up through their circle. Next season is booking like crazy from her referrals. That wedding is almost here. It has to be perfect."

"Wedding. Perfect. Keep the mom happy." He could probably handle that. "What else you got?"

"An opportunity came up this week. *Rosette* is coming to do a spread on Claire and Dean's wedding. They had an unexpected opening, and I pitched their 'Purple Rain' idea to the editor. She loved it. They're featuring the whole thing on the blog and in the magazine…everywhere. The publicity could fix everything."

"What's *Rosette*?" he asked.

"Like *Rolling Stone* but for weddings."

"So, it's a big deal," he said as a statement, not a question.

"It's a huge deal. You sure you can stay in town that long without caving in to the desire to take off?"

"I'll manage. Mom'll be thrilled if I stick around. Your brides have fangs, but they don't scare me."

"Liar." She closed her eyes briefly. "This'll be worse than the time I made you play Fairy Princess Baseball Golf when we were kids."

He chuckled. "I won't wear fairy wings this time. It can't be worse."

"I'll touch base with you. Make sure everything's going okay."

"That's a negative." Jacob slipped through the door, letting it latch quietly behind him. "No stress. That's what the doctor said. No brides. No work. No stress."

"Brek's going to need to consult with me." Aspen got all huffy like she did when she wasn't getting her way. She'd had the same annoyed sigh since she was three. Hell, she'd probably stomp her foot if she wasn't tied down to the bed with monitors.

"Nope. Everything he needs is on your laptop. Brek is a big boy. He can handle things." Jacob usually gave his wife whatever she wanted, but he was clearly sticking to his guns. "Tell her, Brek."

"I'm a big boy. I can handle things." How hard could it be?

"See? He's got it." Jacob crossed his arms.

Brek kissed her forehead. "On that note, I'll go get Ma."

"Brek?" Aspen asked.

"Yeah?"

"Please don't take off," she whispered.

Her plea punched him straight in the gut. Shit, was that what his family thought of him? He would take off without warning? Yeah, so his history wasn't exactly stellar in that department. He had given them plenty of reasons to believe he might leave. Rock shows, fireworks, and stadiums were in his blood. He wouldn't change that for the world, but this time he would stay. Every single one of her brides would get the wedding of her goddamned dreams—even if it killed him. Which, given the nature of some of Aspen's clients, was not out of the question.

"I'll stick around. Promise." He would do anything for his baby sister. Apparently, even plan some damned weddings.

Chapter Three

Velma tugged at her rubber gloves and plunged the last of the plates into scalding water. The hot water stung, but she ignored it and scrubbed off the crusted remnants of mashed potatoes. A night spent faking excitement for her sister's wedding had left her drained.

Not that she wasn't happy for Claire. If anyone deserved to win the husband lottery, it was Claire. Velma just wanted her shot at happiness, too. Maybe not with Dean—for the obvious reasons—but with a guy *like* Dean.

"I hope Brek's sister is okay." Dish towel in hand, Claire glanced to the living room where Dean and Brek huddled after he'd returned.

Dean frowned. Velma's hand would've usually twitched to smooth the creases on his scrunched-up forehead. But he was her sister's future husband. Thoughts like that were not allowed. Besides, tonight her thoughts kept drifting to the rock 'n' roll–loving Brek, not to Dean.

Brek was wild where Dean was stable. Brek was someone for sexual fantasy dreams—not for her current project of finding herself a husband.

"Brek's interesting." Velma handed her sister the plate to dry.

"He's fun. That's for sure." Claire ran the towel over the dish. "I'm pissed he tried to convince you I'm pregnant."

"He wasn't serious. I knew that." Velma stared at the film of bubbles popping along the surface of the water. "I still can't believe you're getting married."

"I know, who would've thought it'd be me? I always figured you'd crack that code first." Claire bumped her hip against Velma's like they'd always done when doing the dishes as kids.

Velma laughed, like she'd always done. Her sister was pretty awesome. She popped by with dinner when Velma's work schedule got nutty. She surprised Velma with theater tickets—they both loved the same old musicals. Claire also never forgot Velma's birthday, given they shared the day. It was nice to have someone always in her corner. And now, she'd do that for her sister. She'd be the best maid of honor Claire could have ever imagined.

"Aspen's going to be okay." Dean strode to where they worked. "Brek's staying in town for a while. He's handling the weddings for her."

"That'll be good. His family misses him." Claire set a crystal wineglass next to the others in the cupboard.

Velma hesitated, tilted her head to the side, and gestured to the biker talking on his phone in her living room. "We're talking about the same Brek. He's planning weddings? Your wedding? That Brek?"

The Brek stalking across her living room toward the kitchen. Toward her. She glanced away from the intensity of his examination.

"Wait. Our wedding." Claire turned to Dean, her eyes huge. "You said no. Right?"

Dean shrugged. "He plans concerts and manages a band. It's practically the same thing."

Velma didn't know much about planning weddings. But it couldn't be the same as managing a band. Not even a little. Not any more than Velma planning finances was like wedding planning.

"You still looking for money, Velma?" Brek tugged on his leather jacket.

Uh. Yes. But the way he said the words sounded slightly indecent.

"Real estate?" he clarified.

"I'm still exploring options for implementation of my five-year plan, if that's what you're asking."

He raised an eyebrow. His lips twitched at the edges.

"I think what Brek's trying to say is that we'd like to ask you a favor." Dean settled his hands in the pockets of his slacks.

Velma kept her expression as neutral as possible. She always felt as though she came across too eager with Dean. She needed to rein that in. "Sure."

Dean dove into full sales mode. "Brek needs a place to stay while he's in town for the next couple of months. We were hoping you'd let him stay in your guest room."

A wineglass slipped from Velma's soapy fingers and clanked against the sink. Um. No. Big ol' negative. She did not need her sexual fantasy living in the room across the hall from hers.

Brek's expression turned serious. "Aspen's out of service for a while. I'm going to stick around and help with her weddings. Figured I'd take your spare bedroom for a few months. Help with the rent and all that."

"Mortgage. I have a mortgage. Not rent." The distinction gave her a grown-up feeling she liked.

"Then I'll help with the mortgage," he corrected.

"That's not a good idea." With him, anyway.

He was rough. Not felonious rough, but still. He was a guy. If she went with a roommate, a female would be better.

Someone who cleaned up after herself, kept to her shelf in the refrigerator, didn't steal chocolate pie or play loud music.

"Way I see it, you're raising money. I have cash. I need a place to sleep, and you have an extra room. Everybody wins." He gave her some serious bedroom eyes.

"That's not a good idea." Claire's expression turned serious.

"Why can't you stay with your family?" Velma asked, rinsing the glass and carefully setting it on a drying mat.

Brek leaned his shoulder against the refrigerator. "Aspen's got too much going on right now."

"Where are you staying now?" There had to be someplace else he could stay. Anywhere else.

"My mom's..." Brek slid a glance to Dean.

"Can't you just stay there?" Claire slid her gaze to Velma and back to Dean.

"His mom's is out of the question long term." Dean stepped behind Claire and laid his hand against her waist in that proprietary way men did when they loved someone.

That was what she wanted, that feeling of being desired. A man who would place his hand on her and guide her into a room. She was going to "Dean" her life—find a man who treated her just like he treated Claire.

She forced herself to stand tall. No moping. This would be her new mantra. "Why is his mom's out of the question?"

"She's trying to set him up so he'll settle down." Dean chuckled. "You should see her when they're together. She's a *real* matchmaker. She's always got prospects marching through wherever he is."

Matchmakers were a real thing? Velma made a mental reminder to check into that. Perhaps a matchmaker was the ticket to her meeting a good guy. Online dating had proven to net a load of not-so-nice guys.

"So, what do we need to do to get a yes on this?" Dean asked.

He had a look he used at the office. An expression he saved for when he wanted something—a ham sandwich from the deli or backup with a difficult client. The look, a combination of pleading eyes like a golden retriever paired with a subtle wink, had always worked on Velma.

Not this time. Things were changing. "You both have apartments. He can stay with one of you."

"I already gave up my lease." Claire stroked Dean's hand.

Velma tried not to stare. She really did.

"And Dean's place doesn't have a guest room," Claire continued.

Because Dean's place had a home gym where Dean worked out. Frequently, Velma guessed, given the size of his biceps. They were almost as muscled as Brek's. Almost.

Biceps were officially going on her list of must-haves. Biceps and the wink thing.

"Your place is close to the hospital," Brek announced. "That's why I thought of it. And the whole five-year thing. Figured we could help each other out."

Oh dear. She was sunk.

"It'll only be for a few months while he's helping Aspen. You're family. He's practically family. What do you say?" Dean dropped his hand from Claire.

No way she could actually be considering this proposition. Then again, Brek wanted a room, not a prostitute.

"Okay. You can stay." The breathy words escaped her lips.

Brek grinned, a flash of white teeth against his lips.

Her stomach flipped over.

"You're the best little sister-in-law ever," Dean said, like she was five. The only thing missing was a gentle noogie on the top of her head.

MAYBE SHE WAS the best little sister-in-law ever. But days of awkward cohabitation with a virtual stranger had Velma ready to tell Dean where he could shove his request.

Velma adjusted the groceries in her arms and kicked the door to her apartment closed. She was rolling with life and doing her best to be flexible. Starting with the roommate situation. No nagging. No telling Brek what to do.

With him across the hall, she barely slept. He'd brought his guitar with him, and sometimes when he'd play late at night, she'd lay awake listening. Even when she managed to drift off, he permeated her subconscious. Things weren't better when she woke up. He walked into the room, and she practically wanted to inventory his ink with the tip of her finger. Memorizing each swoop and line of the tattoos could be her new favorite pastime.

There was one good thing about the situation—with her hormones hyper-focused on Brek, inappropriate Dean thoughts were at a minimum. Those thoughts mostly focused on the broken hopes of her five-year plan, which disappeared the moment Brek walked into the room.

"You have got to be kidding me." She glowered at the dirty plates in her sink and dropped a canvas sack of groceries on the kitchen counter. The dishwasher was right there, for goodness' sake. She pointed at it for good measure—even if she was the only one in the room.

Earlier she had tripped over Brek's muddy boots in the middle of the floor, and his jacket seemed to have a perpetual aversion to being hung.

Claire assured her, Brek would come around to her way of doing things.

Velma wasn't convinced.

Patience. She would need a truckload of the stuff because, no matter what, getting used to each other took time. Brek deserved some leeway while he got situated.

"It's only been a few days," she said in a failed attempt to convince herself.

She yanked open the stainless-steel door to the dish-washer, rinsed and loaded three plates, four glasses, an abnormal number of forks for one man, and a shaker bottle with a little wire ball inside. None of that had been in the sink that morning when she'd left the apartment.

Brek had somehow dirtied enough cutlery to fill the entire basket in her dishwasher.

A splash of whatever the heck the bottle contained dropped on her palm. The thick liquid smelled like vanilla.

"Crud," she mumbled, rinsing her hand under cold water.

She wiped her damp hands on a towel. Something squished between her fingers. Peanut butter.

Okay, they had to chat about this and lay down some ground rules.

"Brek?" she called, rinsing off the mess.

"Hey, V," he hollered from his bedroom.

Her breath stuck against her ribs, and her cheeks heated. The feeling had, unfortunately, become normal whenever he was around. More frequently since he'd started using the nickname.

"What the hell is Bohemian chic?" he asked. "Bride Number Three said she wants it, but fuck if I know what that means."

Cue the cussing, all the cussing. The man invented more ways to drop an f-bomb than anyone she'd ever met.

"I have no idea." She dried her hands and pushed a stray hair from her forehead. "Can we talk?"

He strode around the corner in a tight, long sleeve T-shirt that did amazing things for his arms and a pair of jeans that did even more amazing things for his thighs. First rule of them living together: stop noticing things like that. Easier said than done.

"Hang on, I've got to pin this." He tapped the screen of his phone.

"What?"

"Bride Number One said she pinned something about wineglasses with Skittles in 'em." He dropped the phone next to her purse and made exaggerated air quotes. "They're 'cute.' As are champagne-flavored gummy bears, apparently."

"Wait." Velma couldn't hold in the laugh. "*You're* on Pinterest?"

"Jase already gave me a load of shit about it, right before he followed all my boards," he grumbled. "This isn't my normal gig, but Brides Number One and Two both said I needed to follow them to keep up with their themes."

"Brides Number One and Two?" Velma squinted at him.

He lifted a corded shoulder. "Numbers are easier than names."

"You sure know how to make girls feel special." She forced herself to glance away from the way his shirt highlighted his muscles to focus on his eyes.

"You want me to make you feel special?" The intense way he stared at her gave every indication he was more than happy to follow through if she said yes. Oh, she wanted to say yes. Her subconscious screamed for her to say yes.

She wouldn't say yes.

"No." She tossed him a don't-go-there look. "Let's talk about rules. Starting with your usage of expletive nouns and adjectives."

He scrunched his eyebrows. "What kind of nouns?"

"Cussing. It makes me uncomfortable." She shifted a row of cans in the cupboard to make room for more.

He rested his shoulder against the wall. "You're cute, you know that?"

Gah, it was like talking to a middle schooler. She pressed on. "Roommate ground rules. We need to go over them."

His face went blank. "What kind of rules?"

"Showers and groceries and laundry?" And all of the other things that were driving her crazy about having a roommate.

The sexiest of grins crossed his face. "You want to shower together? I'm down with conserving water."

This man was impossible. And distracting. And heck yes, she wanted to shower with him. But no, she wouldn't.

"That's not what I meant. I mean using up all the hot water. Eating all the groceries. Forgetting to swap your laundry from the washer to the dryer."

"Fair enough. I'll keep showers under five minutes. Throw in for groceries, and only do laundry when you're not home. That work for you?"

"Throw in for groceries?" The way he kept staring at her raised her body temperature past comfortable levels.

"You cook. I don't. I'll toss in cash if you cook extra of whatever you're fixing for yourself."

She stood straighter. He could be reasonable. "There was a bunch of stuff in the sink and peanut butter on the towel. Can you put your junk away and not leave sticky stuff on the linens?"

He glanced to the now-empty sink and a sly smile tickled the corner of his mouth. "Where exactly would you like me to put my junk? And…uh…sticky stuff."

Heat crept up her neck to her hairline. "You don't have to be juvenile about it. If you could just load the dishwasher, that would be great. And paper towels for peanut butter. That's all."

"I can do that." He studied her in that way of his that made her squirm.

"Appreciated." She unloaded a box of pasta from her shopping bag and grabbed the little *B&V* labels she'd made up earlier.

Brek grabbed a mesh bag of tomatoes from the sack and tossed them in a bowl. "What's with the labels?"

"So we know what belongs to whom. Your stuff gets a *B*, mine gets a *V*. Things we share get both." She'd made his *B* labels an appropriate black Hells Angels font, and her *V* labels got a pink swirly curlicue.

"You're dedicated to labeling. I'll give you that. Couldn't we just use the honor system?"

She shook her head. No. No, they couldn't. Her method would keep everything in order and boundaries in place.

He reached over her for a sheet of labels.

Gosh, he smelled good. He didn't wear cologne. The scent was 100 percent Brek. Someone should bottle it and sell it on the black market.

"Labels will make things easier for everyone." She peeled off a *B&V* to stick on the loaf of wheat bread.

"If you say so." He didn't look convinced.

Frankly, neither was she.

"I put extra in here." She tapped the front of a drawer.

"Extra labels," he confirmed.

"That's what we're talking about, right?"

"Is it?" His expression changed, subtly, but she noticed. "Or are we talking about how you're scared to trust me?"

Had he moved closer? No, she still had her space. But holy crud, it didn't feel that way anymore.

"Definitely talking about labels," she said on an exhale, breaking the link between them to finish labeling so she could get the heck out of there.

"You ever think about loosening up? Lettin' down that guard of yours?" His expression softened.

The quiet concern and sincerity in his tone wasn't harsh or mean, but she'd let others in before and it never turned out well for her. Life worked better if she kept her distance.

Especially from guys like Brek who didn't fit into any version of her five-year plan.

"I have no idea what you're talking about," Velma replied.

"Keep tellin' yourself that." Brek's phone rang, facedown on the counter. He glared at it. "It's probably Bride Number Two. She's extra needy today."

"You've got Brek." His lips pressed into a thin line. "Hey, Aspen. Aren't you supposed to be resting?"

He stared at the ceiling while Aspen said whatever she said.

"No. Skittles… That's what I said… Goldfish… She said she wants goldfish now… Well, fuck if I know… I'll find them… I'm hanging up now… Nope… I love you, and for your own good I'm hang—"

He glanced to Velma and rolled his eyes. "I'll talk to the magazine people… I said I'll do it…"

Velma couldn't hear everything that Aspen said, but she caught something about how he better not hang up on her. There also seemed to be a threat about castration.

"Bye, Aspen," Brek said before hanging up and cussing a slew of expletive nouns under his breath.

"Magazine?" Velma asked.

"*Rosette* whatever." He fumbled with a head of broccoli and a label.

The bridal blog? "*Rosette* is covering one of your weddings?"

"Claire and Dean's wedding. Aspen set the whole thing up." He laid aside the produce he'd been unable to label. "You don't happen to know where I can get twenty pounds of Skittles and forty goldfish, do you?"

"No. Why do you— You know what, I don't need to know." She finished loading the cupboard.

"What're you doin' later? Jase and Dean are stoppin' by for a bit. You're welcome to hang out with us." He grabbed a spoon and dove into the new pint of Ben & Jerry's she had just labeled with a *B*.

"I'm headed out for the night." On a first date with a guy named Nathan who seemed nice enough on his profile.

"Big date?" He asked around a bite of Cherry Garcia.

Hopefully. "Something like that. Maybe you could use a bowl for the ice cream?"

"Nah, I'm good like this. Want some?" He lifted the loaded spoon in her direction.

"No, thank you." She rolled the tension from her shoulders. "One other thing. We haven't talked about this, but I think we should. No hookups at the apartment. I don't want to come home to some…" *Random chick prancing around the apartment in nothing but her thong and your leather jacket.* No. Velma couldn't say that. "Someone drinking my milk."

Much better.

"I will protect your milk. And I agree, no outside hookups." His gaze stayed intent on hers.

Wait. Did he mean…? He couldn't seriously be propositioning her. Oh heavens. The heat.

"No hookups at all." Not for her. Nopers. Not with a roommate. Especially not with a guy like Brek. A dangerous guy. The kind who made her question her commitment to finding the right guy to settle down with and make babies. Brek was a *for now* guy. She didn't need that in her life.

"Bummer." He didn't glance away. He simply held her stare. "Guess I'll have to hook up on the back of my Harley."

By golly, she didn't need to sort out that visual. The logistics involved for intercourse on a motorcycle would certainly require preplanning and a diagram.

"Having sex on the back of a motorcycle is impossible." She was nearly certain.

His smirk scared the living snot out of her. "Wanna bet?"

Chapter Four

Two of the many benefits to Velma's apartment complex were the gym and the heated swimming pool. Brek pulled himself from the pool and glanced past the hot tub to the clock. He'd made ample use of both amenities while he settled in at Velma's place. No one else used the rooftop pool late at night. Not that he minded the quiet. In fact, he preferred it. At least until his mind wandered back to Velma —which it always did.

Velma said she was dating, and that declaration sat on his chest like a fifty-pound dumbbell. Sometimes she didn't get home until late.

And who the hell was he to play hall monitor to her dating habits? He shook his head.

He had stayed up, listening for her. Most of the time he convinced himself he was just doing his neighborly roommate duty to ensure she made it home alive. But the number of times he ended up stewing alone in the dark over what she was doing with some jackass grated on him.

Montgomery Events kept Brek so busy he hadn't had time to ask a woman out—not that one had caught his attention. Normally, he didn't have a problem finding a willing partner.

All that had changed the second he'd knocked on Velma's door. His dick seemed to think she owned it.

His dick was a traitor.

He snagged his towel and headed down the elevator, back to the apartment. Velma wouldn't be home for a while. He probably had enough time to watch at least two episodes of *The Walking Dead* while he put together the invitations for Bride Number Three, also known as Velma's sister. Although, tying little ribbons and affixing gold stickers wasn't his idea of a good time. That's why he'd add zombies to the mix. Zombies made everything better.

He shoved his key in the door and turned the knob. His gut took a hit like it always did when Velma was in the room. The lights were on, and she sat at the table with a girly teacup next to her laptop.

She wore pink flannel pajamas and her fuck-me glasses— the rimless kind that sat high on the bridge of her nose. Every so often her glasses would slip, and she would haphazardly push them back, making her look like a librarian. A sexy librarian who did dirty, dirty things to rebels who returned books late and didn't pay their fine.

"Hi, Brek." She glanced up from the light of her computer screen, a sucker stick poking out of the edge of her mouth. She popped the lollipop from between her lips, and his dick stirred to life. *Down, boy.* A few days ago, he'd found a canister in the back of the pantry filled with all sorts of candy. He'd never seen her enjoy her private stash, but he resolved right then and there to keep it stocked.

"Hey." Bare-chested, he tugged his towel around his neck and held it at the ends. He couldn't seem to form a coherent thought, so he evacuated to his room to change into a dry pair of shorts.

With a firm word that his dick needed to behave, he grabbed his post-workout recovery shake from his shelf in the fridge and shook it. Velma had labeled his black mixer bottle with a sticker that read *B*.

Early on, he had decided to find her love of labels cute. That and the swear jar she'd decorated with multicolored ribbons and placed in the center of the kitchen counter. He had already prepaid by dropping in a hundred-dollar bill. She hadn't found that *cute* at all. Nope, she threw a tizzy about it. Didn't matter, though. Her tizzy was fuckin' adorable.

"You're home early."

"Tonight was a bust." She screwed up her face.

"I need to kick the dude's ass?" He would take entirely too much joy in beating the jerk to a pulp.

She shook her head without glancing up from the monitor. "No. Claire and Heather already took me out for a post-date ice-cream-infused dissection. You don't get to flex your caveman muscles on my behalf this time."

"Bummer." He moved to stand behind her. "What're you doin'?"

She pushed the screen closed. "Nothing."

The way her cheeks burned red told an entirely different story.

"Porn?" The idea of Velma watching anything indecent was laughable—she had a thing for old movies with dudes who sang about being in love.

"No." Her nose wrinkled.

Some might call him a bastard for pushing her buttons. Didn't mean he was going to stop.

"Ms. Johnson, please show the class what you're hiding." He reached to open the screen.

She smacked at his hand. "It's a spreadsheet, you oaf. Nothing special."

"A spreadsheet, huh? I don't believe you." He leaned over her to get to the computer.

Her hair smelled like strawberries again. He had always

liked strawberries, but they'd never given him a hard-on before.

"Shouldn't you go shower or something?" She turned her head, and her lips were barely a centimeter from his. Her eyes went wide. Her throat bobbed.

His lips twitched. The attraction wasn't as one-sided as he'd believed.

Without hesitation, he moved closer, brushing his lips in the air over the apple of her cheek. They didn't make contact. Still, though, a little moan escaped her throat that practically broadcast *kiss me*.

His mouth reached her ear. "What's on the spreadsheet, V?"

She pulled her head away, breaking the intimate moment. "Are you always like this?"

"Yes." He straightened and jerked his head toward her computer. "Spill."

A sound escaped her throat that was a cross between "urg" and "gah." She opened her laptop. "It's a dating spreadsheet. See?" She pointed to the screen. "Nothing special."

There were a lot of rows with male names. And by a lot, he meant *a lot* of them. That shouldn't have stung the way it did, but...there it was.

He squinted at the screen. "Velma, the serial dater."

"I'm trying to find the right guy. Unfortunately, it appears my Prince Charming's riding a snail instead of a steed, because he's taking his time."

Each column had a numbered rating and a final score at the end. With an elaborate color-coding system. He couldn't quite pull his gaze away from the insanity on her screen. "You keep a log of all your dates?"

"Well...yeah. I don't want to make the same mistake twice. So, I write everything down and add up the pros and cons."

Her system was crazier than his mother's matchmaking business. And he'd always thought her business was whack. "I thought my mother was the queen of the dating scene." He narrowed his eyes in on the first few columns of the spreadsheet. "But I've never heard of her ranking guys on the diversity of their retirement portfolios."

"Life insurance isn't a joke. Actually, you and I should talk about your coverage." She gave him a look that, in those glasses, made him actually look forward to a conversation about death.

He shook off her suggestion. No way was he talking about retirement bullshit.

"Conversation ability and height?" He continued through the columns. Those were just the first three. There were many more.

"That's a personal preference. Personality is weighted heavier. See, look." She tapped through some screens, her finger clicking the mouse. "Everything gets a rating, and then they feed into the algorithm for a ranking between one and ten. Anything over an eight gets a second date."

Brek let out a whistle. "Tonight's guy is at a three. Poor dude."

Velma studied the monitor. "The formula I created does all the heavy lifting."

She deserved an A for effort, he gave her that.

"What were tonight's cons?" He pulled a chair up next to hers. She had special padded cushions for her chairs that matched the curtains. A lot of work, he figured, but what the hell? They were comfortable.

"Well, he still lives with his parents. That's a big red flag." She tapped on the keyboard to fill out a few more of the columns with number ratings. "He kept checking Facebook and asked if he could post my picture so his friends would believe I went out with him."

"Definite minus. He pay for dinner?"

"No. I did."

"Add a column for that and give him a zero. Guy's a prick, he doesn't pay for dinner." Brek pointed to an empty cell.

She crossed her legs. The flannel made a whisper of a sound that his body responded to as if she were wearing a see-through lace nightie.

"I'm not adding whether he bought me dinner, that's insane."

Right. That would be the insane part of the spreadsheet dating system.

"The man pays for the meal." Didn't everyone know this?

Velma scrunched up her forehead. "That's sexist."

"It's life. Add that to a column and do your algorithm-whatever so it's weighted heavier than the 401(k) bullshit." Brek settled his elbows on a red placemat she'd laid out earlier. It also matched the freaking curtains and the chairs. "What are the pros from tonight?"

"He has a job."

Brek chuckled. "That's it?"

"That's it. Employment is a good thing."

"What about last night's date?" he asked.

"Hmmm?" As she typed, she ran the tip of her pink tongue along her bottom lip.

He ignored the desire to do the same. To her.

"Two. Ouch. Poor guy didn't even have a job?" Brek pointed to the row above.

"Nope." She shrugged.

Brek snagged the box of partially folded invitations from the table and headed for the couch. "Wanna catch a couple episodes of *Dead* with me?"

"Dead?" she asked.

"*The Walking Dead*." He concentrated on the slight dimple he had never noticed before at the tip of her nose.

"I'm not into zombies." She turned off her computer and slipped it into a padded black case. "You go ahead."

"They're not real," he said, the vanilla liquid sloshing against the sides of his mixer bottle. "C'mon, we'll cuddle if you get scared."

"I'm not cuddling with you."

He shrugged. "Your loss. You can help me fold invitations."

"What the heck happened to those?" Velma stared at the mess of gold-foiled cardstock he'd tied pink ribbons around earlier. Tried to tie ribbons around. His hands weren't exactly made for ribbon tying. He'd come up with a sticker system that seemed to work okay. Forget about the tissue-paper envelopes they were supposed to slide into before the mailing envelopes. Who the hell needed two envelopes? Especially with thin-ass paper that wrinkled whenever he breathed?

Her eyebrows fell together. "Are these Claire's? They're all crumpled."

So maybe a couple had suffered collateral damage while he figured shit out.

Velma bit at her bottom lip. "Let me help."

"Thought you'd never ask." He sauntered to the couch and flipped on the television. "And the show's good. Way better than that crap you put on with dudes singing about their feelings."

"Musicals are cultured." Frilly blanket over her lap, she made herself comfortable on the other side of the white leather sofa.

"Eh." Brek brought up the next episode. The start of the third season. "This, *this* is good stuff."

Stack of invitations in hand, she tied the silk around one without any issue.

The damn paper didn't crumple at all. "How'd you do that?"

She held up the invitation in illustration. "It's easy. You make a bunny ear, go over, go under, around, and through. See?"

Fuckin' serious? "I know how to tie my shoes, V. How'd you do it so easy? Around the card?"

"Luck?" Apparently, it was no big deal to her.

"You're in charge of ribbons. I'll put on the stamps."

"You're not using the Love stamps?" She nodded to the stack of American flag stamps he'd picked up earlier.

"What the fuck are Love stamps?"

"They're the stamps with hearts and they usually have 'love' written on them. They coordinate better. I'm pretty sure that's what Claire wants."

The stamps he'd grabbed had Old Glory blowing in the wind. Fuck. Aspen's notes said nothing about special stamps.

"A stamp's a stamp." He stuck a stamp on the corner of an envelope. "They're patriotic."

Velma didn't look convinced.

"You might want to make that a little straighter." Velma reached for the stamp and peeled it off, repositioning it exactly where he'd put it before.

"That's how I had it."

"Yours was crooked."

The zombies on TV were more and more interesting. "You gonna yap the entire show?"

"No. But don't you want to put on a shirt?" She waved a hand at his bare chest.

Sprawled out on the couch, he pressed more patriotism onto the froufrou envelopes. "I'm good. But if you're uncomfortable, you can always take off your top. Won't bother me."

A frustrated gurgling, gagging noise came from her throat. Still, she settled against the throw pillow beside her. Fuckin' cute.

"Velma?"

"Hmm?"

"What happened to that picture over the fireplace? The one with the pansy-ass dude dancing with the hot chick showin' off her legs?"

"Okay, one, that was a limited-edition Jack Vettriano *signed* print. Two, the dude was not pansy-ass. And three, the woman's dress was appropriately modest for living room art."

Living room art had a modesty level?

"Where'd it go?" he asked.

Blanket readjusted, she continued, "I bought it as an investment a while back. I finally found a buyer for it."

They settled in and finished the invitations. One episode morphed into two, and two into three. She stretched out on her side and yawned. Turned out Velma liked zombies after all. She didn't talk the whole way through the show, either.

Her feet crept closer and closer to his cutoff-sweatpants-covered thigh. He took a breath and focused on the images on the television.

This was not a date. Running his hand along her calves would probably land him out on his ass without a place to live.

So, he refrained from touching her. Barely.

Chapter Five

COUNTDOWN TO CLAIRE & DEAN'S
WEDDING: 7 WEEKS

Velma flipped a pancake on the skillet and checked the tomato-bacon-spinach quiche in the oven. *Not ready yet.*

Zombies were so cool. It didn't take much to understand the plot of Brek's show. Zombies are bad, people aren't always good, and when the world ends, you should stock up on bullets and find Rick Grimes. The date-from-heck last night had miraculously transformed into a nice evening at home with Brek. The whole thing was very domestic with a side of comfort she refused to formally acknowledge.

"Morning." Brek emerged from the back hallway.

Oy vey. The man was wearing navy-blue boxers and nothing else.

She stared at the pattern on his arms, abs, and everywhere in between. The amount of ink he sported never ceased to amaze her. It must've hurt like the dickens getting all those tattoos. There really were a lot of them. The tribal doodles even led down to the waistband of his boxers, which led to his—

He cleared his throat. She jerked back to reality. She should probably make a new rule about requiring pants if she wanted to get anything done. Ever.

Velma stacked the pancakes and clicked off the burner. "I made extra if you want, and there's a quiche in the oven. And, Brek...seriously, it's cool if you don't want to wear a shirt, but pants aren't optional."

She liked his chest. He could display it all he wanted. Truly, he could've been a model for one of those marble statues in Rome. Tourists would flock to see him.

He grunted. "Give me a minute to make some coffee before you lay in about dress codes."

"I quit buying coffee and threw out what we had left. I read an article about how bad caffeine is, so I figured we wouldn't keep it in the house anymore. There's some tea in there, though." She pointed at the cabinet to his left with the herbal loose leaf and the everyday mugs.

"You threw out the coffee?" His morning voice was rougher than usual, which she hadn't thought possible until she heard it for herself.

"Uh-huh. Try the tea, though. It's good for you." She lifted her Saturday mug in a mock toast.

He stared at her, unresponsive, his mouth hanging slightly open.

"You shouldn't put that in your body, anyway. The article said too much caffeine causes stomach problems and irritability." It also mentioned insomnia and headaches. She'd given up the stuff a few days ago, and already she felt loads better. Not that her health had been bad before, but, you know, little steps, an ounce of prevention, and all that.

Brek opened the fridge and poured orange juice into a glass. "Know what makes me irritable?"

"Hmm?"

"You throwin' out all the coffee." He downed the juice.

Holy moly, the way the muscles of his throat pulsed as he swallowed. Mesmerizing. Then again, it'd be less mesmerizing if he put on some darn pants so she could concentrate.

"New rule," she declared. "I'll keep coffee on hand for

you, if you wear pants when you're outside of your bedroom."

"I'm wearin' shorts." He raised his hands in illustration, which meant the boxers stretched over his thighs, the bulge in the center on display.

"That's underwear," she pointed out. Not literally. She didn't point or anything. No need to draw more attention to his already on display bits o' glory.

"You're the fashion police *and* the beverage police?" he grumbled.

Before she could respond, the doorbell chimed the special new "Somewhere Over the Rainbow" theme she had programmed yesterday.

"You want to put on pants before I get that?"

"No." He poured more juice, filling his cup up to the rim.

Good. Maybe the juice would raise his blood sugar so he wouldn't be so grouchy. Velma checked the peephole—a woman dressed in a smart blue business suit, complete with coordinated low-heeled pumps, stood on the other side. The Dooney & Bourke purse on her shoulder matched her shoes. Curly, strawberry-blonde hair barely touched her shoulders. Velma pulled open the door. "Hello?"

"You must be Velma." The woman quirked her head to the side. "I'm Brek's mom. Pam."

Well, huh. Pam seemed so…normal. How did a woman with a Dooney bag produce a biker son like Brek?

"Brek. Your mom's here." Velma moved to let her through. "It's nice to meet you."

"Breckenridge Montgomery, where are your pants?" His mother admonished as she walked in the room.

He scowled. "Ma, this is a surprise."

Velma shot him her best I-told-you-so look.

"If you called your mother more often, I wouldn't have to surprise you," Pam replied.

Brek had her blue eyes. They were as striking on her as on him.

He crossed his arms. "We had lunch together yesterday. You hungry?" He grabbed a piece of bacon from the plate. "Velma made pancakes and some French thing."

"Quiche," Velma corrected.

Speaking of… Velma checked the quiche and tugged on two kitchen mitts in the same pattern as her paisley apron.

"If you call it baked eggs, he'll eat it." Pam made herself comfortable on a barstool across the counter.

"I made baked eggs." Velma held up the pie plate and beamed at Brek.

His eyes crinkled at the sides. "Mmm…eggs sound great. You know what goes great with eggs?" He waited a beat. "Coffee."

"Drink more juice, Brek. Get that blood sugar up to get rid of the crabbies." Velma set the quiche on a black metal trivet.

"I'd offer you coffee, Ma, but Velma threw it all out. Juice?"

"Juice would be lovely. Why on earth would you throw out the coffee?" Pam asked.

"She read a dissertation on the problems with caffeine," Brek replied before Velma could answer. "Ma likes to learn stuff, too. You should tell her about it while I get dressed."

He grabbed another slice of bacon and left.

"You want to hear about the article?" Velma asked Pam as she cut into the quiche and served up the pancakes.

"Not if it means I won't like coffee afterward." Pam smiled politely and sipped at her juice. "How is the roommate situation?"

"It'd be great if your son would wear pants more often."

Pam snorted an incredibly unladylike sound. "He's a work in progress, that boy."

"Brek says you're a matchmaker?" Velma asked.

"Indeed I am. Are you seeing anyone?" Pam tilted her head to the side, clearly assessing Velma's potential as a mate for one of her studs. Velma had been through every online dating site, been on blind dates, regular dates, everything— but she had never tried a matchmaker.

"Ah, no. Not right now." Velma pulled off her oven mitts and hung them on their hook beside the stove. "You know how hard it is to meet the right person."

"Velma's got a system, though. You'd be impressed." Brek had tugged on some jeans and a formfitting black T-shirt with a skull on the back and what she assumed was the name of a band on the front.

"How does the match thing happen?" Velma moved her attention to Pam, away from Brek's triceps.

Brek groaned and loaded up his plate. "Why'd you have to go and ask that?"

His mother sat taller. "It's simple. I have a gut feeling when two people are meant to be together." She glanced between Velma and Brek, her face going blank. "Always have. I made my first match when I was eight. I matched our golden retriever with the neighbor's German shepherd. When I was in high school, I set up all my friends. I've been doing it ever since."

The spiel was clearly well rehearsed.

"Ma's got an excellent track record for getting couples engaged. Now, staying married? That's a whole different story."

"Hush. My job is to help them find each other. What they do after that is up to them."

Velma topped off Pam's juice.

"You should ask Velma about her methods." Brek pointed the tines of his fork at Velma.

She glared at him.

"Are you interested in finding a match?" Pam asked.

"Here she goes. Hang on, Velma. You're in for a ride."

Brek sat on the counter, his plate on his lap, bare Neanderthal feet dangling against her maple cabinets.

"Tell me about yourself, Velma." Pam removed a small spiral notebook and pen from her purse, poised to take notes.

"Uh…" Velma started.

"Don't be nervous. I do this all the time. Start with your age. How old are you?" Pam asked.

"Thirty." Velma handed Brek the jar of real Vermont maple syrup.

Pam scribbled something on the paper. "How do you usually meet men?"

"Mostly online."

Pam tsked. "I'm not a fan of online. You can't judge chemistry through a computer screen."

"That's probably why you've had such bad luck." Brek set the syrup aside. "Show her your spreadsheet. She'll love it."

"I'm not showing anyone my spreadsheet." Velma gave him her best attempt at a withering stare.

He smiled at her in reply.

"What spreadsheet?" Pam asked.

"Velma's got a program," Brek said through a huge bite. "Ranks men on the diversity of their portfolios."

"It's more complicated than that," Velma clarified. "The whole thing is part of my five-year plan. I have a spreadsheet so I can compare all the things that are important to me in a man. Financial solvency is a part of that, but it's a very small part. Personality is ranked much higher."

"How do you rank attraction on your spreadsheet?" Pam straightened, her full attention on Velma.

"I haven't gotten that far." Velma cut into her pancake. "No one has gotten past the first stage of compatibility."

"Tell me, Velma. When you're forty years old, sitting next to the man you've married, what do you want to feel?" Pam asked.

Velma blinked hard at the idea of actually finding a

partner who would stick through everything with her. "Happy. I'd like to feel happy."

"And you think a man with a diverse portfolio and manicured fingernails will make you happy?" Pam confirmed.

Sheesh. This was like therapy. Deep therapy.

"No. I just think having someone there to enjoy being happy with me would be nice," Velma said softly.

"You want a guy with manicured fingernails?" Brek paused as he mopped up the syrup from his plate with a pancake. He had abandoned the fork.

"Of course she does," Pam replied. "I don't need to see her list to know that's important to her."

"Velma, shoot your goals higher than a nitwit with nice fingernails and a pension. That's all I'm sayin'." Brek glanced to his mother. "You fix her up, make sure the jerk isn't a total loser."

"Do you think you could really find someone for me?" Velma wiped at a nonexistent speck on the granite countertop with her fingers.

"Would you ever consider…?" Pam glanced to Velma, then Brek, then back to Velma.

"Brek? Like to date?" Velma looked to her roommate. Well, yeah, she'd considered him. All night long. But he wasn't the kind of man who wanted forever. Not with someone like her.

"Leave it alone, Ma," Brek said on a growl.

"A mother's got a right to want her son happy, hasn't she?" Pam raised her eyebrows, practically daring him to contradict.

"I'm happy." Brek grinned. "See?" He pointed at his smile.

Pam smacked her palms together and ignored him. "I love a good challenge, Velma. Come to some of my mixers, fill out the paperwork, and I'll see what I can come up with. It's the least I can do since you're taking care of my son."

"Mixers?" Velma asked.

"Get-together events for singles. I screen everyone before-hand and make sure there's a possibility of a match. Then you meet men and see if there's chemistry—"

"Without having to wonder if he's a serial killer," Brek finished for her.

Pam glared at her son.

Velma agreed with Brek. Serial killer status was good information to have on a potential match.

He shrugged. "It's the truth. Ma screens out all the serial killers and felons."

"Actually, I have a couple of nice girls I'd like *you* to meet, Brek." Pam rummaged through her purse and retrieved a cell phone in a sleek black case. She swiped at the screen and held it up to her son.

"I don't want to meet nice girls. Thanks, though." He didn't even glance at the screen. "Don't try to match me. I'm not staying in Denver."

"Matching people is what I do. And you, Son, need a match." She thumbed through more photos and raised another at him.

He continued to ignore her phone, turning instead to Velma. "Ma's on a tear about finding me a wife."

"Sweetheart, you're over thirty," Pam said. "The time has come."

"What's wrong with a wife?" Velma asked. Falling in love, marriage, family—it'd be wonderful.

"What's right with one? That's the real question."

"I'll crack him yet. We just haven't found the right woman." Pam slipped her phone back into her purse. "It'll happen. Maybe you could bring Velma to the mixers?"

"No." Brek tossed his plate into the sink.

Velma cleared her throat. He got the message and rinsed the plate off before putting it in the dishwasher.

"Ma, what ideas do you have for a 'Purple Rain' wedding

theme? I don't want to bug Aspen, but I'm coming up empty. So far all I've got is lighting the ceremony with black lights."

Whatever the question, when it came to weddings, black lights were never the answer.

"Oh, don't do that," Velma replied. "Some clothes become see-through under black light."

"Like I said, I figure I'll start with a black light. Any other ideas?"

He grinned his darn half smile. Her body responded with ridiculous tingles.

"What if you had Jase hang purple tulips from the ceiling of the church, so it looks like it's raining flowers? You could do that all the way down the aisle." Velma abandoned her breakfast. She dipped her metal tea diffuser in and out of her cup, studying the tea leaves in the bottom. "And at the reception you could use purple candles and those big vase things, fill them with water, and dye the water with food coloring."

"Perhaps you should write this down." Pam raised her eyebrows at Brek.

He cocked his head at Velma. "What else you got in that noggin' of yours?"

"What about a grape juice fountain?" Brainstorming was kind of fun.

"Um." Pam squinted toward Velma.

"I mean if they're going for a 'Purple Rain' theme, you could do lots of things that are purple and drippy. Grape juice. Purple popsicles. Jell-O."

"Grape juice might stain." Pam ran her finger around the rim of her glass.

"V, even I know grape juice and other…purple, drippy things…is a horrible idea." Brek gave her a look like she'd suggested they tie-dye puppies.

"I'm not the one who came up with the theme." Velma shrugged.

She could appreciate that her sister wanted a nontraditional wedding, but she wouldn't choose that for her nuptials. That event would be classic elegance—red roses, her grandmother's white wedding dress, a string quartet, Dom Pérignon, and three hundred of her closest friends, colleagues, and clients.

Now she just needed a groom.

Chapter Six

Velma gripped the metal handrail and slogged up the stairwell to her apartment. Brek's mom had worked fast and come through with a date for Velma in under three hours. The guy, Paul, was perfect on paper. In person? Not so much.

After a day of brainstorming wedding ideas for his brides with Brek, she'd met Paul for dinner. He was a handsome pediatrician who liked salsa dancing and fancy dinners at Brio. Yes, he was Dr. Perfect, down to his chiseled chin and well-manicured hands. They'd chatted about his long-term financial goals and insurance between appetizers and dinner.

Unfortunately, the chemistry piece Pam had mentioned that morning was disappointingly absent. As much as Velma enjoyed Paul's company, it was like having dinner with her cousin. Nice, absolutely, but not in the maybe-we-could-make-babies-together way. When he held her hand, the whole thing was awkward and uncomfortable. No tingles or curiosity as to what lay under his starched white button-down shirt. Probably pale skin with a smattering of hair. Nothing like Brek's menagerie of ink. She could get lost in his tattoos for days.

The fact that she was thinking about Brek's tattoos on a

date with Mr. Maybe Right was not okay. She didn't even like tattoos. At least she hadn't cared for them before she met Brek. Now, if she was honest with herself, she was on the fence about the whole ink thing. Needles were still the devil, and tattoos cost way too much money. But the way Brek wore them? Oy vey.

Thankfully, the hospital called Paul in for an emergency. The relief she experienced was absolutely unacceptable. He had asked if he could call her again. She said it probably wasn't a good idea.

A lavender-scented bubble bath and perhaps a lobotomy were on the agenda for the night—something to help her get over her unhealthy infatuation with her roommate and back into her search for the future.

Key in hand, she walked along the beige carpeted hallway to her door. The television blared through the door of her apartment, sounding ominously like a frat party. She turned her key and hustled inside.

"Brek." She set her purse on the kitchen table, which was almost completely covered with bowls of chips, casserole-style dip, pizzas, and an assortment of beer bottles.

Brek, Jase, Dean, and a guy she didn't know were playing a video game, smashing cars into buildings. Clearly, her life had become part of *The Twilight Zone*—her perfect date having no attraction whatsoever and the hot-guy brigade making messes in her living room.

She glanced from the debris surrounding them to the fireplace. What the heck? A new painting had been hung over the mantel. The colors were right for the room, but it was a canvas print of a pigeon wearing a ruffled lace ascot. The bird was positioned as though sitting for a traditional portrait with a captain's hat on his head and an old-style mariner jacket. The painting looked like something found on the ceiling of one of those kitschy restaurants with all the flair. Definitely not living room artwork.

"Brek." She tried again, but Jase let out a "whoop" as she spoke. Brek didn't hear her.

She stood in front of the television, hands on her pencil-skirt-covered hips. The boys grumbled in unison. One of them paused the game.

"Hey, Velma." Dean lounged on her couch, his controller in hand.

"Everything okay, V?" Brek grabbed the remote control from Jase.

"Fine. Everything's fine. It's just really loud, the apartment's a wreck, and there's a strange picture over the mantel." She pointed to the portrait.

"Figured it'd brighten up the place. Add character." Brek grinned a sly smile that made her knees and her heart all wobbly.

See? Why couldn't she have this reaction to the pediatrician?

"You're home early. Grab a beer and try some of Eli's chips 'n' dip and pizza. He's an artist in the kitchen. We let him hang out sometimes, though that decision is presently being questioned due to his inability to keep his virtual car on the road."

"Bullshit. They adore my wit and humor," Eli said, deadpan, as he crossed his tennis-shoe-covered feet on her Ethan Allen ottoman.

"Eli?" she asked.

He raised his eyebrows in response. His grin could only be described as wicked. Women probably threw their panties at him regularly to see that little bit of a lip twitch.

"Take your shoes off my furniture, please?"

Without shifting his gaze from hers, Eli slipped off his tennis shoes and dropped his sock-covered feet back on the furniture.

Jase smacked Brek's shoulder. "You're right, man. She's totally fuckable."

"Dude." Dean glared at Jase.

Velma's heart stumbled inside her chest. She dropped her hands from her hips. "You did not just say that."

"What? Am I not allowed to go there?" Jase asked.

"No." Dean rubbed his forehead.

Brek dropped his elbows to his knees, controller dangling in hand. "Don't say it in front of her. Hey, Velma, glad you're home. Sorry dickhead here's bein' a dickhead."

Velma opened her mouth to reply—with what, she had no idea—but Brek spoke first. "Jase, you owe money for the swear jar. Gotta pay to say 'fuck' around her."

That was nowhere near what she was going to say.

Brek tossed his controller to the side and rose. He grabbed the beribboned jar from the counter and moved back to Mr. Cussy McCusserton.

Jase grudgingly tugged out his wallet. "You've been cussing all night."

"I prepaid for the month," Brek said seriously.

He had, and he wasn't even trying to keep his potty mouth under control.

Jase shoved his wallet back into his pocket and winked at Velma. "Sorry if I offended. I'll use a different compliment next time."

"Using the f-bomb is never a compliment," Velma replied.

"Whatever you say." Jase pointed his finger at her and made a clicking sound with his tongue.

Brek moved the jar to Eli. "You, too."

"What'd I say?" Eli lifted his shoulders in defiance.

"Not what you've said, but what's gonna come out of your mouth at some point tonight." Brek shook the jar so the dollars and change rattled.

Eli reluctantly dropped in a crisp ten-dollar bill. "Can I say she's fuckable now that I paid?"

"No. No one says she's fuckable." Brek set the jar on the

coffee table. "Dean, the jar's here if you feel the urge to say 'fuck.'"

"Noted." Dean nodded.

"Brek's the one who said it first." Jase slipped off his shoes and set his feet on her ottoman.

"Did you really say I'm f-able?" Velma couldn't hide the shock from her tone.

"I'll take my Fifth Amendment privilege not to incriminate myself by answering." Brek shifted uncomfortably. "What happened to your date, V?"

"He had to go to the hospital." She evacuated from the television to the food table so they could continue burning brain cells with violent video games. She took a bite of Eli's casserole. Artichokes and melted cream cheese. Oh man, it really was yummy.

"You sent a guy to the hospital?" Jase asked with what sounded like awe.

All four of them focused their attention on her.

"He's a doctor. He got called in." She dipped another tortilla chip, the homemade kind, into the pan.

Jase took a swig of his beer and set it on her end table—without a coaster. "Bummer. See, now, if I had a girl like you, I wouldn't let anything call me away. Because, as Brek pointed out, you're totally—"

"Dude." Dean glared daggers at Jase.

"Is that all you guys think about?" Velma asked.

"Yes," three of them replied in unison.

An eye roll and she grabbed her laptop bag from the counter. "I'll leave you to rot your brain cells with senseless violence."

"Much appreciated." Jase fist-bumped Eli, and they went back to their game.

A bubble bath sounded better and better. Velma could escape to her room for the night so she didn't get anxiety over the lack of coasters and the abundance of feet on furniture.

She shut her door, propped her coral-colored throw pillows behind her on the bed, turned on her laptop, and clicked open her spreadsheet.

Someone knocked lightly against her door.

"Come in," she called.

Brek poked his head into the room. "You're not havin' all the fun without me, are you?"

He clicked the door closed behind him and strode to her bed with a jar of Nutella marked with a *B&V* label in one hand and two spoons in the other.

"Fun?" she asked as he crawled onto the bed beside her.

"Fillin' out your spreadsheet. I'm here to help." He stretched out and propped the Nutella between them. "What've we got so far?"

"Nothing. I just turned it on." Velma wiped at a fleck of dust on the monitor with her thumb.

"Perfect." He rolled onto his side so he could see her screen and dipped one of the spoons into the jar before lifting it to her lips.

She moved her head back. "What are you doing?"

"Sharing."

When she literally didn't bite, he moved the spoon to his mouth. The way that man ate. She could watch him lick cutlery all day long.

Ack. No. No. No. Not her focus tonight. "Shouldn't you go play with your friends?"

"Nah. Usually Dean and I team up against Eli and Jase. Dean had to take off. Which means we're down a player. Which means, they're playin' one-on-one. I'm guessing, since you're here, you didn't get your post-date dessert with your girls. So here I am." He glanced to her screen. "Whatcha got so far?"

"Okay. So, we have height, which was acceptable. Employment, he's a pediatrician. Bonus points there. A good investment firm manages him. I'll give him an eight on that. I deducted two points because it's not my firm. Housing, nine. He said he's got a place in Cherry Creek." She tapped in the scores.

"Transportation?" Brek read the heading in the next column.

"Definitely a nine. He drives a Mercedes. Sleek but not the highest safety rating." She clicked away on the keyboard, adding up the numbers. Her heart dropped. He was already at a nine-point-five, which really wasn't a surprise.

Brek shoveled more Nutella. "What's the 'style' column for?"

"Like does he wear a suit? Regular haircuts. That stuff."

"Well?" Brek asked.

She sighed. "Nine. And attraction is at a big ol' zero."

"His name's Paul. You should deduct points for that." Brek pointed at her screen with his spoon.

"Why would I deduct points for that?"

"It lacks creativity. A name like Breckenridge. That's creative." He nodded along with his assessment.

"Where'd your mom come up with it anyway?" She continued adding numbers in the columns.

"She named both of us after where we were conceived. A condo in Breckenridge for me and Aspen...well, you get the idea."

Velma giggled. "You're serious?"

"Not something I'd lie about," he said, deadpan.

She picked up the other spoon and scooped a small amount onto it, licking off the hazelnutty chocolate.

His gaze fell to her lips.

"What?" she asked around the bite.

"I don't get it," he announced.

"Get what?"

"Why you don't have a guy." His eyes didn't move from her mouth.

"I'm not exactly tons of fun, Brek."

"See, that's where you're wrong. It's official. I'm gonna teach you the hokeypokey." The light in his eyes twinkled dangerously.

"Is that a kinky handcuff game?" Knowing him, that was exactly what it'd be.

"Nah. I'm just gonna help you turn yourself around. Your life, anyway."

She caught his gaze. He was serious. "Thanks, but no thanks. I'm fine."

"Nah. But you will be. Especially once you help me with all these damn brides." He rubbed a hand down his face.

"What are you talking about?"

"I need help. I'm glad to tell you, you're gonna be that helper." He was totally serious.

"Are you insane?" She knew next to nothing about planning weddings.

"Possibly. But I still need help, and I'm hoping since you like me, and I like you, you might take pity. Don't you plan things all day, Ms. Financial Planner Lady?"

"I move stocks and set up individual retirement accounts. That's not the same thing." Not even close.

"Maybe you could make me a spreadsheet? Run interference with Bride Number One?"

The whole room held his scent—the one that made her mouth go dry.

Funny, when she was around Brek, she didn't think about her quest to find a man like Dean. And when she was around Brek, even things that had never made sense before started to make sense. Like Nutella in bed. Who would've thought?

"How about I teach you how to make your own spreadsheet?" she asked.

They could start with that.

His phone buzzed in his pocket. "Hang tight. It's Aspen. She's been harassing me all day." He held the phone to his ear. "Hey, Aspen. You're not supposed to call me. Jacob said—" He leaned away from Velma and squinted. "Whoa. Calm down… I didn't know they had special stamps for that. Does it matter?"

Uh-oh. Those stamps were a horrible idea. Everybody knew to use the special wedding stamps when sending wedding invitations. You didn't shove them in the envelopes and affix the ribbon with an abundance of gold stickers. Some of the ones he'd put together had so much gold foil stuck to them, they looked like they should be dancing over at Pistol Polly's strip club. She'd confiscated those.

Brek flinched at something his sister said. "Tell her to chill, it's not like—"

Velma could hear Aspen all the way on her side of the bed. And Aspen did not sound happy about those invitations. Velma's phone beeped with a new text. She glanced at it. Claire. Velma's heart dropped. Oh no. Brek had found the invitations Velma pulled—and he'd sent them.

"They weren't all like that. Velma tied some… The stickers held the bows on… I improvised… I know this is a big deal… I'll apologize… I won't fuck it up… Right."

Aspen apparently hung up. He stared at the phone in his hand. "I'm fucked."

"Claire's really upset." Velma ran her thumb through the messages bouncing back and forth between Claire and their mother.

"That's the understatement of the year," he growled.

He had the look of a guy caught in the headlights of one of those Ford Super Duty trucks. "What's it gonna take for you to help me?"

"I did help you." Not that it had worked.

"Long term through these weddings. You know things about stamps." His expression was one of total seriousness.

Velma shifted on the bed. "Brek, I have a job."

"I need your help so I don't screw up Claire's wedding."

Well…when he put it like that. Gah. "Fine. I'm in."

He nodded. "What's it gonna take to get your help with Brides One and Two?"

She sized him up. He really was worried.

"Please." His eyes were the embodiment of sincerity.

Apparently, she was powerless against needy bikers with Nutella. "You have to wear pants when you're home."

"Agreed." He inched closer to her and gestured to her laptop. "You gonna see this guy again?"

She stared at the numbers on the screen. "No. I don't think so."

"Great." Brek closed her computer and moved it to her nightstand. "Now that we're working together, I propose you drop the spreadsheet and we hash out a friends-with-benefits situation."

Her belly went all fluttery. He couldn't mean those benefits. Not the bedroom kind. Except they were on her bed, in her bedroom.

"Are we friends?" The words came out breathy.

He gestured his spoon to the jar between them. "We sittin' on your bed eatin' Nutella?"

She moved to lie on her side so they were face-to-face. "We're *friends*, then. No need to ruin that with…benefits."

"As your friend, I feel it's my duty to inform you that you're high-strung."

Well, that wasn't very nice. "That's not kind."

"You need to chill. Lucky for you, I have a certain skill set to help with that." He put the lid on the Nutella, took her spoon with his, and set it all on the nightstand with her laptop. He scooted closer to her.

She resisted the urge to move backward, because she would end up on the floor. Besides, he only scared her a little bit with this whole conversation. And it wasn't like he had touched her or anything.

He rested a hand on her waist and moved his head closer

to hers. Her heart hammered loudly in her chest. Surely, he could hear it, too.

"What do you say, V?"

"You want to be friends who sleep with each other?" That couldn't possibly be what he meant.

"I want to be friends who have sex with each other. Sleeping is optional."

Okay, so that *was* what he meant.

"Way I see it, you need to relax. I can help with that. I won't be in town long, so no long-term expectations. No weirdness when it's over."

Wow. That sounded super rational.

"Really, I'm flattered. I…we're so different. I'm…me. And you're…you know…you."

He grinned right up close to her, and, Holy Hannah, the wattage of his smile. "Feel that between us? It's called chemistry."

"I don't like rock music. There. I said it. I think it's loud and obnoxious," she declared.

His eyebrows dropped together. "What music do you like, then?"

"Country, mostly. A little Justin Timberlake…" Her voice trailed off as his eyes sparked with humor.

"Won't listen to music while we do it, that's fine." The edges of his lips twitched.

"You have tattoos and I wear sweaters," she continued.

"What's wrong with tattoos?" he asked, moving his hand away.

"Nothing. No, it's just we're different. I haven't even seen them all. What if you have one that I really don't like, you know?"

"Take off your top." He tugged at the hem of the pink-striped sweater she had paired with the skirt.

He wasn't making any sense. "What?"

"You take off your top. I'll take off mine. You can check

out my tattoos, make sure you like 'em. I'll check out your girls, make sure I like 'em. Tit for tat."

"You're such a pig." She crossed her arm across her chest and tried to stand, but he caught her and pulled her back to him.

He ran a hand through her hair and pressed her to him so their foreheads touched. She shivered—in a good way. In a maybe-I-should-reconsider-my-stance-on-this-proposal way.

"Oink."

She laughed, pretty much against her will, and shoved him away.

"Holler if you change your mind about our situation." His thumb grazed her bottom lip. For a moment, only a moment, she seriously considered allowing him to have his way with her right there in her bedroom while his buddies played video games in the other room.

Luckily, she came to her senses.

"Clean up the living room before you go to bed," she whispered instead.

He chuckled as he stood. "Next time Ma sets you up, tell her to be sure the guy's schedule is clear for the evening. You deserve his full attention."

He left. She glanced out the window at the clouds that covered the stars before she hauled herself out of bed to finally take that bubble bath.

Chapter Seven

COUNTDOWN TO CLAIRE & DEAN'S
WEDDING: 6 WEEKS

Velma had slathered on makeup and, at Claire's insistence, slipped into a pair of tight jeans. Their friend Heather had picked the girls' night location. Heather rocked the pinup look with her red lipstick and cleavage-baring vintage top. Hank's Bar, she promised Velma and Claire, had an amazing band on tap for the night. The place was a dive, but clean—sealed concrete floor, long wooden bar top, and a scattering of tables throughout the room. The tables along the wall were countertop height, so patrons could watch the band. Standard neon alcohol signs lit the wall alongside triangle pennants declaring the various beers on tap. They were quite festive.

"Another?" Heather asked, tipping her forehead toward Velma's nearly empty Shirley Temple.

Velma rested her elbow on the table and propped her palm against the side of her head. "That'd be great."

Heather headed toward the counter.

"Thank you for dealing with Brek on the invitations," Claire said.

Velma had helped smooth everything over. She'd promised Claire she'd be involved with the rest of the details, and she'd report any issues immediately. After a chat with

Aspen, she'd made Brek a spreadsheet of all that still needed to be done.

"Okay. Dish. You're overthinking something." Claire took a sip of her drink.

Velma was overthinking Brek. And his proposal. And her refusal. Which she was now questioning on an hourly basis.

"Brek propositioned me."

"Again?"

"He wants to be friends with benefits." Velma stirred her drink—the swirling cubes of ice matching the feeling in her chest.

"Yeah. And?" Claire stared at Velma with an absurd amount of interest.

"And I said no." Velma's hand fell on something sticky along the edge of the table.

Claire raised an eyebrow and Velma flinched. That look. The one that told her Claire was ready to pounce for information. "But you thought about saying yes?"

Velma nodded.

"Oh my God, Velvet. This is crazy."

Gah. Velma had done more than think about saying yes—she'd nearly brought it up to him twice. Nearly. Both times she'd caught herself. Nowhere in any of her plans did a short-term fling with a guitar-playing biker come into play.

"I can't blame you. I mean, have you seen him?" Claire licked her lips. "The other day when he was with Jase showing me options for our flowers... I mean, don't get me wrong, I love Dean, but, you know, Brek's not hard to look at."

Velma squirmed. She shouldn't care that her sister checked out Brek. Not when she, herself, had admired Dean. Still, though, it felt wrong. "I want a guy like Dean. Like what you two have."

Heather hopped back onto her barstool. "They're bringing our drinks over. What are we talking about?"

"Velma wants to hook up with Brek." Claire grinned like she'd won the lottery. "And the feeling is mutual."

"Get out." Heather smacked Velma's shoulder. "You totally should. I would. You could use a little of Brek's brand of fun."

Claire sat taller. "Agreed. It's like a reset button. To help you get over the whole Tommy thing."

Velma's heart dropped at the mention of Tommy. The last guy she'd seriously dated forever ago. The last guy she'd gone to bed with.

He'd told her she was boring.

In bed.

The hit to her pride pierced a lasting sting.

"I want a relationship. A husband. Not just a roll in the sheets with Brek. I want what Claire has with Dean." Velma dropped her head to the table. Her forehead fell into the stickiness. Regret immediately followed the move.

She was midwipe with her napkin on her forehead when the door to the joint opened and—fudge, Brek had found her bar.

Her heart tripped over her ribs. She glanced to Heather. Then to Claire.

Heather looked to the door. She rubbed her hands together. "Tonight just got so fun. You're gonna go press the reset button."

The waitress pushed two new Shirley Temples in front of Velma. "A regular Shirley Temple and a vodka Shirley Temple."

"Oh, Velvet, I fixed your drink order. You're welcome." Heather beamed.

Velma was going to need vodka to get through the night. She took a long sip from the straw.

Her gaze slid back to Brek in time to see a look of shock pass over his features.

She focused on her spiked Shirley Temple.

"You should go over there," Claire encouraged.

"Say hello." Heather was practically bouncing on her barstool.

"Tell him you changed your mind," Claire continued as though this conversation were totally normal.

Velma wasn't going to do that. But it was probably better to just say hello and move along than to stare at each other across the bar. That'd be awkward. She trudged to the table Brek had claimed.

He fixed his eyes on the cleavage peeking out from her black V-neck T-shirt. Slowly, he raised his gaze to her face.

Her toes curled in her high heels at the way his eyes ate her up.

"What're you doing here?" He glanced to the door and back her way.

"Girls' night. What're *you* doing here?"

"Drinking." He nodded to the bar, the movement causing his hair to brush against the collar of the leather biker jacket. "Scouting the band." He glanced again at the door and rubbed the back of his neck. "And meeting a friend."

Oh geez. He was on a date. Velma's heart plunked straight down to her patent leather Jessica Simpson sling-back heels. Apparently, she had a jealous bone (or ten) in her body, because the idea of Brek with another woman made her stomach hurt. Of course he was with a woman. A guy like him didn't spend quality time alone with his hand on a Friday night.

She scraped her heart back up to her chest and flashed her most sincere you're-my-roommate-and-everything-is-fine smile.

"We'll go somewhere else." His apologetic gaze landed on Velma. He began to stand, but she didn't budge.

"No. You're here to have a good time. So am I." She cocked her hip and tried to look sassy. She was pretty certain she failed.

A piece of hair escaped the tight bun at the nape of her neck, but she didn't fix it. He stared, fixated on the chunk of escaped in-desperate-need-of-highlights blonde.

Her ovaries practically sighed.

That's when the world turned topsy-turvy. A gorgeous biker babe hit the bar wearing a tube top under her leather jacket that matched her tight pants. And by tight, the pants were painted on. She definitely was wearing a thong, because there was no panty line. Either that or she was going commando. But that couldn't be comfortable in leather.

Still, the look worked on her. Or she worked the look. Either way, Lordy, the amount of hair spray to tease hair that big must've raised Denver's emissions to hazardous levels. Sheesh.

Velma was wrong. She hadn't plastered on makeup. Nope. This chick had the market cornered on that.

Biker girl's painted lips ticked into a full grin as she stalked toward Brek.

He stood but he didn't smile. Not until Tight Pants said something in his ear. Then he gave her a half grin and a side squeeze.

Velma hadn't moved at all since Brek's date had walked in. She should've moved, though. Should've gone back to her table. Or to Minnesota. Anywhere but there.

"Who's this?" Biker chick gave Velma a once-over that would've chilled the entirety of the Breyers Ice Cream factory.

"Velma. Chelsea. Chelsea. Velma." Brek shifted uncomfortably, but his hand still rested on Chelsea's waist.

"Nice to meet you." Velma infused her tone with warmth to counter Chelsea's winter blast.

"Hey, Brek." Claire hooked her arm through Velma's. "You crashing girls' night?"

Velma warmed with her sister beside her. Taking her back. Well, her side, in this case.

Chelsea kept her expression neutral. The kind Velma knew well from her high school days when the pretty, popular girl was dismissing her.

"Not tonight. Another time." Brek glanced to Chelsea, his intentions for the evening absolutely clear.

Which was totally fine, because Velma had her friends. "We're just going to ah…go back to our table."

Head high, Velma looked Chelsea straight in the mascaraed eye before heading back to her barstool. She didn't even glance back as the band began to set up on the small stage.

"I don't think any of us saw that coming." Heather squeezed Velma's forearm. "It'll be my personal goal to find you a guy tonight. Ignore Brek. Don't look over there."

She didn't need to, because she was a confident woman. A confident woman who studied a chip missing from the table-top. Except, one last look and then she'd be done.

Brek moved to shake hands and smack the drummer on the back. Much better than his hand on Chelsea's waistband. The guy handed him a guitar. Brek played a few chords.

He was pure rock 'n' roll in that moment. Long hair, guitar strap around his neck, playing some song Velma recognized but couldn't put her finger on. And when he glanced up and caught her looking? It felt like he played only for her.

She ripped her gaze away.

"Holy crap, he played that for you. Right in front of her." Claire sucked in her bottom lip. "Like, *right* in front of his date."

"He's got an amazing voice." Heather's expression went dreamy. "We need to help him ditch her."

Claire nodded in agreement. "Nicely, of course."

Brek had stopped playing.

Velma couldn't bring herself to look back to the stage. "This is ridiculous, he's on a date. He doesn't want an offer of bedroom benefits from me when he's on a date."

The waitress dropped three red plastic baskets filled with oversized hamburgers and fries on the table.

"This is a complication, that's all." Heather squirted ketchup on the waxed paper lining her basket.

"I should go home." Velma couldn't think about food right now. "Deflated" was the word of the night.

"No. It's girls' night. We'll eat and go somewhere else. I'm thinking massages at that place in the mall." Claire swirled her ketchup with a fry.

Velma held the burger to her lips and dropped it without taking a bite, her gaze shifting to Brek and Chelsea. He'd left the stage. Now he had his arms crossed, feet propped on a vacant stool, listening to something Chelsea said. Chelsea was a hand talker. It didn't seem to bother Brek, but she'd better be careful or she'd knock over his Coors.

Velma's chest rose and fell quickly. Fight or flight and no way was she taking on a biker babe.

"I need to use the ladies' room." Velma slid off the stool and headed down the hall leading to the bathrooms.

Get it together, Velma.

Brek was allowed to date. Of course he was. She just didn't want a front-row seat.

An intoxicated guy poured himself from the men's room, stumbling straight into her. He wobbled a finger in her direction, but even his finger wag looked drunk. "Watch your step, sweetie."

She reached out to steady him when he tottered backward.

"Plans for tonight, muffin?" His drunkard smile looked more like a sneer.

"Yup." She laughed what she hoped was a dismissive chuckle and turned on her heel to go back to the table, grab her friends, and get out of there.

The guy's hands wrapped around her hips, twisted her, and he pulled her against his crotch.

"Stop." She lurched forward to get away, but his fingertips ground in, holding her in place while he rubbed himself against her backside. The bile in her stomach curdled.

"Let go." She steadied her breaths while she shoved at his hands. He gripped her harder. Her pulse sped, and she kicked at his shin with the heel of her shoe.

"You heard her." Brek pushed past and wrapped his hand around drunk guy's neck. Apparently, he squeezed, because the guy gasped for air, released his grip on her, and clawed at Brek's hand.

He pushed forward, the idiot smashing against the Bud Light sign on the wall. Brek forced the guy's chin in her direction. "See her?" Jaw tight, Brek jerked his head toward Velma.

Drunk guy nodded, his glazed eyes huge.

Well, huh. She had never had someone growl on her behalf before.

Brek slammed his palm against the wall next to the man's face.

Velma jumped at the sound. "Brek, stop. You don't need to hurt him."

Brek ignored her.

"Brek. Let the guy go." Chelsea sounded decidedly pissy that her date was taking time to defend Velma's honor.

Honor that Velma was perfectly capable of defending herself with a strategically placed knee to the douchebag's fly.

Brek ignored Chelsea, too.

"She's a lady." He got right up in the guy's face. Deep down, Velma knew this wasn't going to end well.

"Velma? Are you okay?" Heather shoved through the small crowd forming at the entrance to the hallway."

"Velvet, let's go." Claire stood right beside Heather.

"Seriously, you have to stop." Velma moved forward, but Brek stopped her with a furious glare.

Or, you know, she could just wait here.

Brek waited a beat and turned his face back to the squirming drunk in his grip. His nostrils flared. "I said, she's a lady. You get that?"

Brek's fingers still wrapped tight around the drunk's throat, the guy nodded.

Sheesh, someone was actually going to get hurt. "Brek, you have to let him go," Velma said with as much conviction as she could muster.

Brek ignored her, his face maliciously close to the other guy's. "We need to talk more about how to treat a lady?"

Drunk dude's eyes bugged to cartoon status. He shook his head.

Brek released his grip and patted him on the shoulder like they were old friends. "Then we're done here. You okay, V?"

Velma shoved her hands onto her hips. No. She wasn't okay. "I'm fine."

Now free, the idiot made an attempt at a drunken fist, and, holy crud, he lunged at Brek. Velma pushed Brek out of the way.

A wild swing grazed her cheek. She dodged and fell to the floor with a very unladylike *thunk*. Pain radiated up through her shoulder. *Crud, that hurt.*

Brek twisted back to the guy.

Oh no. With the murder in Brek's eyes, drunk guy didn't stand a chance.

"Well, shit," Chelsea said under her breath.

Before Velma could scramble to her feet, Brek had him pushed up against the wall again. "I guess the lesson wasn't finished."

Claire and Heather flanked Velma, pulling her backward.

"Brek. No," she said with a gasp. "I'm okay. He didn't hurt me."

Too late. Brek raised his fist, and it connected to the other man's face with a sickening *thud*. Blood spattered across the wall and onto Brek's shirt. Drunk guy whimpered and slid to the ground.

Brek cussed a string of creatively combined curses. He curled his fist around the guy's collar and yanked him back up. "You need more schooling? Or we done here?"

"Done," he whimpered.

Well, thank goodness for small miracles. At least one of them was finished.

"What the hell?" the bartender yelled, pushing through the group of people. "You with this guy?" He glanced from Brek to Velma.

She opened her mouth to explain, but Brek got to it first.

"Yeah. She's with me." Brek spat the words.

"Wow, Brek. Nice." Chelsea huffed and walked away.

Drunk guy stumbled, one hand against his nose, the other pointing to her. "They assaulted me. I'm pressing charges."

The idiot could not be serious.

The bartender shifted uneasily. "We don't need the cops involved."

Blood flowed between the guy's fingers. "They broke my nose."

Brek grabbed napkins from the wait station and threw them so they rained down all around the bleeding jerk. "That'd be me, asswipe. But if you want Velma to get the credit for knocking some sense into you, I'm sure she'd oblige."

He didn't just say that. She absolutely wouldn't "oblige." Blood thumped uncomfortably in her temples.

Velma glanced to Brek. He had turned a strange shade of pissed-off red. Not good, not good at all.

"Hey." Idiot guy grabbed Brek's arm. Velma may not have been schooled in bar fights, but one could guess that was not a good idea.

"You got something to say?" Brek jerked his arm away.

"This." The man scrunched his hand into a fist and drunkenly aimed for Brek's face.

Fortunately for Brek, he had absolutely no force behind his punch.

Brek made his fist, pulled his arm back, and landed another blow to the guy's nose.

Bone crunched as his knuckles made contact.

"Now there's no question who broke it."

SHE WAS GOING HOME. And when she got there, she was going to have some serious words with her roommate. Velma plopped her derriere onto the cold bus bench. They'd all been tossed out of the bar. Brek had disappeared. Claire was on the phone with Dean—their designated driver for the night—calling for an early pickup.

"Dean's on his way. I can't believe you got kicked out of a bar." Claire slipped beside Velma, her arm draped around Velma's shoulders.

"Be real, who thought we'd get tossed out on girls' night because Velma got in a bar fight?" Heather leaned against the bus stop sign.

The roll of an engine cut her off as a motorcycle pulled up to the bus shelter.

Brek's bike.

Now, she wasn't into motorcycles, but his was vintage cool. Like something James Dean would have ridden—shiny black and loads of chrome with one large circular headlight. His spectacularly male set of thighs nearly covered the Harley-Davidson nameplate.

"On the bike, V." Brek handed her a half helmet that would cover the top of her head and nothing else.

Um. No. She absolutely wasn't getting on his death trap, especially without a full helmet.

"What happened to your date?" Velma pulled her purse over one shoulder and stood.

"Bike. Now." Brek shoved the helmet toward her more forcefully.

"I don't do motorcycles." She glanced between him, the helmet, and the ground.

"You should get on the bike," Claire chimed in.

"If you don't, I'll totally get on the bike." Heather grinned like a loon.

"Swear to God, V. Get on the bike, or I'll toss you on the bike." Brek's glare turned fierce.

"You wouldn't dare." She glared right back.

"Five bucks says she doesn't get on the bike," Claire said from behind.

"I'll take that bet," Heather replied. "If he tosses her on the bike, I get double."

Velma turned and hushed them. "You're not helping."

"I kinda think we are." Heather shrugged.

The bike motor seemed to get even louder. Oh dear. Given the expression that crossed Brek's face, he absolutely would toss her on his bike.

Velma took the helmet, put it on, and clipped the chinstrap.

"We all need to go out more often." Heather sighed.

Velma stepped closer to Brek, so they were nearly nose to nose. "Why are you doing this?"

Exasperated waves of frustration poured from him. "You wanna talk this out? We'll do it at home."

"You think they're really going to *talk* this out?" Claire stage-whispered to Heather.

Velma ignored her.

Brek did have a point. Bickering on the corner made no sense. She gestured to the seat. "I've never been on a bike before. How do you…you know?"

"I feel like my baby sister is growing up before my eyes." Claire laughed. "I'm so proud of you, Velvet."

"Climb on. Hang on. Don't let go." Brek held Velma's gaze with his own.

"Right." She could do that. She fixed her bag to cross-body and not so gracefully swung her leg over the seat to settle against his back, attempting to keep a modest space between them.

He pulled her arms around his waist, erasing any space. She tried to move farther back, but the engine growled, sending interesting vibrations between her legs.

Okay, so she was beginning to understand the draw of motorcycles.

The bike lurched forward. Fine. That worked, too.

"Have fun with your talk!" Heather shouted over Brek's engine.

Velma squished her eyes closed and held on tighter.

The first block flew by before she finally peeked out from beneath her lashes. They stopped at a red light, and Brek stuck his foot against the pavement to hold them up. She gripped his waist harder. She wasn't going to biff it at a red light wearing only half a helmet. His jacket was unzipped, and sheesh, he had amazing abdominal definition—the ridges prominent even through his shirt. Of course she had seen them before. But she'd never *felt* them.

Perhaps the Brek Express was a good option. A car ride had never turned her on like this.

Brek pulled into his parking space, right beside hers. He cut the engine and put down the kickstand. She climbed off, lost her balance, and fell helmet-first against his chest.

His arms caught her, and he didn't release his grip. Her rapid heartbeat echoed in her ears. Surely, he could hear it, too. She clutched the soft leather of his jacket as his hand at her waist slid higher. His other hand unclipped her helmet and tossed it to the asphalt. She focused on where it landed near the painted yellow stripe delineating their parking space. Brek's finger traced her chin and lifted it so her gaze met his, which was a really bad idea because the heat from his anger melted into a different kind of fire. A warmth that somehow amplified his intense blue eyes.

She stood frozen in his gaze as he dipped his face until his lips barely brushed hers. Testing. Examining. She opened her mouth to tell him this was a bad idea. Supremely bad. Epically bad.

He must have misinterpreted her response because his lips urged for more and opened further. Perhaps this wasn't such a bad idea. Nice, actually. Perfect amount of pressure. Oh, some tongue. Dear goodness, he tasted delicious. Cardinal sin, mistakes, and all the things she never let herself feel. In other words, he tasted amazing. Amazing with a subtle hint of wintermint gum. She adored wintermint gum. Of all the mints, that one was her top choice. He pulled his tongue back, and that was no good. No good at all.

She tilted her head and sought him out again with her mouth. He responded with a vengeance, tongue and hands everywhere. Her fingers still clutched him close and, oh my, she was panting. Whatever. She blamed it on the motorcycle engine purring between her thighs for three miles.

Except, they were roommates, and this was inappropriate. She broke the kiss, still breathing hard and more than a little shaky. She could blame it on the bike ride, but the truth was the Tilt-A-Whirl inside her had nothing to do with a motor- cycle and everything to do with the man she was still hanging on to.

Step one. Release Brek.

Step two. Apologize for leading him on.

Step three. Insist it never happen again.

Step four. Well, she would figure that one out eventually.

She dropped her hands. Miraculously, she did not fall over. "I, um—"

"Don't say it." The fire in his eyes turned angry again.

"Say what?" She tugged at the hem of her shirt.

"Whatever bullshit you were about to say to ruin what just went down," he clipped.

Oh. No apology this time. Onto step three.

"That can't happen again."

"There it is." He pressed his lips together and shoved his hands in his pockets.

"There's what?"

"Your bullshit."

"It's not baloney. I'm serious. That was a lovely kiss."

"Lovely?" He looked less than impressed.

"Amazing. It was amazing," she corrected. Well, it was. "Also inappropriate."

He narrowed his eyes. "Inappropriate?"

"What would Dean think about us?" she asked.

His expression went dark. "Why would Dean have anything to say about us?"

Velma held herself back from the urge to lick her lips. "Nothing. I just mean..."

"Wait." Brek's eyes widened. "No. That couldn't be."

His whole vibe changed.

"What?" she asked.

"It'd make sense though," he continued.

"Brek, what?" He was putting the pieces together for something.

"Your reaction when your sister got engaged."

Oh no.

His palm hit his forehead. "Tell me you're not into Dean. Is that what this is about?"

"What? No." Not anymore. She shook her head for good measure.

She needed to deflect this conversation. No way could she tell him about her previous Dean-plan. "This is about tonight.

I wasn't your date. What about her? How would she feel about what happened just now?"

"You're serious?" He glanced up to the stars. "She's fuckin' serious."

"I am serious," she confirmed.

"Chelsea left. I was a shitty date because I couldn't get my mind off you."

"Oh." She bit her bottom lip. Everything was so messed up. All because she'd actually considered his proposition. "Let's go back to the way things were before," she heard herself say. The words sounded hollow and vacant.

The lines at the edges of his lips turned down, then smoothed. "That's what you want? Because that's what you say, but thirty seconds ago, your lips told a whole different story."

She sucked in a breath but didn't respond. The air between them hung like an itchy wool blanket.

"That's what I thought." He moved away to pick up the helmet and tuck it in one of the saddlebags. "Go on ahead."

She didn't linger. Step four officially involved hustling to the entrance of their building without further contact. The security door was nearly within reach when the engine on his bike rumbled. She entered her code, and a pull she couldn't quite decipher stopped her. She turned, but Brek was already gone.

Step five was apparently disappointment. In herself.

She went through her nighttime routine and crawled into bed, tossing and turning, waiting for him to return.

He didn't.

Chapter Eight

Brek was over the bullshit of the night before. After spending the night at Jase's, Brek rolled the tension from his shoulders and studied the license plates on the ceiling over Jase's couch. Jase had collected a motley assortment from all fifty states, and then some—enough to cover all the plaster. The result was impressive, and a decent distraction from Velma. Brek had needed space to think.

Jase's family owned a slew of flower companies throughout Denver, Fort Collins, and Colorado Springs. Jase managed the Cherry Creek store.

The whole florist thing was very *not* Jase. But when he had returned from Afghanistan, he was done with defusing road-side bombs and tossing grenades. Swore he needed simplicity.

"Roses don't blow up," he had said. "They're simple."

After last night, Brek needed a little simplicity. Chelsea had found out he was back in town and called yesterday. He'd met her to purge Velma from his head. The last thing he had expected was to find the woman he was trying to forget serving up attitude three tables over. Chelsea was pissed about the whole night. Rightly so, because, hell, he hadn't even kissed her.

He'd saved that for Velma. She was a siren wrapped up as a good girl. But only girls with a streak of bad could ever use a tongue the way she did. Which was why he had needed to get out of there, away from temptation and the taste of her. The story of his life: distance was a good thing. Freedom meant not being tied to anyone. He itched again for the independence that came on the road, traveling between gigs.

Funny thing, if he ever decided to stay in one place, he'd always figured he'd buy a bar just like Hank's. Great bands. Good booze. A solid location where he could settle down.

It was a good thing he didn't have any desire to stay in one place.

"Don't you have clients to meet?" Jase emerged from his bedroom, yawning and scratching at his tee.

Brek groaned. "Yeah."

More brides. They were killing him. How Aspen did this day in and day out, he would never understand. He rolled off the couch and reached for his boots. Velma was supposed to help him out today, but after last night, who knew? Pre-kiss, she had not only created a color-coded spreadsheet of all that still needed to be done for each of his brides, but she had also organized a calendar of individual items to be confirmed and had cross-referenced each of them to the wedding date, venue, and theme. Then she'd printed everything and tucked the pages in bound, laminated covers.

He loved it. Even if he did give her hell about it.

His only regret was not begging for her help earlier.

"How's the life of Denver's finest wedding planner?" Jase asked.

"Bride Number Two propositioned me at her cake tasting last week." Brek tied the long black laces on his boots. "Between the coconut cream and the chocolate decadence, she not-so-tactfully suggested we exchange bodily fluids. Her words, not mine."

He hadn't realized a person could choke on coconut cream.

"And since you have a hot roommate and decided to adopt a code of ethics, you didn't jump at the chance?" Jase ran the tap to fill the coffee carafe with water. Apparently, he didn't read articles like Velma did.

"I prefer to keep my dick out of other people's relationships." That and Brek's one job over the next couple of months was to ensure every one of Aspen's brides made it down the aisle, happily ever after. If he nailed one, Aspen would murder him in his sleep. He enjoyed life, so he'd declined. "Did you find out about those lilies Bride Number One wanted?"

"The orchids?" Jase clicked on the coffee maker.

"Sure."

"Still working on it. Her old man's gonna keel at the price tag." Jase sat against the card table he used as a kitchen table.

Bride Number One, Sophie, had what could only be described as an "episode" when she learned the flowers she wanted were out of season and, therefore, cost twice as much. Tears and a substantial amount of wailing quickly ensued. Her father finally pitched in the extra cash to have Jase bring in whatever she wanted. Turned out she could live without out-of-season dahlias if she could get exotic in-season orchids for the same price.

Brek ran a hand through his hair. "Make it happen. Whatever you've got to do."

Jase opened the fridge, took a swig of milk from the container, and offered the jug to Brek.

Brek scowled. "Pour it in a glass. You're not an animal."

"The little piece you're living with is rubbing off on you, isn't she?" Jase grinned.

Last night, she had rubbed her tongue all over his. So, yeah, she'd rubbed off on him. "Don't call her a 'piece.' Her name's Velma."

"Aw, you've got a case of feelings. Best cure for feelings is getting laid. Get on top of her to get over her, I always say." Jase eyed the coffee as it dripped. "Bonus, you'll have fun doing it."

"Your advice is crap." Brek grabbed his keys from the beer box Jase used as an end table.

"You're welcome to the couch next time you and the missus have a falling out." Jase moved closer to Brek, his arms wide. "You want to hug it out, Stud Muffin?"

"Asshole." Brek frowned at his phone. Velma hadn't texted or called. Not that he expected her to wonder where he went. Chelsea, however, had left five voice mails since she'd left him at the bar last night. Likely a variety of rants, chewing him out.

"Coffee before you face the morning after?" Jase held up a cup.

"Nope. I gotta run. I'm meeting a couple to discuss tablescapes and sample kah-naps." Not his idea of a good time.

"Kah-naps?" The lines on Jase's forehead squashed together.

Brek nodded. "Yeah."

At least there would be food—even if they were presented in miniature. He'd tried a few the other day, and the ones with the apricot and cream cheese weren't shit.

"What the fuck's a kah-nap?"

That was exactly what Brek had said when he'd read Aspen's e-mail with instructions for sampling them. "Small appetizers. They're a thing."

"Canapés?" Jase asked.

Brek tagged his wallet and tucked it into his back pocket. "Yeah. Whatever."

Jase fell against the wall in a fit of laughter like they were in a comedy club. "You are so fucked."

Yes, he was.

With traffic, he would barely make it on time to the party rental warehouse to meet with Bride Number One...and maybe Velma.

BREK WAS LATE by the time he got to the event warehouse off Colfax. He hurried through the entrance and headed straight for the showroom. Velma stood with the bride and the groom. A weight of stress rolled off of him at the sight of her.

Bride Number One held what he could only imagine was a dog—one of those teeny-tiny teacup canine things. A tornado of fluff and yap.

They all focused intently on one of the place settings Aspen had requested for the big tablescape decision. Sophie, the soon-to-be Mrs. Murtz, was a young, pretty, rich girl used to getting her way. Her groom? An aspiring junior partner at daddy's law firm who had no clue what he was getting himself into.

The groom, Troy, studied a fork like it was engraved with Megan Fox's personal phone number. Velma's expression puckered in concentration at something Sophie said.

Velma's white dress getup had an entirely too-high neckline, a skirt that brushed her calves, and a thin belt that cinched her waist, accentuating her ass nicely. One glance at her, and his pulse beat against his throat and lower in his—

"Brek, you made it." Velma beamed at him, her expression covering the clear concern in her eyes. "I explained to Sophie and Troy about how bad traffic has been downtown today."

"Yeah. Sorry, I got caught up."

Velma hesitated for half a second before putting on that fake grin she liked so much.

He might've been pissed at her. But she was still V, and he was still Brek.

The future Mrs. Murtz didn't glance up from the place settings. Her oblivious groom gave a little wave and set down the Megan Fox fork.

"We were discussing napkin rings." Velma held up a gold one with thin silver wire twined through it.

He fuckin' hated napkin rings. Fold the damn thing and lay it across the plate. Or, better yet, save everyone the trouble and wrap a paper napkin around some silverware.

Velma slipped the dog into his arms. The thing smelled like fancy perfume. The dog glanced up to him with the biggest eyes he'd ever seen on a canine, and son of a bitch, he was a goner. So, he liked the dog? It wasn't that big of a deal.

"Hey there, little miss." He tickled under her chin.

"Little dude," Velma corrected. "He's a boy."

No way.

"His name is Buttercup." Velma practically dared him to say something.

Brek tucked the little guy under his arm like a football. "What'd you come up with so far?"

Velma hesitated and glanced to Sophie, who, for the first time in his presence, went quiet.

"Sophie mentioned the flowers changed to orchids, so she's feeling more of a tropical vibe now." Velma's attempt at cheerful didn't work.

Brek let out a breath through his nose. *Sophie* was two weeks away from her big day at a mountain resort in Estes Park that Aspen had reserved over a year ago. How the hell would they make a log cabin *tropical*? Then again, given Sophie's ability to pitch a fit, it wouldn't shock him if she requested all the pine trees be uprooted at the resort so they could transplant palm trees.

"We're brainstorming ideas." Velma dropped the rings into a bowl.

"Tropical log cabin?" he asked Sophie, using his best you're-a-bride-so-I-have-to-be-nice tone.

"Exactly." Her face brightened. "I *knew* you'd understand."

"Troy?" Brek asked her groom. "You okay with this?"

"Whatever she wants." Troy shrugged and went back to investigating spoons.

"Could you get some of that grass thatch and cover the roof of the cabin? We could hire some of those hula dancers to perform at the reception. Maybe even roast a whole pig? Would your caterer do that?" Sophie was on a roll with ideas. Which would've been great—six months ago.

Brek held in the sigh threatening to spill out. Aspen had booked the band Sophie insisted on last fall, and Eli had spent the last month sourcing the ingredients for her extremely specific menu. "You don't want the swordfish and grass-fed buffalo steaks anymore?"

She shrugged. "Buffalos aren't tropical. Swordfish is still good, though."

He pasted on his best attempt at a placating smile and scratched at his temple.

"It's like Swiss Family Robinson in the mountains?" Velma piped in. "You could keep everything the same, but we have Jase add palm leaves to the table decorations and Eli can have the bartender add umbrellas to all the drinks?"

Sophie's eyes went dreamy. "Champagne with little umbrellas?"

"We could even have a tree house. Everyone could take photos with it. Wouldn't that be fun?" Velma was on a roll again. The kind that went right downhill.

The little dog squirmed in his arm. Yeah, he could relate. "There's no way I can build a tree house that quickly."

"Oh." Velma pressed her teeth into her top lip.

"I think I want a tree house. It couldn't be that hard to

put together. It's just wood." Sophie worked her I'm-going-to-talk-to-daddy-about-this tone.

"Maybe we could just get some estimates. See if it's even possible?" Velma suggested.

Fuck a duck. "I'll see what I can come up with."

On no notice.

"This will be so amazing!" Sophie shrieked a shrill "eeek" sound. Troy grimaced.

Brek officially gave them three months before Troy filed for divorce.

"Why don't you and Troy take a look at tablecloths. Velma and I will talk about the plan?" Brek suggested.

"You're the best, Brek." She snatched Buttercup away from him and made kissy noises at the dog's face. "Isn't he the best?"

"Of course he is." Troy's cell beeped as he spoke. He retrieved it from his pocket and scowled at the screen. Sophie, securely back in in her cocoon of happiness, pulled him behind her across the warehouse.

"Sorry about that." Velma twirled another napkin ring on her finger, this one dark wood with burnt-on initials. "I didn't think about how much work it would make for you."

She slipped off the ring, and, damn, why did every movement she make feel like an erotic invitation to tango naked?

"Major party foul." He growled. "It's a good thing you're pretty."

"Do you want to talk about what happened last night?" She swallowed hard.

Absolutely not. "Nope, but thanks for being here this morning."

She paused. Took a deep breath. "I want to tell you… You're right. I used to have a thing for Dean."

This was not news to him. But it still made his heart shrink.

Her brows furrowed. "I never told anyone. Not even

Claire. So, when they hooked up, what was I supposed to do?"

He did not want to discuss her infatuation with his friend. "I shouldn't have said anything."

"No, you're right to say something. The thing is, I haven't even really thought about Dean. Not since you moved in."

Without breaking the thread of their gaze, he stepped toward her, boxing her in, and dropped his voice low. "That so?"

Her mouth opened slightly. "Yes."

His blue jeans went two-sizes-too-small in the crotch.

"You want to reconsider how things went down last night?" He grinned his best smile. The one he generally reserved for picking up women.

"Your Jedi mind tricks don't have power over me." Her voice faltered.

He chuckled. Once again, her mouth said one thing, but her body betrayed her. "I guess we'll see."

"We should, uh, go help the bride and groom pick out their linens." She pushed at his shoulder to get by.

Fuck, she was cute.

He planted his new motorcycle boots wider. "V, you can keep denying what's going down between us. But we both feel it."

She made an odd noise in the back of her throat. "I like you. But you're my roommate and you're Dean's friend and—"

He cleared the anger from his vocal cords. "So, it still comes back to Dean?"

The world stopped spinning for an instant. Not enough to throw it off its axis but enough to throw him off his.

"No." She shrugged her deflated shoulders. "Yes. I mean, it's complicated." Her face flushed, and she looked away to the porcelain serving bowls.

Apparently, the elaborate options for silverware held

particular appeal to her as well.

His heart skipped several beats. "You said you didn't think about him."

She backed up. Her thighs bumped a frilly tablecloth and rattled the wineglasses. "I don't. I haven't. But you're…you're you."

His throat went uncomfortably thick.

"I mean you're not here permanently. You're leaving soon. And while you're here, we have to cohabitate. We can't risk messing that up."

"You're shitting me."

She stared him down. "I assure you, Brek. I'm not *shitting* you."

He flinched at her choice of words. Cussing didn't fit her. He wanted to shove the dirty word back into her mouth. "He on the fuckin' spreadsheet?"

"Who?"

"Dean," he clipped.

Her shoulders dropped further as she gripped the round table behind her, her knuckles matching the white lace. "He's the reason I started the spreadsheet."

Blood rushed in his temples. Now the universe was just screwing with him. "That so?"

What a clusterfuck.

"Brek!" Sophie squealed from across the warehouse. "I think we've found the linens."

He ground his teeth together. "Be right there."

"I'm sorry about all this." Velma's cheeks flushed. She smoothed her skirt. "You've got clients."

"I'm not giving up on you."

"Brek?" Sophie called again.

"I think we need to be done here." Velma pushed past him, heading across the warehouse to their overbearing bride.

Velma was right about a lot. But she was wrong about this. They were not done. Not even close.

Chapter Nine

After surviving a tedious planning session with Sophie, Brek hopped on his bike. He rolled the tension from his shoulders. He needed a day of open road followed by a night of rock 'n' roll. Unfortunately, he would have a day of cake tasting followed by a night of figuring out how the hell to create a Swiss Family Robinson tree house from swizzle sticks, coffee filters, and Elmer's glue. Okay, there would be lumber involved, and possibly a chain saw. But the whole thing felt like an excercise in futility when Sophie would change her mind again in a week.

Brek stepped inside Jase's flower shop. The metal cowbell Jase used to announce customers clunked heavily against the glass door, and an old Cyndi Lauper song played through the overhead speakers. Two glorious hours before he had to go meet up with Dean and Claire and shop for wedding cake. And he needed a beer.

Jase glanced up from clipping stems using brown-camou-flage-patterned shears.

Eli apparently had the same idea as Brek. He already had his ass planted at Jase's workstation shooting the shit and generally not dealing with the bridal crap that had enveloped Brek's life.

Brek settled onto a stool across the table from Jase.

"Trouble in paradise?" Jase continued working on a vivid pink arrangement.

Brek grunted in reply. "Bride Number Two wants tulips tied to the pews with that tulle stuff. You think you can handle that?"

"That's a negative." Jase pulled on some of the petals on the flower in his hand.

"No. See. I say *the bride wants tulips*. You say *okay*."

"Tulips won't work on the pews. No water. They'll go limper than a dick at the Shady Acres Retirement Home. I could rig up some vases, but she's already over budget."

Shit.

"Tell her to stick with roses," Jase continued. "They'll match her bouquet."

Brek had a feeling that conversation would go about as well as any other conversation he'd had with brides lately.

"I'll talk to her." Not like it would do any good. "You two still coming to the cake tasting this afternoon?"

"Will there be cake?" Jase lifted his hand in a fist bump to Eli.

Eli met it. "There's cake. We're there."

Claire and Dean had asked the entire wedding party to help them pick flavors. Jase was appointed as a groomsman, so he'd gotten the invite. Eli was in charge of the wedding catering, so he'd offered to attend, as well.

"So, Brek. Velma, huh? Serious?" Eli paced to the mini fridge Jase kept near the register and grabbed a beer.

"Not as serious as he'd like," Jase mumbled, fluffing a white bud and slipping it into the vase.

"I see you've been chatting with G.I. Joe over there." Brek snagged the beer from Eli's hand as he walked by, sloshing a bit onto the rim. "Thanks, man."

Eli glowered briefly and went back for another. "Not like you to chase a skirt."

True, generally the skirts chased him. Velma, however, was not a typical skirt. She was a lady.

"She's got an idea of her perfect guy." Brek took a long pull of hops, Rocky Mountain water, and magic.

"Aw, c'mon. With your bone structure and witty personality? How can she resist?" Jase scooted a trash bin against the edge of the table.

"Ma's trying to match her." Brek's index finger tapped a rhythm against the bottle. "Find her a guy who wears fingernail polish."

Jase scraped the pile of flower debris into the trash bin. "Why the hell would she do that?"

"Velma's got a type, apparently." Brek grabbed his beer and stood to pace between the garden art and the potted plants. "And it's not me."

"Well, if you ask me, I say it's better not to get tangled too tightly. Women are like grenades." Jase pointed a finger at him. "They seem fine, sure. But one day, without warning, they'll blow up your house."

Brek sighed.

Eli popped the top off his Coors. "Don't you have somewhere to be? Rock stars to sober up?"

He did. But so far no one had needed bail money. His early morning call to Hans—his assistant manager, and his eyes and ears with the band at the moment—hadn't been returned. He hoped that meant the boys had partied all night, and not that Hans was handling a crisis. "Yes. And yes."

Eli tipped his head to the side like he always did before saying something profound. The guy didn't talk much, but when he did, people generally listened. "I haven't gotten to know Velma well. But in the two seconds we talked, she didn't strike me as a booty call. She's the kind you hand your balls to on a silver platter with a diamond ring."

So, yeah, he was profoundly stupid today.

Brek would keep his balls for himself, but Velma had settled under his skin. He liked her there. Wanted to keep her close. For now.

Besides, there was more than enough time for them to get their kicks. By the wedding, they would both be ready to go their separate ways. She could return to searching for a weenie husband, and he would head back on the road for the Dimefront tour.

He only had to convince her that spending time with him could be a good thing.

"Try flowers," Jase said.

Brek glanced to the bouquet in front of him. "What?"

"You want in her pants. Buy her flowers. Women dig 'em." Jase pointed to his current project. "Not these. They're sold. Other flowers. And ask her nicely."

"You want me to give her a dozen roses and ask her nicely to drop her panties?" Brek's pulse spiked, apparently on board with that idea.

Eli shrugged. "Always works for me."

"This your latest way to drum up business?" Brek asked Jase.

"It works, and everybody wins. I usually start with a bouquet of lilies and ask nicely. Very, *very* nicely. With extra tongue." Jase moved his current creation to one of the walk-in coolers near the cash register.

"No one wants to hear where your tongue's been," Brek replied.

Jase removed an oversized bouquet of large white flowers. "Here."

"What the hell are these?"

"Madonna lilies." Jase laid the flowers on the table.

"Why lilies?"

Jase tied tissue paper with a bow. "Women like 'em. They mean purity."

"Isn't purity the opposite of what I'm goin' for?"

"Reverse psychology." Jase cut the ends of the ribbon and folded the edges of the tissue.

Brek crossed his arms. "You're cracked."

"They're also pretty and they smell nice." Jase lifted them to his nose and inhaled.

"Fine." What the hell. Brek reached for them.

Jase rubbed his index finger and thumb together. Brek sighed and took out his wallet, dropping a hundred-dollar bill near the cash register.

THE WHOLE CAKE shop held the delicious scent of sugary sweets.

"There are a million flavors." Velma glanced from the menu in her hand to the oversized art deco prints that hung on the teal walls. Cupcake-shaped chandeliers dangled from the ceiling over petite white tables throughout the tasting room.

"Five hundred." Brek tapped his finger at the top of the menu where, sure enough, the writing announced *five hundred flavors*.

Velma gestured to several wedding cakes in an array of themes, from whimsical to traditional, decorating the counters along the walls. "How does this work?"

"Bride and groom pick five options before we get here. Maggie brings 'em out. We sample and then support the bride in her poor decision-making when she picks the wrong one."

Brek rested his palm against Velma's bare shoulder.

Brek seemed to like her sleeveless blouse; he had been more touchy-feely than ever. He'd even brought her flowers. Lilies were officially her new favorite.

He rubbed his hand over her elbow with a tender familiarity she wouldn't allow herself to get used to. A trail of goose bumps followed his fingertips, igniting nerve endings throughout her body that had no business perking up in public.

"What are you doing?" She shifted her arm away.

"Warming you up." He continued his exploration by massaging a pressure point at the base of her neck.

She swallowed a moan. "I'm fine."

He raised his eyebrows, clearly not buying her declaration. The pads of his thumbs did things to her muscles that should probably be outlawed.

"We're in public." She didn't need to look down to know her nipples had pebbled beneath her silk blouse. Air conditioning did that to a girl. Also, Brek's hands working their magic. Not a whole lot she could do about either.

"No one's here." Brek's breath whispered against her earlobe.

"Which flavors did they pick?" Velma shrugged off his hands.

He let them drop. "Chocolate, vanilla, lemon drop, coconut cream, and confetti cake."

"Did they really ask for confetti cake for their wedding?" Velma asked.

"Yep." Brek slipped the menu from Velma's fingers and placed it on the counter. "I've got a theory about cake and marriage."

Velma laughed, the sound uncomfortable to her ears. "I bet you're going to tell me all about it."

He shrugged. "You read articles. I have theories."

"What's your theory, then, Mr. Montgomery?" She flipped through a photo album filled with pictures of multi-tiered wedding confections.

"Vanilla? Boring. They'll be divorced within a year," he replied.

Sheesh. His body remained only millimeters from hers.

The scent of him mingled deliciously with the frosting and carbs. She fixed her attention back on the album, shuffling through the pages.

"You still with me?" No touching, but the lack of contact was nearly as erotic as the neck massage.

"Chocolate?" The word was a tad squeaky.

He chuckled. "Passion. The marriage will be filled with it. Kitchen table. Washing machine. Everywhere."

"Like sex *on* the kitchen table?" He couldn't be serious. That was highly unsanitary.

"All. The. Time."

Oh.

"See now, lemon?" he continued. "They'll hit their fiftieth wedding anniversary without issue."

Lemon cake sounded lovely. Respectable. Not at all dirty. Lemon cake would be served at her wedding. Someday. When she found a groom. "And the…uh…confetti cake?"

"Means they're swingers."

The air weighed heavy against her. No way would her sister pick a swinger cake. "What about coconut cream?"

He scratched at the back of his neck. "Infection. Avoid that one."

A laugh rattled her chest. She held the back of her hand to her lips.

His expression gentled. "Good to see you laugh, V."

She fiddled with a plastic edge of the photo album.

His phone chimed. He glanced to the screen. "I've gotta take this."

He strode outside, stopped at the picture window, and leaned against one of the pillars.

"You must be Velma?" a woman asked, hustling from the back room. She held a tray of cupcakes and set it down at a table near Velma.

Velma looked from Brek to the young, petite redhead with striking green eyes. "Yes. Hello."

"I'm Maggie. Brek said you'd be helping him out today. I understand you're the maid of honor?"

"That's me." Velma scooted the chairs out of the way as Maggie pushed two tables together.

"Hey, Maggie." Brek reentered the room and tucked his phone into the pocket of his jeans. He dropped an air kiss on Maggie's cheek.

An unreasonable sting of jealousy settled in the center of Velma's chest.

"Brek." Maggie's eyes sparkled. "Always good to see you. Everything's set. Let me know when your couple arrives. I've got a few projects in the back I need to wrap up. Nice to meet you, Velma."

"You, too," Velma replied, refusing to further acknowledge the possessive streak that had come over her.

Brek stared at the screen on his phone. His expression had gone tight.

"Everything okay?" Velma asked.

"Band problems." He thumbed through his contacts.

"Anything I can do to help?"

"Not unless you can figure out why my drummer wants to sell his drum set and move to Belgium. Or my lead singer wants to try out for a Food Network cooking show when we've got a tour starting soon. I knew things were too quiet. They need to be practicing and relaxing. Not threatening to jump ship."

That was bad. "What are you gonna do?"

Brek cursed inventively under his breath. "I have no idea."

"I am here for cake." Jase's announcement boomed through the little shop.

Eli stood beside him at the doorway. "Let's do this."

Where were Claire and Dean? Velma glanced to the parking lot. "We should probably wait for the bride and groom."

"Alternatively, we could pick their flavor for them. Save them the trouble." Jase sat at the table, apparently ready for his cake.

"They're here." Brek strode to the door and held it open for them.

Claire, Heather, their mom and dad, and Dean all hit the cake shop, ready for sugar.

SO FAR, Claire preferred the coconut cake and Dean liked the vanilla. The motley crew of helpers sat around a table at Maggie's bakery, helping Dean and Claire pick their final choices.

Brek didn't seem to have an opinion, as long as they said, "I do."

"Maybe we could do two tiers of each?" Claire suggested, wiping a stray smear of frosting from Dean's lips with her thumb.

"As long as there's vanilla, I don't care." Dean kissed the pad of Claire's thumb.

Velma never would've pegged Dean as a vanilla guy— more of a vanilla with a chocolate swirl guy.

Dean whispered something to Claire. She grinned.

Velma looked away. That was what she wanted—someone to kiss the pad of her thumb when they ate cake. And smile at her the way Dean smiled at Claire. And whisper things that made her smile.

"Don't you think vanilla's a little dull for a wedding cake?" Velma's mother asked as though she'd read Velma's mind. "I mean, it's your *wedding*. The cake should exemplify all you are as a couple."

"That is a lot of responsibility to put on a cake, Mom." Velma flipped through the flavor menu. Perhaps they'd just narrowed their choices too far. Cookies 'n' cream looked yummy.

Dean helped himself to another sample. "Vanilla's not dull when it's done right."

Oh.

Well, lucky Claire.

Velma tossed Brek a look. He was holding back a laugh.

She held the menu for him to see and whispered, "I like the cookies one. What do you suppose that means?"

Brek's breath whispered across her cheek. "Whatever you think it does."

She shivered.

"Tell Eli about your work, Velvet," Dad said around a bite of confetti cake. "He's a chef, did you know that?"

"I did, his artichoke dip is really good."

"Ah, so you've had his dip. That's lovely." Her mother looked between Eli and Velma and gave her dad a knowing look.

"Velvet is a financial planner. Isn't that right, sweetheart?" Her father was ready to lay it on thick, she could feel it.

"No one wants to hear about me. Today's about cake." She lifted her fork. "Yum!"

"Nonsense." Her father wrapped an arm over her mother's shoulder. "We couldn't be prouder of both our girls. Velvet's made a name for herself in Denver. Works with all the high-up mucky-mucks and all that. All the big names. She handles their accounts. Don't you, dear?"

"You're embarrassing her, Walter." Mom loaded Dad's plate with another sample of the sprinkle-filled confection. "Have more confetti cake."

"Oh yes. That one's my favorite." He shoveled it into his mouth like a man who hadn't had cake in a decade. Which, Velma knew, given his sweet tooth, was not true.

"I thought you liked the lemon one?" She didn't want to

think about her parents being into confetti cake. She glared at Brek. This innuendo was all his fault, putting thoughts of what cake might mean in her head.

"Not a fan of lemon." Her father hadn't touched the lemon sample Maggie had added to his plate. "You'll really like our Velvet, Eli. She's quite the catch. Doesn't ask for anything. Always self-sufficient. She put herself though school, got herself a mortgage. Now, Claire. That's another story."

Gah. Her father had to stop. Claire had enjoyed her twenties, and her parents hadn't let her live it down.

"We're just pleased as punch she's found Dean so she'll settle down—"

"Dad," Velma said, lowering her voice in warning.

"Walter. Knock it off." Velma's mother poked at her samples with a fork.

"Velma's funny, too," Brek added. "And she can cook."

Aw. He thought she was funny?

"Indeed." Her father beamed. "Indeed. Indeed."

"You two aren't shoving cake in each other's faces, are you?" Velma's mother asked the bride and groom.

No, of course they weren't. This was Dean and Claire.

"Isn't that the point of getting married?" Brek asked.

Velma kicked his leg under the table. "They're not doing the cake thing."

"Claire is in charge of the shoving of the cake. If she wants to do it, I'll play along." Dean was totally serious. "Do you think Maggie could make purple vanilla cake?"

"I bet she could. I wonder what that might mean, though? Hmm." Velma pinched her lips together.

"I think I've created a monster." Brek ran his boot gently over her calf.

Crud. That felt nice.

She absolutely would not consider how nice it felt.

Like their kiss.
He caught her gaze. The moment stalled.
And she refused to let the feelings inside sink her.

Chapter Ten

Brek had crazy-ass rockers to manage, but first he had to deal with weddings. The first wedding. Sophie's wedding. He'd built a fucking tree house for her. Well, he'd helped build the damn thing.

They'd transformed the outside of the Estes Park Community Church into a bridal venue that would make Aspen proud. He snapped a final picture and texted it to his sister. Maybe that would keep her off his case during the final prep.

The inside of the chapel wasn't big enough for Sophie's guests, so they set up a chapel outside with taffeta-covered fancy bamboo chairs, the makeshift tree house, and a pergola for the vows. Jase had decked everything out with the orchids-from-hell. The fact that Brek could now distinguish taffeta from silk and orchids from dahlias was a testament to the vise grip these brides had on his balls.

Velma trotted around the corner of the church with a cardboard box filled with chocolates. The dog-slash-ring-bearer trotted beside her in his miniature tuxedo.

Brek had her on dog babysitting and goldfish centerpiece duty. Also, hanging-around-to-keep-him-sane duty.

She'd found a source for goldfish centerpieces and Skittles for the champagne glasses. How her guy had both, Brek wasn't gonna ask. Some things were better left unknown.

"The chocolates have arrived." Velma set the box down on one of the chairs. Hands on hips, she took in the scene. "You did good."

"Thanks." He took the leash from her. The dog yapped and did a whole body shake in his tux. The damn thing couldn't be comfortable, especially in this heat.

Aspen had told him to wear a tux. He'd told her hell-to-the-no. The best she was gonna get was black jeans and a collared shirt.

Velma's getup matched his—black pencil skirt, white tank top thing, and one of her perpetual sweaters to match. Sweaters in the summer made no fuckin' sense to him, even if they were thin. Then again, if she wore the thin sweater without the tank top underneath, he could be 100 percent on board with that fashion trend.

Velma cleared her throat.

He glanced up from her chest and his daydreams about sweaters.

"Check it out. Aspen gave us these headset radio things. Isn't that fun?" She held up a set of the two-way radios that clipped on the ear. He used something similar at concerts to talk to roadies and keep tabs on band members.

"What's next?" Velma placed the headset in the box with the candy.

"You got the pearls?"

Sophie had been abundantly clear about the importance of the pearl necklace. It had belonged to some long-lost aunt, and apparently the happiness of the marriage hinged on her wearing them when Troy tossed his life into the Dumpster and promised her forever.

Velma grabbed the sleek wooden necklace case from the box of individually packaged truffles and handed it over.

He shoved the case into his back pocket. "Chocolates go on the chairs for the guests."

"Here?" Velma asked.

"Aspen said chocolates go on the chairs for the guests. These are chairs. Those are chocolates." One plus one equaled two.

Velma didn't look convinced. "Do you think maybe she meant the reception chairs?"

"No." He was mostly sure. Guests got chocolate before the wedding while they waited. Yep, that made sense. "Then we've gotta head over to the reception hall. Make sure everything's done. Then we've gotta pray Troy doesn't bail at the last minute." He started unloading the foil-wrapped truffles Sophie had picked out. "You check on Sophie?"

"I did. She's getting her hair and nails done in the choir room." Velma took a handful of the chocolates and laid them out on the chairs. He followed suit along the next row.

"V?"

"Yeah?"

"Thank you. For all you've done to help me." He stared at her a long moment, his gratitude a very real thing.

Velma went still, her expression gentled. "You're welcome."

His phone buzzed in his pocket. He tugged it out.

Aspen.

"You're not supposed to be calling me," he said into the mouthpiece.

"The venue looks great. Did you check on Sophie?" Aspen asked. He could hear her clicking away on her laptop in the background.

"Velma did." He held the phone against his cheek while he continued tossing truffles on chairs.

"And Troy, somebody check on him?"

"He'll be here later. I took him coffee earlier." As Aspen had insisted in her ten-page list of the things-that-must-happen-at-this-wedding. "Bachelor party was epic, but he's not trashed anymore."

"You have eye drops in case his eyes are still red?" Aspen was all business.

"No. His eyes are red? That's his problem. He can be a normal person and wear sunglasses." Brek was a wedding planner today, not a frickin' babysitter.

"Absolutely not. That'll wreck the photos. If his eyes are red, that's *your* problem. He can't have red eyes for pictures. Send someone for drops."

"Hey V." Brek held the phone away from his mouth. "We have to run and get Troy pussy-ass eye drops. Aspen says he can't wear sunglasses like a normal pers—"

"Don't say 'pussy,'" Aspen cut him off. "Don't say 'fuck.' Don't say 'shit.' You're in a church."

"I'm outside of the church." Therefore, cussing was still fair game.

"Technicality. You got the stuff I told you to pick up? Tylenol. Granola bars. Sewing kit. All that?"

No, he did not. She'd sent him a ridiculous list of things—including a shower cap, a variety of Band-Aids, and double-sided tape. These were adults who could take care of themselves. They didn't need him passing out headache tablets and Hello Kitty bandages—that had been one of the specifics on her list. "Everything's handled."

"Let me talk to Velma," Aspen insisted.

Gladly. "V, Aspen wants you."

He handed the phone over. Velma straightened one of the chocolate boxes so it was perfectly centered. Buttercup ran around her heels as if chasing an imaginary moth.

"Hey, Aspen." Velma frowned. "I don't think so. Hang on." She put her palm over the mouthpiece. "Did you get the stuff Aspen asked you to get?"

"Tell her it's handled." He didn't need Aspen's heat added to the day. The temperature was already well into the nineties.

"But did you get it?" Velma pushed.

"Tell her it's handled," he said again.

"I'm pretty sure he didn't get it." Velma flinched at whatever Aspen said in reply. "I'll work on it... Okay... Sure... I can't do that to your brother... Then I'd have to touch it... I'm not touching it..."

Velma hung up. "Jacob came home. Aspen had to go. You should turn off your phone and stop answering."

He tossed a box on the next chair. "If I stop answering, she'll panic, pull her ass outta bed, drive over here, and then Ma will be pissed at me because she's not in bed. Jacob will be pissed at me because she's not in bed, and I'll be pissed at her because she's not in bed. So, I keep answering her calls and everyone's only minimally annoyed."

"Mr. Montgomery." The mother of the bride's nasally voice was hard to miss.

He turned.

Mrs. Winthrop had enough work done on her face to age her down at least twenty years. He knew her type before she set foot on the grass in her red custom Versace gown that came with an honest-as-fuck cape.

"Be a dear and get me an aspirin. I have a killer headache." She sat and draped herself on one of the chairs.

Velma raised an eyebrow at him. She needed to stop turning him on with her facial expressions when he was in the midst of the wedding of the century without any aspirin for the mother of the bride.

"I have something in my purse. Hang on." Velma gave him a pointed glance and strutted toward the building.

So, they'd make a pit stop and get everything on Aspen's ridiculous list. Point made. Although he had no idea why anyone might need a shower cap at a wedding.

"Coming, dear." Mrs. Winthrop stood and followed Velma.

He finished placing the chocolate in his hand, glanced up,

and…shit-fucking-son-of-a-bitch. The woman had sat on one of the chocolates. And by the look of how her ass was covered, apparently the chocolates had melted. Aspen thought the truffles would withstand the heat. She was wrong.

His heart stopped. Just quit. Boom. No more beating.

When the lighting at a show wasn't just right, his drummer could toss a tantrum better than anyone he'd ever known. When the guitar pick wasn't the right shade of blue, his bass player had a tendency to lose his mind. Put the whole band together? The energy that made their music top the charts was the same energy that made their fights turn into full-on brawls. But he had a feeling the fit Mrs. Winthrop was about to throw would top anything his boys could've imagined.

And she was headed for Velma.

He grabbed the dog's leash and hightailed it to the door. Buttercup kept up beside him.

Then the scream. The scream that made his blood clot on impact. He yanked open the door and saw that Velma had spilled aspirin all over the Berber carpet tiles in the foyer.

If fury had a color, it would've been the shade of Mrs. Winthrop's face in that moment—mottled red with splotches of pink, white, and even orange. "My dress."

Little white pills crunched under his boots. "Mrs. Winthrop, it's gonna be fine. We can fix this."

How? He had no idea. Nothing would fix this.

The woman's mouth opened and closed like one of the goldfish Velma had gotten for the tablescapes.

Velma's eyes were massive round orbs. "The chocolate melted."

Yeah, he'd gotten that. He snatched up the dog and set him on a nearby table to keep him out of the painkillers. He tossed the necklace box next to Buttercup and started unbuttoning his shirt.

"Okay, here's what we're gonna do." He pulled his arms out of the sleeves.

Mrs. Winthrop sucked in a breath.

He didn't think it was possible, but Velma's eyes got bigger. "What are you doing?" she demanded.

He shoved his shirt to her. "Go take off your clothes."

Mrs. Winthrop puffed up like a peacock. "Mr. Montgomery. I don't know what you're getting at here—"

"Velma's gonna give you her clothes. She's gonna put on my shirt. I'm going to take your dress to get the chocolate out." *Was he the only coherent one of the bunch?*

He was the one standing there with no shirt, but he had a plan. Still, the women didn't move.

"I didn't sign up for this." Velma crossed her arms.

"Excuse us." He nodded to Mrs. Winthrop and scooted Velma to the side.

"Look. This lady has the power to ruin Aspen's business, and she's got melted chocolate all over her ass. I need you—I'm asking you—to let her borrow your clothes for thirty minutes while I figure out how the hell to get it out."

Velma pursed her lips and glared at him.

"Please." He wasn't above begging at this point.

"Fine." Shirt in hand, she marched toward the bathroom.

He let out a relieved breath and dialed Eli. Eli was at the reception hall kitchen, and Brek needed a favor.

"Hey," Eli said.

Brek stared at the bathroom door, listening to his heart try to beat out of his chest, waiting for Velma. "Need a favor."

"I have three hundred steaks we're prepping. So now's not a good time." There was a decent amount of pan clanking and activity in the background.

"Need you to run somewhere and grab me a shirt. I saw a tourist shop on the way into town."

There was a long pause.

"Three hundred steaks," Eli said again.

Brek was cutting it short before, but now he was running out of time. "I need to preempt the steaks and call in a favor."

"Why do you need a shirt?" Eli was not grasping the intensity of the situation.

"Don't ask. How quick can you grab me something?" He glanced down to his bare chest. Aspen would lose her ever-loving mind if she saw him here without his shirt.

"I'm the caterer not your personal assistant."

Enough was enough. "Remember that time you got your ass tossed in jail, and I bailed you out? Callin' in that favor."

Eli heaved a sigh. "Fine. The shirt for you?"

"Yeah. See if they have a dress or somethin' for Velma, too."

"What the hell is going on over there?"

"Said not to ask. See you in ten."

He clicked off his phone and turned his attention back to the bathroom door. Velma came out with a stack of neatly folded clothes. His shirt barely skimmed past her thighs. The air in the room buzzed in his ears and his mouth went dry.

He may have had a pissed-off mother of the bride. He may have had a ticked-off Velma. Hell, even the dog was probably mad at him for something. But the way Velma looked in his shirt? None of the rest mattered.

"Give me your belt." She set her clothes down and held out her hand.

"Why?"

"Because I'm giving my clothes to someone for you, and I'm wearing your shirt that barely covers my tush. I need your belt." She made a gimme wave with her fingers.

He pulled the damn thing off. What did it matter at this point, anyway?

She took the belt and tied it around her waist. "Now at least it sort of passes for a dress."

She was right, if one squinted and turned their head to the side.

"Eli's on his way." He snagged her outfit. "He's bringing us clothes."

"I *have* clothes. You're just giving them away."

Fair point. He tossed his phone to her. "Look up how to get chocolate out of designer dresses."

She tilted her head to the side and pretended to be Brek while doing a nearly perfect impression of his sister. "Hey, Velma? Would you be a dear and help me out yet again? I know you're barely wearing any clothes because I didn't listen to my sister and pack a wedding planner bag, but would you mind looking something up for me?"

Clothes tucked under his arm, he moved toward her, settling his hands on her shoulders. "Thank you, V, for rolling with this. I owe you. And I'm going to make this whole day up to you."

"See how much nicer that was? You know what I'm going to do for you? I'm going to figure out how to get chocolate out of satin." She started scrolling through the Internet on his phone.

He wanted to kiss her—full on the mouth, with tongue, everything, but he also didn't particularly want to be nutted, so he only squeezed her shoulders. "Thank you."

Velma started her search. Mrs. Winthrop changed and left her gown with him.

"It says we should take the dress to the dry cleaner." Velma sauntered into the foyer, still swiping through the pages on his phone.

"There's no time." A handful of tissues in hand, he poked at the chocolate.

It smeared, doubling the size.

"See, I think that's why Google wanted us to take it to a dry cleaner." She was lucky she looked hot in that getup. "Maybe get the tissues wet?"

He grabbed a vase of flowers, chucked the orchids, and

drenched another handful of tissues. Using more force than probably necessary, he scrubbed at the chocolate again. The mess smeared more, this time leaving a wet ring around the edges.

"Fuck." Wiping only made it worse.

"What if we run it under a faucet?" Velma asked. "Hot water might work better than plant-food-infused water?"

"Good idea."

They headed for the bathroom.

Buttercup made what could only be described as a gagging noise behind him. He turned. The dog had chewed through the box and attacked the pearl necklace. Beads were strewn on the table and fell to the floor among the little white pills.

No. This day was unraveling faster than he could keep up with.

"Oh my gosh." Velma rushed to Buttercup and pried open his mouth. "I think there's one in there."

Buttercup coughed and gasped. Brek threw the dress on the table and grabbed the little dude, holding him against his chest. The dog coughed again.

Brek's whole body went numb and the energy in the room pulsed. He'd never had official CPR training, but he knew the basics of what he was supposed to do on a human. A canine couldn't be that different. He put his fingers under Buttercup's ribs, doing his best attempt at the Heimlich maneuver on a teacup poodle.

Buttercup gagged some more.

"Maybe stick your fingers in there and see if you can grab it?" Velma sounded as panicked as he felt.

"That's not what you do when someone's choking." He continued with little thrusts on Buttercup's chest.

"He needs oxygen." Velma's voice was getting higher and higher.

Normally, Brek wouldn't consider giving mouth-to-mouth

to a canine, but today his boundaries had gone to shit. One more try. "C'mon, little dude."

Another thrust and the dog did a gag-cough combo. He vomited kibble and three heirloom pearls all over Mrs. Winthrop's dress.

"What in the actual hell?" Eli asked from the doorway. A plastic grocery sack that read *Thank You* on repeat across the front hung from his hand.

Funny how as life was fucking you, you noticed the little details.

Buttercup licked Brek's chin in apparent thanks for saving his life.

"Now that's gonna need dry cleaning," Velma said on a gasp from behind her fingertips.

Brek ran a hand over his face. "You at least bring us clothes?"

"Yes. Yes, I did. The tourist shop I found had a limited inventory, but I managed to get something for each of you." He held up a nightgown with the words *Colorado: The Altitude Isn't the Only Thing High* written across the chest and a T-shirt that read *Colorado's Okayest Tourist* over an outline of the state.

"I'm not wearing that," Velma announced.

"Brek, we've got an issue." Jase maneuvered through the door and paused, glancing from Eli's ridiculous tourist apparel, to Brek without a shirt, to the ruined dress, to Velma's thighs. "I can come back later."

"Just say it." Might as well get it all over with at once.

"The goldfish aren't making it. Not all of them, anyway."

Say what?

"I'm not sure where you got them, but they're like geriatric goldfish. We've got quite a few floaters."

Brek glared at Velma. "Where'd you get the fish, V?"

"From a guy a lady at work knows about. He gave us a great deal."

Brek closed his eyes and took a few deep breaths. This wasn't happening. This whole day wasn't happening.

"How many goldfish do we have per table? Can't you just go back and redistribute them?"

Jase shrugged. "They'll be uneven."

"Does that look like the biggest issue we have today?" Brek gestured around the room.

"Point made. I'll see what I can do." Jase took a look at the Versace gown. "What'd you do to the dress?"

"Mrs. Winthrop is coming." Velma snatched up the damn thing and shoved it behind a potted plant. She positioned herself in front of it and crossed her arms.

She looked like a bride who'd gotten caught doing the dirty with the best man.

"Mr. Montgomery." Mrs. Winthrop was red in the face and huffing and puffing as she hurried toward them. "Sophie's missing. She's not with her bridesmaids. No one can reach her."

His heart jumped clear up to his collarbone. His sister was gonna kill him.

The phone in his back pocket buzzed. He tugged it out and glanced at the screen.

Aspen.

Chapter Eleven

"Velma?" Brek's voice echoed through the headset.

"Still here." Velma pushed behind a rack of choir robes in her search through the Estes Park Community Church. Sheesh, the place wasn't huge. How had they managed to misplace the bride in a building this small?

"Did you check the pastor's office?" The sharp concern in his voice exposed his nerves.

"That's where I am. She's not under the choir robes. Are you sure she didn't leave?" Velma adjusted the belt on her makeshift dress. She'd added the ridiculous nightgown Eli had brought her underneath Brek's shirt, so at least it fell above her knee and didn't threaten to show the world her underwear when she bent over.

"Valet's on alert. No way she could've gone that way, and Jase is standing guard at the back door." Brek sounded out of breath.

The window creaked open. A small thread of lace flew from the hinge.

Velma clicked her talk button. "I've got a lead. Stand by."

"I'll be right there—" Brek continued speaking, but Velma

pulled off the earpiece so it dangled at her shoulder. She climbed onto the bench in front of the window to search outside. Sure enough, a trail of beads and pieces of lace led across the pine needles through the evergreens. Crud-ola. A runaway bride.

She blew out a long breath. Brek would lose his ever-loving mind.

He had been on edge since the chocolate fiasco. The Buttercup incident had threatened to push him over. But the last hour since Sophie's disappearing act? He'd been a total basket case. He'd held it together, but with each second that passed, he moved closer to tumbling over the precipice of his temper.

Well, Velma didn't have much of a choice. Heaving a breath, she wrenched her body over the windowsill—one leg, then the other. Her balance precarious, she kicked her low-heeled pumps below, said a prayer, and jumped unceremoniously the six feet to the ground.

She slipped on her shoes. Her headset crackled against her shoulder. She ignored it. Best she find Sophie and get her bum down the aisle before Brek went bananas.

Stiletto footprints led to a clearing where Velma discovered the white silk Louboutins abandoned. Carefully, she picked them up and wiped dirt from the heel. The dang things, which retailed for over a thousand dollars—half Velma's mortgage, for goodness' sake—were tossed aside because a bride had short-circuited in the eleventh hour.

She hurried around the building, following the tracks Sophie had left in the soft dirt. Mountain air wasn't generally this hot in the summer. Today was the exception. Brek had been certain Sophie wouldn't leave the building—not decked out in a ten-thousand-dollar wedding gown. Apparently, Sophie had other ideas.

Velma held the headset microphone to her lips. "Brek?"

"Do you have her?"

"She's outside. I'm not sure where. Looks like she went toward the road. You go north, I'll head south."

Brek cursed a slew of colorful words. Velma dropped the headset to her shoulder again and trudged forward, moving aside branches and calling Sophie's name.

"Sophie," she called again, her voice scratchy from all the hollering.

Velma paused for a moment to catch her breath. She glanced around. Nothing but an older white house across the road. Sophie couldn't have gotten far with bare feet. Velma pulled the headset on and pressed the button. More nothing. Apparently, Brek had trekked past the limit of reception. Fantastic. She hurried to the tree house Brek had built near the ceremony arch. A distinct sniffle came from inside.

"Excuse me," she called. "I'm looking for a bride. Have you seen her?"

Silence.

Louboutins in hand, Velma carefully climbed the boards nailed to the tree as footholds.

"Sophie?" she asked as she came through the opening to the primitive tree shack. The place was beyond cramped. Sophie had squeezed herself into the corner, a half-full bottle of sauvignon blanc in hand. She'd dropped the designer shoes but kept the wine? Sophie definitely had her priorities mixed up.

"May I join you?" Velma didn't wait for an answer as she heaved herself into the tight space.

Tears trailed down Sophie's cheeks, smearing her meticulously applied eyeliner and blush. First thing when they got back to the church, Velma would grab the makeup artist. Hopefully she had something in her bag of tricks for red eyes and tear-stained cheeks.

"This is cozy." Velma squeezed next to Sophie.

Sophie offered her the wine, and Velma took it, setting it aside with the shoes.

"Everyone's really worried about you." Velma adjusted her legs beneath her.

Sophie doodled a fingertip along the beads of her dress. "I'm making a mistake."

Considering the two of them were shoved into a tree house while several hundred guests anxiously waited for their pineapple-topped steak dinners, Velma agreed with Sophie's assertion.

"You told me you love Troy when we were picking tablescapes." A trickle of perspiration dripped down the center of Velma's back. "You love him. He loves you. That's what today is about."

"It's not about love. It's about Dad showing off to his friends. It's about Troy being inducted into their boy's club. I wrote him a note and went to slip it under his door at the church." Sophie hiccupped and handed the crumpled piece of paper to Velma. Velma unfolded it and smoothed the crinkles—a love note that was absolutely none of her business. "Do you know what he said?"

Velma handed it back, but Sophie shook her head. "He and Dad were talking behind the door. They didn't know I heard them. Dad told Troy once the marriage certificate is signed, then he'll have paperwork ready to make him a full partner." Sophie paused. A new onslaught of tears slid from her eyelids. "That's why Troy's marrying me. Not because he loves me. He's marrying me so he can be a partner."

That explained so much.

Velma tucked the note into her pocket.

"Have you ever been married?" Sophie asked.

Velma shook her head. "No."

"Engaged?" Sophie continued.

"Nope. I'm holding out." *For a man like the one who got away —straight into the arms of my sister.* "There was someone once, though."

"What happened?"

Dull pain settled under Velma's ribs. "Turned out he was really into my sister."

Sophie slumped against the wooden wall. "Do you think any of them are good?"

Velma's mind drifted to Brek. "I think so."

"What do I do?"

Velma was definitely not the one to be dishing out relationship advice. "Do you love Troy?"

"I thought I did. Now, I'm not sure."

"When you have that thing that makes you want to be with someone, I think you act on it." Velma brushed away a sticky thought of what that might mean for her in regard to Brek.

"But how do you know if you really love them?"

Velma shrugged, the knot in her stomach tightening. "I guess if you have to ask, then the question's already answered."

"I think I fell in love with the wedding." A sliver of light traced its way across Sophie's tear-stained face. "I spent months worrying what our guests would want to eat and drink, and I don't even know how Troy likes his steak cooked."

"What?"

Sophie's chin trembled. "We're having steak at the reception, and I'm supposed to marry a man when I don't know how he likes his steak? What if he likes them well done, and I only like medium well?"

"Then I suppose you'd compromise," Velma replied.

"What if I don't want to compromise?" Sophie asked, her words serious.

"Then I guess your decision is made, you know?"

"Velma? Sophie?" Brek's panicked voice sliced through the stifling air.

Velma leaned over the opening. "Up here. I found her."

"I'm coming up," Brek replied immediately.

"There's no room." Velma shook her head. "Give us a minute."

"I'm ready. I know what I have to do." Sophie stood as best as she could in the cramped quarters.

"We're coming down." Velma extended her hand to Sophie.

Sophie squeezed her hand. "Thank you for listening."

"You go down first." Velma helped Sophie adjust her dress so she could climb down the steps before gathering the shoes and the wine.

Sophie cleared the opening and Velma checked to ensure she made it down all right.

"On my way," Velma hollered. She dropped the shoes. Bottle of wine gripped in one hand, she carefully stepped down the makeshift ladder.

Brek met her at the bottom and took the wine with raised eyebrows.

Velma shook pine needles from her sleeves. "Don't ask."

"Let's head back for the ceremony." Brek herded them toward the church.

"No." Sophie stopped midstride. "Like Velma said, if I have to ask if I love Troy, then the question's already answered."

Velma's pulse stopped beating for three solid seconds.

"That's what Velma said?" Brek's glare lanced straight through Velma.

"That's not what I meant. I meant for me. Not for you." Velma looked to Sophie and hurried to correct herself.

"What you said makes loads of sense. I can't marry Troy. I'm sorry. I'll be the one to tell him." Sophie wiped her eyes with the back of her hand, smearing mascara across her temples. She reached for her shoes, slipped them on, and headed for the church.

Brek turned on Velma. "You told her if she has to ask, then she doesn't love her fiancé?"

A sinking feeling settled in Velma's stomach. "Not exactly like that, no."

"It's their wedding day. She's stressed and confused. How could you add to that?"

"She misunderstood—"

He held up a hand. "You're done."

His words weren't harsh. They were spoken calmly, but with such a certainty that Velma's heart ached. "Brek…"

"I've got to figure out how to salvage this." He shook his head and walked away.

BREK TOOK in the remains of the chaos that had ensued after Sophie's declaration that she wasn't getting married. He wanted to throttle Velma's pretty little neck. He wouldn't, because he was wrapped around her beautiful little finger.

Sophie and Troy sequestered themselves in the pastor's office to talk. Troy's perfect exterior cracked when Sophie told him she wasn't his bride anymore. Brek felt for the guy. Sophie was wrong. Troy did care.

On damage control, Brek sent the guests to the reception to eat hundred-dollar steaks instead of waiting for a wedding that wasn't gonna happen. Jase dismantled the orchid archway where the vows were supposed to take place, and Brek waited for Sophie and Troy with the parents of both the bride and groom. He arranged for cars to take them wherever they wanted to go once they finished.

"Sophie is taking some time." Hands in his pockets, Troy moved along the aisle to where the parents waited. "I saw her to one of the cars. Thanks for arranging that." He nodded to Brek.

Brek rose from the chair and moved to Troy's side. "Really sorry, man."

Troy swallowed forcefully. "I didn't realize she was so

unhappy. I'll go to the reception. Tell everyone the wedding's off."

He left with his parents. Brek moved to the altar to touch base with Jase about the teardown before heading to the reception hall himself.

"It wasn't her fault." Jase climbed down the ladder to stand with Brek.

"Sophie?"

"Velma." Jase replied. "I know you're blaming her for telling it like it is, but you're wrong."

Velma hadn't intended sabotage. Still sucked she had talked to Sophie without him.

"Are you quoting bad rock lyrics to me again?"

"No, sir. That is a Jase Dvornakov original." Jase taped a box of flowers closed. "Sophie would've walked no matter what. Saw it in her eyes when she couldn't pick the flowers. Your girl's taking it hard, though. Thinks you blame her for Sophie walking away. You should go ahead and make that right."

"When did you become my conscience?"

"Fourth grade, when you looked up Catherine Bracken's skirt on the playground, and I told you not to be a perv." Jase went back to boxing up another large batch of orchids.

"Like you never looked up Catherine's skirt," Brek huffed.

"Never got caught," Jase replied.

Brek headed for the door. He had amends to make with a certain blonde.

Sophie's pissed-off parents stood cross-armed in the foyer. Mr. Winthrop wore a tailored tuxedo Brek estimated cost around five thousand dollars. Maybe more. Mrs. Winthrop still wore Velma's clothes.

"Mr. and Mrs. Winthrop." Brek cleared his suddenly thick throat.

He'd nearly asked, *How are you?* But that didn't seem like the best idea at the moment.

"May I ask a question?" Mr. Winthrop had the same edge to his voice that guy on that legal show got when he interrogated someone on the witness stand.

"Absolutely." The tension in Brek's shoulder blades strung tight.

"Do you handle all of your engagements with such an exemplary disregard of decorum?" The fury in his expression countered the saccharine-laced tone of his words as Mr. Winthrop sauntered forward.

Shit fucked as it was, these people held the connections keeping Montgomery Events afloat. Brek squared his stance. "I'm sorry the day went sideways."

Apologize. That was a good start.

"No. You're not sorry." Mr. Winthrop had to look up to meet Brek's stare. Sometimes height had its advantages. Like, when one needed to reach something off the top of the refrigerator, or when a pompous prick with too much extra spending money had to stretch his neck to make eye contact.

Winthrop never blinked. "I expect there will be a refund."

Brek steadied his deteriorating nerves. "There's time to discuss all of that once the final numbers come in."

"Nothing to discuss. Services were not rendered, due to the willful disruption of this wedding by your staff." Winthrop hooked his thumbs at his belt, elbows wide.

"Sir, with respect, your daughter took off before any of our staff talked to her." Brek held up his hands. He did not want to argue with this guy. "We'll go over it all once things have settled."

"I'm very disappointed in how this day has turned out. I'm certain you understand there are consequences to actions of this sort. Be prepared for them." With that, Winthrop headed out the doors to his waiting limousine like the goddamned King of Screw You, his wife on his heels. The only thing missing was her cape.

Well, shit. The guy had no power over Brek, but he and

his wife could make business impossible for Aspen. And fuck if Brek would let that happen on his watch.

The reception hall was only about five minutes away. He made his way through the packed parking lot and the somber banquet room. Velma stood in the hallway near the kitchen, holding a clipboard against her chest and carrying on a conversation with Troy.

"Hey, V," Brek said as he got closer.

She looked at him, her eyes void of emotion. "Hi. I, uh, had the bartender put away the champagne, and he said he will give a refund on the other unopened drinks. The guy who runs the hall understood our situation and said he'll give a partial refund, as well. That'll at least take care of some of the costs."

Troy dropped his shoulders. "I'll head off now. Sounds like you've got everything under control."

"Yeah," Brek replied. Even though he had nothing under control. "We'll handle it."

"Troy?" Velma pulled a crumpled note from her pocket and handed it to him. "Sophie gave this to me. It's addressed to you. Given everything, she'd still want you to have it."

Troy took the paper and stared blankly. He stuffed it in the pocket of his tuxedo jacket without glancing at the words. "Thanks."

"There's an exit that way," Velma suggested.

Troy nodded and slipped out through the kitchen.

Velma pinched her bottom lip under her teeth. Brek's lungs squeezed tight. Velma hadn't said anything that shouldn't have been said. Sophie would've left anyway, with or without their conversation.

"I haven't talked to the band about money. I figured that was your department. But I asked them not to play right now. Not until you gave them direction." Velma paused. "I'm so sorry, Brek."

Brek tucked a stray hair behind her ear, his fingertips

lingering there. "I'm sorry I blamed you for Sophie. Wasn't fair. Wasn't right."

She slumped to one of the benches lining the hallway. "I screwed up."

"Not our place to force someone to get married. She walked out long before your conversation. I'll talk to Aspen about everything. She wouldn't have pushed Sophie, either."

Velma hugged the clipboard close. "They picked cheese-cake. What do you think that means?"

"That they'd never make it down the aisle, apparently."

"Sophie worried she'd be making a huge mistake by marrying Troy."

Velma hit him with those gray eyes of hers, and his pulse stumbled over itself.

"I understand the whole not-making-mistakes thing," she continued.

"What mistakes have you made, V?"

"I have a professional knack for dating horrible men." The back of her head dropped against the wall.

"That's because you want them to paint their fingernails." Brek laid his hand across the back of the bench and leaned in.

Velma was silent. The only sounds came from Eli's catering staff in the kitchen.

Brek glanced away to the empty bulletin board along the wall.

Her hands went limp against her lap.

He slung his arm across her shoulder and pulled her into his side. She fit perfectly. "I get it. You know what I think?" He inhaled the scent of her hair.

"I bet you're going to tell me."

She leaned into him, her hand against his chest. Fuck, that was nice.

"You're trying to control things that are out of your control instead of embracing what can be."

"Are you shrinking me?" Arching back, she caught his gaze.

"Nah. But I get it. You're scared as shit to move forward with anything other than what you already know." The hair along her temple practically begged to be touched.

"Are you using your mind powers to manipulate me?" Her hand was still on his chest.

"Silly girl, I don't have mind powers."

"Brek?" she asked.

"Velma?" he replied.

"You keep touching me," she pointed out.

He ran his thumb along her jawline. "You're very touchable."

She gurgled a frustrated sound. "We're professionals."

"You're touching me, too." He wrapped his hand around hers—the one on his chest—and moved his mouth to her ear and whispered, "Do something different. Something crazy. Get a tattoo. Your plan hasn't panned out, so do the opposite."

"Mistakes cost. Planning works. It just takes time."

He set her clipboard aside and settled his hand against her waist. "Or...we could make out in the hallway and see where that takes us."

Her eyes went wide, but a nearly imperceptible smile ticked the corners of her lips. He focused there and settled in, his lips brushing lightly against hers, testing the waters before diving in headfirst.

She responded, opening her mouth and gripping his triceps with the pads of her fingertips, hanging on because she spent her days scared as hell that life would continue tossing her like a rag doll. Their tongues met, and she made the little squeak of a sound he felt in his dick. He wanted her.

Their mouths pressed together, forcing a jolt of desire straight through him. He traced his hand to her neck and rubbed his thumb behind her ear. She moaned into his mouth. He took the kiss deeper, drinking in all she had to give.

"Fuck, you can kiss," he said against her mouth.

Her response was to kiss him again, pressing her tits against his stupid tourist T-shirt. The wedding was already fucked. Maybe the wedding planners getting caught fooling around in the hallway wasn't the worst thing that could happen at this point. He moved his fingers to unbutton her shirt.

"I love it when mommy and daddy make up." Jase's voice sliced through the moment, severing Brek's reality and bringing him back to the present.

Velma pulled away and pressed the back of her hand to her mouth. Her cheeks flushed a deep red.

Jase officially had the absolute worst timing.

"Hope he apologized for being a dick to you earlier." Jase sauntered by and paused at the doorway to the kitchen. "Don't put out right away. He needs more time to grovel. Tell him to buy you more flowers first."

Brek prepared to beat the shit out of his best friend.

"Don't mind me." Jase lifted his hands in defense. "I'm just the poor schmuck trolling for leftovers and finding my best friend and his girl in a clinch."

"Get your dinner, asshole," Brek hissed, holding Velma so she wouldn't take this as an opportunity to run.

"Roger that. Enjoy your evening." Jase gave a two-finger wave and disappeared into the kitchen.

"He thinks I'm your girl?" The little creases between her eyebrows deepened.

"Seein' as my tongue was in your mouth and you were squeaking, he's got a point."

She wiggled in his grasp. "I don't squeak."

"V, I haven't had lots of time to explore the interior of your mouth. But both times I've had the pleasure, you squeaked."

"I did not," she huffed.

"It's adorable." He brushed his lips over hers once more. "One of my favorite things about you. Makes me wonder what noises you'll make when I'm inside you."

She gasped. "You need to go talk to the band."

"Yeah." He traced her lips with the pad of his thumb before he stood and offered his hand to help her up.

She took it.

The length of her pressed against him. "V, you're all kinds of fucked up when it comes to what you think you want. But we're gonna make some mistakes and sort you out."

"What mistakes?" she asked cautiously.

"The naked kind."

She stilled. "Oh."

"Either that or we get you a tattoo. Your call." Brek headed to the stage.

"What tattoo should I get?" she asked his back.

"Whatever you'll regret most," he replied without glancing behind.

Chapter Twelve

COUNTDOWN TO CLAIRE & DEAN'S
WEDDING: 4 WEEKS

Velma continued to mull over Brek's proposal. She had said no, but the more she thought on it, the more she *did* want to do something out of the ordinary. Different. Crazy. The world was moving along, and she was getting left behind.

The sales lady emerged from the back room of the bridal shop with a garment bag. "The designer got started on the concept we discussed. They'll take it in this week. There will be a few more fittings afterward."

Velma frowned. When they were kids, they'd talked about wearing their grandmother's gown in their own weddings. Their mother had worn it, too. Every once in a while, their grandmother let them try it on and pretend to be brides. Velma loved that dress.

Their grandfather, Pops, had given the gown to Claire for her wedding.

Claire was updating it. Making it modern.

Velma paused, blinking away the dryness clouding her vision.

They could still let it out again someday when Velma got married. Put it back the way it was. That would be okay.

Not all changes had to be permanent.

"Let me get the room set up for you." The sales lady ducked into the dressing room marked with a glittery number two on the door.

"This is exciting." Claire lifted her plastic champagne flute in illustration, but her enthusiasm was absent. "Trying on dresses. Drinking fake champagne."

Claire had been off all day. Distracted. Not chatty.

"Everything okay?" Velma asked.

Claire released her breath as the sales lady dropped the tape. "Everything's peachy."

"She hasn't been herself all week," Heather called from the dressing room where she tried on yet another option for their bridesmaid and maid-of-honor dresses.

Velma hated trying on clothes, so she was happily delegating the task of finding their bridesmaid gowns to Heather.

"Dean and I had a talk, and I'm still figuring it out."

"What'd you talk about?" Heather hollered over the top of the dressing room door marked with a glitter-encrusted number four.

Claire's face went blank. "Kids."

In Velma's Dean Dreams she had planned on three kids within the first few years of marriage. That way they could get the diapers done all at once. Those were steps five, six, and seven of the five-year plan. The free spirit in Brek probably didn't want children and—holy crap, she did not need to be thinking about Brek's babies.

"Dean doesn't want kids." Claire sounded defeated. "He wants to travel. Maybe move to Europe."

Whoa. Europe was not a house in Aurora.

"Don't you want kids?" Velma was certain she did.

"I don't know." Claire lifted a shoulder and stood still while the sales lady continued with her measurements. "I never thought much about them. I don't *not* want them. But it's Dean, and he's the most important thing in my life."

Velma dropped to a white tapestry chair. "I can't believe Dean doesn't want kids."

Really, with a face as handsome as Dean's, procreation should be mandatory.

Next thing she knew, Claire would be telling her how Dean's financial portfolio was all high-risk and not diversified.

"We'll figure it out." Claire flipped through a veil catalog. "I want to have fun today. I need to shake it off."

"What do you think?" Heather emerged from the dressing room in a short, tight purple tube dress that only fit women without any curves. In other words, it wouldn't work on Velma.

"I love it." Claire perked up at the sight of the dress.

"It's the best, isn't it?" Heather's eyes lit up.

"Totally *the one*. Velma, this is going to look awesome on you." Claire was genuinely excited about the dress.

Except, it would look awful on Velma.

"That dress is not going to work with my chest size." Velma shook her head. Or her tush size.

"Give it a try. I bet it'll look amazing when you get it on. You don't give yourself enough credit. You will rock the hell out of this dress," Heather insisted.

Maybe…Velma could try a hemline that short. It might even be fun.

"We're all ready for you, Claire." The sales lady stuck her head out of the dressing room.

"I guess it's time." Claire turned to Velma and made an "eeek" sound before she disappeared into the dressing room with the sales lady.

"I have gifts for you and Heather," Claire said over the rustling of the garment bag in her fitting room. "Can you grab them? They're the white boxes on the counter."

Heather picked up the two white boxes from the counter and handed one to Velma.

Velma untied the ribbon from her box and removed the

lid. An ache formed in the center of her chest. She recognized the handmade Italian lace that had once covered her grandmother's entire wedding gown.

But the piece in her hand was not on the dress. It had been sewn into a dainty handkerchief. Velma couldn't seem to move. She wasn't breathing. She opened her mouth, but air wouldn't come.

"You okay?" Heather asked, her expression concerned.

"Yes," Velma croaked, taking in the devastation that was once her grandmother's bridal gown. Claire was making changes to the dress. Velma knew this. She'd even encouraged it when Claire couldn't find a dress she loved.

Everything was changing.

Except Velma.

"Ta-da." Claire emerged from the dressing area.

Gramma Velma's dress had a train, poufy sleeves, and yards and yards of handmade Italian lace. The version Claire wore used some of the same lace, but the sleeves had been removed and the fabric cut short so it fell at the knee.

Velma's heart tumbled to her toes. This dress was beautiful. Totally Claire. But it wasn't her grandmother's. Not anymore.

Everything was different. Velma had gone blurry from tears forming on her eyelids.

"Velvet?" Claire's face fell.

Velma hiccupped and pressed the back of her hand against her lips. "You're so pretty."

Claire started to cry, too. "You don't think I ruined it?"

"I think sometimes an update is in order." Velma stared as the sales lady tugged at the fabric of what had once been a family heirloom, holding it tight and pinning it in place.

Velma's world was crumbling like the huge sandcastle they'd built too close to the tide when they were little. The whole thing was lost to a saltwater wave.

She gulped against the gritty feeling of losing the dress

her grandmother had worn. Claire loved the changes. This was Claire's wedding. Velma's job was to support her, not freak out over a cut-up family heirloom. Her heart rate slowed. She could do this.

"What are you doing later, Velma?" Heather sifted through a rack of bridesmaid dresses. "We were thinking about grabbing dinner."

Velma hedged. "I have plans tonight."

Downtown at a matchmaker mixer.

"With Brek?" Heather paused, giving Velma the side-eye with a dash of smirk.

"Brek's overwhelmed with brides at the moment," Velma dodged. Actually, he was alone, using his mom's empty garage to change the oil on his motorcycle.

Claire gave Velma a good once-over, the sales lady still pinning the material into place. "How's helping him out with planning going?"

Well, given that the last bride had bailed, not so good. "It's going."

"And the friends-with-benefits situation you've been working on?" Heather plucked a mint from one of the crystal bowls.

"We're just friends." She needed to keep repeating that.

"A guy like Brek needs a woman ready for adventure. I think you could be that woman." Claire grinned wide. "You know it's going to happen. Ditch the dating spreadsheets. Do like the Prince of Pop and *just go crazy*."

"I think you mean 'Let's Go Crazy,'" Velma corrected.

"What?" Claire turned so the sales lady could pin the side of her dress.

"That's the title. *Let's Go Crazy*."

Claire rolled her eyes. "Now you sound like Dean."

"Either way you say it, I think you should *do* it." Heather held up a purple chiffon dress. "Yay or nay?"

"I think we should do the one you're wearing," Velma

replied. Claire loved it. Heather wouldn't pick something that would make Velma look bad.

Heather beamed. "Really? You're going to look amazing in it. Brek's going to be all over you."

Velma sighed. Maybe doing something crazy wasn't such a bad idea. And doing Brek would be *crazy*. Also, probably fun. She could run her tongue along his abs and all those muscles over and over again. And she trusted him.

Besides, if her grandmother's dress was getting an update, didn't she deserve one, too?

Velma's phone buzzed in her purse. She tossed the used paper cup into the bin and pulled out her phone.

Brek.

"Brek?" she asked into the phone.

"Dinner. You want Chinese?"

"Are you at your mom's?" Velma's voice cracked. She was going to do this.

"Why? Everything okay?" he asked immediately.

She gulped back the intensity of all the feelings inside her. She switched the phone to her other ear. "Where are you?"

Heather and Claire paused while she spoke. They hadn't moved since she'd picked up the phone. They just watched her.

"She's gonna do it," Heather whispered. "Our baby girl is all grown up."

"Changing my oil. V, talk to me. What's going on?" Brek's tone sharpened.

"I'll meet you there." She clicked the phone off, shoved her purse onto her shoulder. Claire had driven Heather and Velma to the shop. Velma's car was still at the apartment, so she'd need a cab.

"Do not put this on your spreadsheet," Claire said with a wink.

With that, Velma let out a breath she'd been holding for nearly thirty years.

Chapter Thirteen

Brek dried his fingers on the grease rag in his hand. Where the hell was Velma? She wouldn't pick up her damn phone. He tried again. Nothing.

This time he tried Claire's number.

"Brek?" A female—not Claire—answered.

"Velma there?" He shoved a hand through his hair.

"Hi, Brek. It's Heather," still-not-Claire replied.

"She there?"

"No. I think she's headed your way." Shuffling in the background, and he was pretty certain she said, "It's him" to someone.

He cursed under his breath. "Call me if you see her?"

"Absolutely," Heather replied.

Another incoming call beeped in his ear. He glanced to the screen. Aspen.

"Yeah," he said into the phone as he clicked to take Aspen's call. "You've got Brek."

"Would you explain to me why six of my brides have cancelled for next season?" Panic laced her should've-been-staying-calm voice. She wasn't supposed to be getting status reports, and she sure as hell wasn't supposed to be getting upset about them. Sophie's parents had wasted no time bashing Montgomery Events. "The last one cancelled for this season. I only have Claire and Dean's left."

"Everything is under control." He winced as he spoke.

"I don't believe you." A note of hysteria tinted the words. "Brek, I needed those weddings."

Life was so much easier with pill-popping guitar players and their groupies. If he made it out of this mess without having a stroke, he'd forever consider himself a lucky man.

A taxi pulled into the driveway, Velma in the back seat.

"Aspen. Swear to God, I'll sort this."

"You swear on your Harley you'll fix everything?"

"Yeah." Because if he failed, he'd be selling the thing and everything else he owned to get his sister back on her feet.

He clicked off the phone to head straight toward Velma.

She fumbled with her purse, but he handed the guy a twenty through the window before she even opened her wallet. He snagged the door, opening it wide so she could climb out.

"What's going on?" He glanced over his shoulder as the yellow taxi backed out of the driveway and turned down the street.

"I'm here to accept your proposal." She'd gone pale.

"What are you talking about?"

She bit at the side of her lip. "Do you still want to have sex with me?"

Uh. Of course he did. He was a heterosexual male with an abundance of fantasies about her...well, all of her.

This, however, was not a conversation to have in front of his mother's neighbors.

"Come inside." He guided her with his palm against the back of her shirt. She was wearing another skirt. This one shorter than her others, midthigh. He stepped behind her into the garage and pressed the black button to close the door.

She drew a quick breath. He helped her sit on the top step

heading into the laundry room of the house and then plopped down next to her.

"Well?" she asked. "I mean, if you've changed your mind. You don't have to—"

"I haven't changed my mind." He moved his hand to the skin of her thigh and traced his fingertips there.

"Is your mom coming home soon?" She set her purse behind her on the step.

"No, she's out for the day. Some business thing tonight she's all wound up about. Won't see her until she comes up for air when it's over." Ma always disappeared before her big functions.

"Okay." Velma began unbuttoning her shirt.

"Okay?" He couldn't move his eyes from where her fingers were undoing the buttons.

This was new. He usually made the moves on her…and failed. The last button undone, her shirt fell open. She shrugged it off. His mouth went dry, and he couldn't pull his gaze from her lacy bra and the rack he'd dreamt about for weeks. The holy grail of breasts presented to him in silk and lace—and it wasn't even his birthday.

"I think we should set some ground rules, though." She scooted toward him. He stilled, and thanked fuck his mother had a climate-controlled garage. How far was Velma going to go with this?

When Velma tugged his shirt out of the waistband of his jeans and ran her palm up his abs, he got the idea.

He cleared his throat. "You want to tell me what you're doing?"

"Setting down the boundaries," she said against his temple.

His dick responded to boundaries like it had never responded before. "What kind of boundaries?"

"Well…" She scrunched her forehead and gestured to the

fly of his jeans. "I guess we should probably be exclusive while we do…this."

He could be on board with that. "Sounds fair."

"And I think it's just friendship and sex. Anything else should be discussed beforehand."

Maybe it was the blood flow rushing to his zipper, but he had no clue what she was blathering about. "Discussed beforehand?"

"Like sleeping together…without sex. And, you know, if you wanted to take me to a movie or something and hold my hand. We should discuss that first."

He glanced to her exposed bra. Her hand was not what he wanted to hold at the moment. His salivary glands worked overtime. Pretty soon, he'd be like one of those huge mastiff dogs, dripping slobber all over her. But in a good way.

"No sleeping. Got it." He focused on her eyes. It was hard. "What, uh, were you thinking? We could go back to the apartment?"

"Can you really have sex on the back of a bike?" She glanced uncertainly to his Harley.

He nodded. "Yes."

"If I'm going to do something crazy, I should go all in. You want to show me how?" She moved her palm over his pec, brushing his nipple, and fuck it. Yes, he did want to show her the many different ways one could hook up on a motorcycle. She'd been upset, though, and she wasn't a quick fuck. He couldn't take advantage.

Scruples really sucked sometimes.

"You're upset," he said, moving her fingertips from under his shirt and threading their hands together. He was always ready to go *there* when it came to Velma. But her abrupt change of heart gave him whiplash.

"You make everything better." She moved over him, straddling his thighs on the top step, her knees pressed against his hips.

He dug his fingertips into her ass, tugging her closer. His body responded in kind. But where the fuck had this come from? "What's with the one-eighty?"

She shrugged, but something passed across her face he couldn't read. "I think it's time. You want me. I want you. Isn't that enough?"

He had a dick, so that was enough.

His mouth met hers, and he deepened the kiss to the point she squeaked. His hand slipped along the lace cup of her bra and tugged it down. He finally got a handful of her tit and moaned into her mouth. Her nipple pebbled under his thumb. She gasped and arched her back, basically presenting herself as tribute. Bonus, it also provided opportunity for him to unclasp her bra. One of those handy front clips he appreciated in moments like this.

Not that he'd ever done a chick in his mother's garage. Ah well, first time for everything.

She pulled the hem of his white tee up. With a bit of help from him, she got it over his head. And there they were, chest to breast, ready to carnally christen his bike.

"Stand up," he directed her.

Another something he couldn't quite understand passed over her face when she complied, but he was too far gone to be a gentleman and ask. Unless...fuck.

"I don't have a condom." He swore. Maybe he'd left one up in his old bedroom from when he was a teenager and thought it was a sign of awesome to keep a store, just in case. Those couldn't still be any good. Condoms likely had a shelf life.

"You don't need one." She covered her breasts with her arm.

"Thirty-two years old and nobody's baby daddy. Pretty proud of that record." He stood and moved to her, so she had to drop her arm. A rack like that shouldn't be covered unless absolutely necessary.

"No, I'm…it's just…sheesh…" She blushed deeper than he'd ever seen before. "I'm on the pill, okay?"

He raised his eyebrows at her. He was clean, but he'd never made it a habit of not using backup protection. Little Montgomerys running around all over the country weren't his only concern.

"My periods have always been wonky…" She glanced away. "And now I'm officially mortified."

"V, when it comes to anything you ever want to tell me about yourself, don't be ashamed. Sorry your periods are… wonky." He hugged her close, the lower parts of his anatomy glad to be back in the game. "Don't need to go into a full sexual history here, but do you make a point of relying on the pill for protection?"

Her soft body went stiff. "Yes. I mean, no. What?"

He could tell the second she realized what he'd asked because her eyes got huge and then…she fuckin' laughed. "You're asking if I'm diseased?"

Apparently, that was amusing. She laughed so hard against his chest, he thought she'd pop a kidney or something. "Breckenridge Montgomery is asking if I've got an STD?"

He set his jaw. "Not something people usually find amusing. Yes or no question."

She sobered and glanced up from under her eyelashes. "No. I'm healthy. Other than the period thing. Anything else?"

Nope, that about did it.

"For the record. I'm clean, too." He leaned his face to hers and gave everything he'd held back before. She didn't just squeak, she fuckin' groaned into his throat as his tongue slid along hers. He lifted her so her legs wrapped around his hips and moved to his bike. She stood panting before him. Her skirt lifted easily, and he shoved her cotton panties down to her knees, running his hand up the inside of her thighs on the trek back up. He growled when his fingertips grazed the apex of her thighs and found her drenched sweet spot.

She mewed a small sound and gripped at his shoulders. His breaths came rapidly, and his dick prayed that soon it would follow suit. Whatever. Next time he'd go slow. This time was all about basic need and desire.

Until she broke the seal of their kiss. "I'm worried I won't do a good job."

"Less worry. More action." He turned her so that her hands splayed on the seat of his bike. He shoved at her skirt, spreading her legs in the process. His erection throbbed for release. For her.

She stopped his exploration, straightening and grabbing his hands in hers. "I've had a bit of a dry spell."

"How long we talkin'?" He asked around leaving a hickey on her neck.

"Just awhile. I…I don't want to mess up." The way her eyes got big and her face pale hit him straight in the gut. She was not a groupie looking for a good time. Not a hookup on his bike and never call again chick. This was Velma. His Velma. The thought hit him right in the stomach.

His pulse. His breath. Even his dick hiccupped.

"Fuck me," he said on a breath.

"Okay," she replied.

Everything inside him had stopped. He couldn't use her as a distraction. She deserved more than that.

"Did I do something wrong already…" Her words trailed off, just like his punch of lust.

He paused, stepping back and pushing her skirt back down over her ass. He wasn't about to pop the cherry on their relationship over a muffler. "We're not doin' this."

Not here. Not like this.

Without glancing to her, because he didn't trust himself to be a gentleman for very long, he moved to snag her shirt. He tossed it to her, unsure about anything in life at the moment.

"I've gotta check the house. Lock up. Then I'll take you home." He couldn't bring himself to look at her. Instead, he stalked through the doorway to check the dead bolts on the doors.

Clearly, he had to treat her with more respect than he'd been known for. He wasn't staying in town. She searched for forever and wedding rings. He searched for an easy lay. No, he couldn't do that to her. Wouldn't do that to her.

He finished up inside and returned to the garage. The big overhead door was open, and Velma was gone. He jogged outside, glanced up the street, and cursed as the bus pulled away from the corner stop.

A gentleman. That's what he'd been. And he'd done the right thing. But doing the right thing had never felt so wrong.

Chapter Fourteen

The last two hours had been the longest of his life.

"Velma, pick up your phone." Brek hesitated, his hand resting on the door handle outside Jase's shop. "Please."

He clicked off his cell. The cowbell clanked against the glass when he slipped inside.

Like always, loud eighties music blared from the overhead speakers. He stepped around a precarious display of ceramic angels and miniature crystal flowerpots.

Jase emerged from the back room lugging a tub of white roses and singing along to Van Halen.

"Hey." He nodded to Brek and danced like an idiot to the walk-in display refrigerator.

Brek leaned a hip against the white marble-top counter. Doing the right thing had drained any hope of happiness.

Jase emerged from the cooler, brushing his palms on his green apron. "Uh-oh. I know that face. That's the face of you and Velma after another spat. Do you two do anything but play tongue twister and fight?"

"Do me a favor, would you?" Brek asked, rubbing at the creases in his forehead. "Don't be a jackass."

"Spill it." Jase gestured to the stools surrounding the

worktable in the retail space. Brek always thought it was a stupid place for an arranging station, but Jase insisted customers liked to watch him while he put the flowers in vases, so whatever.

Brek checked his phone again. Nothing. He had sent Velma five texts and called her three times. Once from the driveway as the bus pulled away, once from the garage right before he left, and then again when he pulled up to Jase's. He'd gone straight to their apartment. She wasn't there.

Doing the right thing had never left him feeling like such a failure. Brek gave Jase the breakdown of Velma's one-eighty, her willingness to do the dirty with him, and his sudden surge of conscience.

"She was really ready to put out for you?" Jase's expression remained unconvinced.

Brek glared at him. "Yeah."

"So, to be clear, you had Velma—willing—bent over your bike, ready for you to take her, and you decided *that's* the moment you've got scruples?"

That about summed up the situation. "Pretty much."

Jase leaned forward, elbows on the stainless-steel table. "You do realize you're the dude who once took me to a beauty pageant where the girls all went down on each other for the talent competition?"

Not one of his finer moments, but yes. Brek had received an invite to the local motorcycle club's annual beauty pageant. He had dragged Jase along. Neither had expected the evening to take that turn. Neither of them had minded much, either. Which was reason number one thousand and twenty-six why Velma deserved better than being bent over his bike in a dirty garage. And a dirty garage was all he had to offer. A woman like her needed more.

"That was a fan-freaking-tastic night." Jase put his knuckles out to fist-bump Brek.

Brek made a face at Jase's outstretched knuckles.

"You wanna know what I think?" Jase rubbed his eyebrow.

Not particularly. "No."

"Good. I'll tell you." Jase leaned in further. "Since you're here instead of out there tracking down Velma, I think she scares you. Because you know when you get in deep with chicks like her, you don't come out on the other side."

He should've talked to Dean. "That so?"

"Woman like her? You set up house, buy some doilies, and hand over your balls. Like Dean." Jase smiled bigger than a chick in a room full of lilies. "He's happy as a clam with Claire's wire strippers holding tight to his nuts. You, my friend, are scared that's the direction you're headed."

Brek shook his head. "Aspen pushes out this kid, and I'm out of here. That's my problem. Not because I'll want to stay, but because no matter what, I'm leavin'."

"Ahhhh…so it's about you not wanting to hurt her? This is an interesting development." Jase rubbed his hands together. "And the plot thickens."

"Yeah, I don't want to hurt her." Brek's heart already felt like it was in a combat zone when she was nearby. He couldn't do the same damage to hers.

"But by walking away with her already hot and bothered and ready to go, you hurt her anyway." Jase pointed out.

Shit. "Yeah."

"Well, I'm not Freud." Jase wiped a clump of dirt from the tabletop. "Thank fuck for that. But, in my estimation, you both want to do this thing. So, you lay out some guidelines, toss her on the bed, and show her the ways of the sexually inclined."

"That, right there, is why you're a fuckin' florist and not a therapist." Brek stood and walked to the window of the cooler. Jase's idea wasn't bad. They would set more rules, understand where the other was coming from, and move forward. Communication and all that shit.

"The alternative is to get used to your right hand." Jase followed him. "We both know that's not gonna happen. Now, lilies are my go-to for *please let me in your pants*. I think in this situation we're going to have to layer them with a handful of hydrangeas because you got her all hot and bothered, then walked away. Nothing says *sorry I was an asshole* quite like hydrangeas."

Brek pointed to some small blue flowers. "What about those?"

"Ahh…those are agapanthus blooms," Jase slid open the door and stepped inside. "The most expensive flower we carry. These are the *I'm sorry I slept with my secretary* flowers."

"Now you're just makin' shit up."

"Making shit up is my gift," Jase replied, grabbing a handful of the stems. "Will you be paying with cash or credit?"

"Cash." Brek pulled his wallet from his back pocket and counted out some bills. Time to talk to Velma.

Jase wrapped the flowers.

Brek tucked them into his jacket and headed back to the apartment. He'd wait for her there.

HE TURNED his key in the door and pushed it open.

No Velma. The apartment was silent. He did the only thing he could think of to find her.

He dialed her sister.

Claire picked up on the first ring. "I'm not happy with you."

"I messed up."

"No kidding." Claire was in a huff. He couldn't blame her.

"Do you know where she is?" He filled one of Velma's vases with water and set the flowers in it.

"She's on a date," Claire replied.

His stomach did a nosedive.

"Some matchmaking thing your mom put together," Claire continued.

Brek cursed under his breath. "She say where this thing's happening?"

"If I tell you are you going to muck it up again?"

"No."

"Pinky swear promise?"

"Claire." He practically growled at her.

"Elway's," Claire said, matter-of-fact. "Don't hurt her or I'll send Dean to hunt you down."

"Fair enough." He wouldn't hurt her. Not again.

He tapped the phone off and hustled to the hallway. With no time to wait for the elevator, he jogged down the steps two at a time. He had to get to Velma before she made an even bigger mistake with someone who cared a hell of a lot less about her than he did.

OF ALL THE men Velma expected to meet at the matchmaker mixer, Wayne Marsh was not one of them. And yet, Brek's mom, Pam, had matched Velma and Wayne for the first thirty-minute date of the night.

Wayne and Velma had grown up together. He was the literal boy next door.

Velma's throat constricted. She had hurried out of the garage after her humiliation with Brek. No way could she face him after what happened. Nope. Avoidance was key. She'd ignored his calls. His texts. What was left to say?

Wayne sauntered toward her, winding behind tables and chairs and other attendees. All six feet two inches of police officer handsome. Darn it. Why couldn't he make her all tingly like Brek? All those little feelings that made her uncomfortable, happy, and adventurously naughty hit her in the belly, only with the one man she had embarrassed herself with and could never, ever see again.

"Velma, dear. This is Wayne. According to your question-naires, you two are incredibly compatible." Pam squeezed Velma's arm in reassurance. "Really, it's very rare to find two people as compatible as the both of you."

His eyes twinkled as he got closer. Honest to goodness, they twinkled. Like a freaking cartoon hero. "Velvet."

Ugh. No. Not Velvet.

"Hi, Wayne." She made every effort not to wring her hands or suck on her lip. She failed and glanced to Pam. "We, ah, actually know each other. We grew up together."

Pam clapped her hands in delight and waved to someone across the room. "Wonderful. I can feel the chemistry already. You two are in the far booth. Thirty minutes and then I'll introduce you to your next partner. Talk about the things you both enjoy doing and relax. Remember, this is fun!"

Wayne wasn't bad. He was goodness personified. He should probably get his own sunshine halo and the key to the city. It wouldn't ever cross his mind to have sex on a motorcy-cle. Wayne would have rose petals and champagne. Probably strawberries. Dipped in chocolate.

He stood there, eyes sparkling, an ear-to-ear grin. Nothing like Brek. Which was a good thing. A great thing. Especially since she wasn't presently talking to her roommate.

"Should we go sit?" Wayne cleared his throat and gestured to a corner booth set for two.

"Yeah. Yes. Yup." Velma ran a hand over the skirt of her teal dress. He held out his palm, clearly waiting for her to grasp it. But she couldn't touch him. Not when she had thrown herself at Brek earlier in the day. Brek, who had changed his mind about her…because she was boring, boring Velma.

Brek had to get *out* of her head.

She took Wayne's cool hand and…nothing. Absolutely nothing. His thumb stroked the fleshy part between her thumb and pointer finger and, well, still nothing. The familiar cologne he wore was a comforting balm on an otherwise rough day, but that was it.

"This is my first time," Velma said, the blood promptly draining from her face to pool in embarrassment within her chest. "I mean, here. My first time at one of these things."

"I came last month." They skirted the tables and Wayne helped her as she stepped up into her side of the booth. Aside from the lack of tingles at his touch, he could make an exceptional date.

"How did it go?" she asked before choking on a gulp of water. She pounded a fist to her chest and smiled.

"I'm back this month. That tells the story, I suppose." He chuckled at himself. "So…"

"So." She sipped a bit more, avoiding the ice cubes. "We should have wine. Let's have wine. I think we should."

Snatching the wine menu beside the salt and pepper, she flipped through the laminated pages. She glanced up when he remained silent.

His eyes caught the low light from the sconce on the wall beside their table. "All right."

He hailed a waiter. Velma ordered the house white. He ordered a Coors, from a bottle. Like Brek always ordered. Ugh. Brek.

"I have to admit, I'm surprised you're here tonight." Wayne leaned against the back of the booth. His long arm sprawled along the edge.

"Me, too," Velma said under her breath. She fiddled with the fake leather cover of her menu.

"I guess it's my lucky day, then." Wayne dropped his arm and poured his newly arrived beer into a frosted glass. "I've had the steak. It's good. But probably just time for appetizers tonight before they move us along."

Oh. Right.

She refused to look at the label of his bottle. As far as she was concerned, Coors was now the beer of Wayne. Not that other guy. The one who always drank straight from the bottle. No frosted glass for him because it probably broke biker code.

Velma toyed with the stem of her wineglass. Her phone buzzed in her purse. Her fingers itched to check and see if Brek was calling again. She already had several voice mails from him. She couldn't bring herself to answer the phone or listen to his messages. That would make it real. Every time she picked up her phone, she got all dizzy and out of breath.

Wayne leaned forward, concern evident in his expression. The low hum of the restaurant cocooned them in time and space. "Are you all right?"

"Fine." She smiled her best smile and glugged a drink of fortified grape juice. "How's work?"

"Busy day." He relaxed against the bench once more, but the concern in his eyes remained.

"Caught some bad guys?" she asked over the throaty laughter from the woman in the booth behind her.

"Yeah. You could say that." His elbows rested on the table.

She should make a column for that on her spreadsheet. Elbows on the table meant an automatic three-point deduction. As would ordering Coors in a bottle like Brek. Right now, Wayne was at a negative six. But he caught bad guys, so that added some points. She should add a column for that, too. "Did you get to put them in handcuffs?"

"As a matter of fact, I did." He scanned his menu.

A deep breath didn't help the discomfort of the moment. She and Wayne had always had an easy air between them. He was an amazing guy. Kind. Steady job. Polite. Her parents adored him.

But he wasn't Brek. And that was the crux of it. If she married a guy like Wayne, she would be miserably comfortable for the rest of her life. A guy like Brek would never get married. Yet, he had managed to weasel his way into her life in the most comfortably obnoxious way.

But he didn't want her. And Wayne was safety. Stability. Kindness. Boredom. They had that in common.

"I have tickets to see *The King and I* at the Buell next weekend," Wayne said.

Oh. He definitely got extra bonus points for *The King and I* tickets. The Buell was hands down the best place to see Rodgers and Hammerstein.

"Interested?" Wayne asked before taking another drink of his beer and setting it carefully on the cardboard coaster with the logo of a craft beer company.

"Sure. No. Actually, could you give me a second?" Velma forced her hands to stop shaking. "I need to use the ladies' room."

"Something's wrong." Wayne's forehead scrunched.

"Yep." Velma slid out of the booth, snatched her purse, and hustled to the restroom before he could say anything more. She stood over the white porcelain sink and splashed cold water against the red splotches forming on her cheeks and neck. She needed a plan—a strategy to get out of the next twenty-five minutes with Wayne.

She stared at her reflection, waiting for inspiration to strike.

Nothing. Darn. Firming her resolve, she pushed her shoulders back, tucked her black clutch under her arm, and headed back into the lion's den. With barely one foot around the corner to the main restaurant area, she walked smack into Brek.

An extremely unattractive "oomph" escaped her lips. Brek's hands steadied her. She shoved them away.

"What do you think you're doing?" She gritted her teeth so she didn't say more.

"Finding you." His intense gaze lanced her to her core.

That, right there, was why she'd chosen to avoid him. Even looking at him hurt.

He stepped to the side to let a couple of women move past. "What're *you* doing?"

"Finding someone else, since you decided you're not interested." She huffed out a breath. "See that guy over there?" She pointed to Wayne. "His name is Wayne and he's very interested in me."

"Wayne?" His expression went tense.

"You're off the hook." Darn it, her voice trembled. Heat rose in her chest. Absolutely unacceptable. She would not fall apart. Not here, not now. Not in a hallway outside the ladies' room when she was on a sort-of date with Wayne. Definitely not in front of Brek.

"If you'd pick up your damn phone, you'd know that's not what I want."

Oh no. He didn't get to be pissed. He had no right to be angry. To *cuss* at her. He was the one who had gotten her all kinds of turned on and then left her with her panties around her ankles.

Mortifying.

She focused on the back of Wayne's head across the room. Brek stepped in front of her. "Hear me out. Please. I'm sorry about the bike. I'm sorry I didn't handle that well." He shoved his hands in his jeans pockets. "I'd like to make it up to you."

"You'd like to make it up to me?" she asked, incredulous.

This time she shoved past Brek, but he whispered from behind. "You're on a date. With someone else, V."

She spun around. "You told me to do something crazy. To try something new. So, I did, and it was scary. It was scary, Brek. And then it was humiliating."

Great. Now she was whisper screaming. She jutted her chin in defiance, glaring with all she had.

"I made a mistake. I'm sorry." Brek held his hands palms up.

"Is everything okay over here?" Pam asked, her eyes darting between Velma and her son.

Velma turned her head toward the restaurant and shoved her hair out of her face. The room had gone silent. Everyone stared at them.

Maybe she had screamed more than whispered?

Oh God.

A blush of itchy hives crept up Velma's chest.

"I should leave." Velma's cheeks burned. Turned out, yes, this day could, in fact, get more embarrassing.

"Right. Let's go home," Brek agreed.

Everyone in the room seemed focused on them. No, she couldn't look anymore. She wanted to crawl under the nearest table and hide. She wouldn't, but she wanted to.

"Ma, thanks for the fun time. Velma's comin' home now," Brek said calmly. "Would you mind letting her date know?"

"Please tell Wayne I'll call him," Velma said as carefully as she could, being that her love life was flipped upside down.

"Nope. Don't tell him that," Brek corrected.

"Have you two finally decided to see each other?" Pam lifted a manicured brow. "Officially?"

"Negotiations are currently taking place," Brek replied.

Velma shot Brek a look, daring him to say anything more.

He didn't. He just shrugged at his mother.

She pressed her hands together and tapped her index fingers to her lips. "Well, then, I'll find someone else for Wayne."

Pam's eyes sparkled. She patted Brek's arm on her way to apparently have a chat with Wayne.

"We need to talk." Velma grabbed Brek's arm and pulled him outside to the sidewalk next to his bike. She stood as tall on her toes as she could. "Have you lost your mind?"

He closed the gap between them, his mouth on hers,

kissing the stuffing right out of her. Everything she had built up in her head melted away as she kissed him back furiously.

He broke the seal of their kiss. "I'm sorry. About before."

She swallowed down all the emotion from the day. "Why did you stop? In the garage? What did I do wrong?"

"This is all new territory for me—the whole caring thing. So that was me respecting you." He was all hard muscle and kind eyes. "We both know what this is. I won't leave you hanging again. Now's the time to say no if you don't want this."

She remained silent and kissed him again.

Chapter Fifteen

Velma held on to Brek's muscled abs as he parked the motor-cycle at their apartment building. His spicy scent overpowered her senses. The whole ride, she'd rehearsed what she might say. She hadn't said no, and this time he seemed intent to see this thing through. So, they would talk about boundaries and create a plan.

Velma's breaths turned shallow while she fought with the thick black clasp on her chinstrap.

Brek climbed off and unhooked his helmet easily.

Her clasp wouldn't release. She pressed and pulled harder. The strap bit further into her jaw as her breathing became erratic. "I can't get this darn thin——"

"Here." Brek's warm grip surrounded hers. With barely a flick, he released the clasp and removed her helmet.

Shaking, and with no grace, she climbed off the bike. Velma ran her hand over her hair and glanced to the variety of pebbles scattered across the asphalt. She studied them like they held the solution to all her life's problems.

Brek placed his hands along her jaw, one on each side, and tilted her head up. "You can change your mind. Anytime."

His thumbs stroked her temples.

Her stomach did a little flip at the sensation. "No. I just… I'm not good at this stuff."

"Okay."

"Okay?" she asked.

"Yeah."

What was he even saying? "Yeah?"

"V, you're overthinking things. Catch your breath. I'm still me. We're still us." He settled both hands against her shoulders, and the fingertips of his right hand brushed little circles against the sensitive skin just below her jawline.

She nodded. "Let's go home."

Focused on the sidewalk, she hustled toward the building and inside the elevator.

He stepped into the elevator and pushed the button to their floor.

"Havin' second thoughts about us?" he asked, his expression genuine.

"No." She wasn't.

"Then don't run from this." The words were practically a plea.

The silver doors slid open. He looped his arm around her waist, his long strides propelling both of them down the hall.

Brek shoved the door to their apartment open. She hurried to her bedroom. Brek kissed her as soon as they got there. All fire and tongue, melting her against him.

He pulled back and winked. "Don't move."

She blinked as he disappeared behind the door and immediately popped his head back in.

"Don't freak out, either."

She opened her mouth to respond when he turned on his heel and left once more.

This time, her chest heaved full-on breaths. Each inhale drew excitement, and a dash of fear. What had she gotten herself into?

She should go and see what the heck Brek was doing.

Gosh, the room had gotten uncomfortably hot. Carefully, she removed her sweater and dropped it into the wicker laundry bin.

Her gaze moved to her bathroom, her only escape. She just needed a minute to get herself together.

She pulled the pocket door closed and glanced to the garden tub. An impromptu shower seemed like a better idea. Unzipping the side of her dress, she stepped out of it and pulled open the plexiglass door to the walk-in shower.

Warm water did little to rinse away the turmoil raging inside her. Not confusion about Brek. She understood down to her marrow that he would never hurt her. No, they would figure out their limits and discuss rules, and then she would learn everything she could from him.

The spray of water pounded against her as she lifted her face to the stream, closing her eyes and bracing her hands on the dark-gray tiles of her shower.

The rattle of the shower door opening jolted her attention away from the showerhead. She covered her breasts with an arm and shook the droplets of water from her eyes.

Brek.

Not just Brek. *Naked* Brek. Sure, she had felt him up over his T-shirt when she rode on the back of his bike. And, yeah, the definition of his back was etched in the recesses of her mind from the times they kissed and she had held on tight. She'd seen him without a shirt countless times, but, totally bare, he was a Greek god with brilliant ink across his arms, chest, and down his right leg. Her gaze moved back to his arms. Arms that led to abs with muscles defined into a V leading to—she forced her eyes to meet his.

"You want me to leave?" A sly smile tilted at the corners of his lips.

At the husky purr of his words, she was pretty sure she almost had an orgasm right there. The warm water poured over her, circling the drain like her commitment to boundaries.

She pressed her palms to her eyes and shook her head. "No. Stay."

"Then I'm coming in. You good with that?"

Finally, she dropped her hands and smiled a shaky smile. She nodded. His eyes were soft, his body rigid.

He prowled through the small space between them, turning her so his chest brushed against her back. The air shifted in the quickly steaming stall.

"This is how it's gonna go," he whispered into her ear, the length of his erection settling in the cleft of her bottom, pressing up toward the center of her spine. His wet hands slid along her elbows and over the sides of her breasts. "I'll take lead, but you've gotta tell me when I do something you don't like."

She moaned when his fingertips stroked lightly over her nipples. At the moment, certainty took over that she would enjoy everything he chose to do to her body.

Fine, so she didn't have loads of experience in this department. Handling things alone in her bedroom at night hardly counted. No, the things they were about to do, or rather *were* doing, were carnal, instinctive. She had never been confident with a man this way. But there were no mistakes here. Just Brek.

He ran his hand over the slope of her breasts, down her belly to the wisp of curls at the apex of her thighs. He slid a finger inside as his other arm braced her so she didn't collapse into a puddle and slip off down the drain. "You with me?"

This was new. Sure, she had made herself come, but this…this was something totally foreign. Different. Exciting.

"What?" She hitched her leg slightly to give him better purchase, his fingertips venturing farther.

"I do something that doesn't feel good, you talk to me." He continued his beautiful assault on her senses. "I do something you like, you talk to me. I'll return the favor. For example, right now, the water bouncing off your tits is fucking with my head. Makes me want to do this faster so I can play with 'em. But, see, that's not the guy I am. I've got a problem because I really want to touch your tits, but my hands are busy."

"That is a problem," she said on a breath.

"Looks like you're gonna have to help me out here. Touch your nipple." He slid another finger against the one already between her legs.

She followed his command and ran a hand over her breasts, like she did when she was alone and doing this to herself. The friction elicited a moan from the depths of her.

The hardness of his erection twitched against her backside.

She cleared her throat. Her head lolled back against him. "I like that. A lot."

"Which part?" His hand continued doing magnificent things to her.

"Mmm." Words escaped her as his thumb rubbed against her sweet spot. The sensations of the water, her hands, *his* hands, were overwhelming.

"We should go to my bed." She had no idea where the words had come from. She would gladly stay in the shower forever. They could just live there, the two of them, alone in the water.

He turned her to face him. "That's what you want?"

She nodded. His mouth crushed down on hers. Finally, he let her go, and she turned off the water to follow him out. He immediately wrapped a bath towel across her shoulders and dried her off, before doing the same for himself.

Holding the towel in place, she followed him to the bedroom.

He'd pulled the blackout curtains closed and laid out all of her candles from the living room—even her emergency the-power's-off candles from the hall closet. They flickered in the dim light.

Her breath caught. "You did this for me?"

"Thought you deserved special." He held a hand out to her. This was it. Deep down, she understood he was asking her to trust him. He was Brek. Her Brek.

She released her grip on the towel and stepped across the invisible line to meet him in the center of her flannel sheets. Laying her back against the pillows, he knelt over her body, his hand stroking the length of his erection.

Holy crap. The vision of Brek with his hand on his...it... would be forever burned into her mind. She could watch him do that for hours.

"We'll go slow. Tell me if you need a break." His kissed her quickly, and then all she saw was the top of his head as he moved his lips down the slope of her chest.

This was nice. "Nice" being the least appropriate word ever. "Fantastic" was more like it. His mouth covered her left breast, and he sucked on her nipple, groaning along with her moans. She massaged her fingertips against his scalp, and he released her nipple. A mew escaped her lips, but he continued kissing her torso, down to her thighs. He stopped at her knee and opened her legs. They fell easily apart. Oh dear, he was really going for it.

She wasn't boring Velma anymore, not with Brek. "I feel like I'm falling."

"V," he said, the word a command for her to look at him. "You feel like you're fallin'? Eyes on me. I'll catch you." Brek's fingertip trailed along the inside of her heat, his breath against her most intimate place.

He spread her legs further and brought her just to the cusp of unraveling before he stopped with the tip of his erection against her entrance.

The feel of him there, the stretch of skin and, oh, the heat.

His hips slid firmly against hers, his erection joining them together. The coarse hair of his legs was a contrast to her smooth calves.

"Eyes," he said, gentler than she'd ever heard him before.

Her gaze locked onto his. Her lips involuntarily parted as he invaded her senses, inch by inch. This felt right. *He* felt right. She reached between them, trailing her fingertips down his abs to where they were together. She gripped his erection and guided him in farther.

"Brek," she whispered his name like a prayer.

"Eyes," he grunted, seating himself firmly inside her.

He didn't move. Muscles in his arms twitched. His gaze never faltered. "Ready?"

She wasn't ready for this. The back of his bike was a hookup, but this. This was not. This was her bed and her room and her life.

"I can hear you thinkin' all the way up here." He nuzzled his nose against her shoulder, his thickness still hard inside her.

To heck with it all. She ran a hand over the muscles of his shoulder. "I'm ready."

Slowly, he pulled out and gently pushed himself back in. She arched into him and moved with his body. The length of him pulsed inside her.

His expression remained fiercely protective. "Relax against me."

She tried, she really did. The beauty of all that was Brek overwhelmed her. Gosh, he felt so good. His skin, his mouth…everything.

He reached his thumb between them, rubbing the sensitive nerves. A coil inside her tightened.

"Relax," he whispered.

How could she relax when his body did things to hers that should be illegal in forty-eight states?

He slowed his persistence, keeping hold of her gaze.

"Pulled into your parking garage. Prettiest woman I ever saw gave me lip about parking in her spot. Those moments? I prayed harder than I've ever prayed for anything that you'd open up and let me in."

The coiled spring inside her tightened further but refused to release.

"You let me into your world, and for once, I didn't want to leave. I *always* want to leave, V. Always." His mouth found hers, gently nipping her bottom lip. "'Til you."

She moaned into his kiss. Gosh, he was good at this.

"That's right, V. Give yourself to me."

She opened her mouth to say something. What? She wasn't sure. Instead, she clenched her thighs around him, her ankles involuntarily lifting to his lower back to give him better purchase.

"You're mine. We're from the second I saw you."

"I can't relax." Even as she spoke, her body disagreed with her words. His continued persistence sent her higher, the tension building.

"Mine." His hand moved to her hair. "You're mine."

"Yours," she muttered, her head falling to the side. The tension inside became more than she'd ever imagined.

The pressure continued to build.

She relaxed, and without warning, everything in her contracted, releasing on a wave of intensity. His fingertips brushed her nipples and then pinched. Another wave overwhelmed her, her core pulsing around every part of him.

He cursed. The pleasure was so intense, she didn't even care. He trailed intimate kisses along her neck, to her collarbone, down to her breasts. Yet, somehow, he continued thrusting in her. Then he met her stare and held her hand as they fell together.

Chapter Sixteen

COUNTDOWN TO CLAIRE & DEAN'S
WEDDING: 3 WEEKS

The last thing Brek wanted to think about was reality outside of the bubble he had created around himself and Velma the last week. He fixed the messy bed in Velma's room, pulling up her sheets and her comforter with the little roses printed on it.

He slept next to her and held her hand. She was scared of getting close to a guy who would be leaving. He understood. That didn't mean he couldn't take her out to a show at the Buell Theatre.

She had enjoyed the date he planned, too. He hadn't told her where they were going. But her face went soft and her eyes got misty when she saw the playbill for some pansy-ass old musical. It hadn't slipped his notice how afterward she'd moved his pillow next to hers, his soap to her shower, and his guitar to her bedroom.

The fact remained that she would stick around Denver after he left. More and more, he began to think of Denver as his base. His adult life had consisted of living out of hotel rooms, planning concerts, scoping out venues, and managing one of the most popular bands of the decade. He'd been the glue that kept Dimefront together this long. He traveled cross-country, celebrating the roar of the engine, the open road, and his freedom to do the job he loved.

Dean's wedding was coming along. Dress was done. Flowers, catering, country club—everything was on track. Still, he'd braced for something to go wrong.

It hadn't.

Velma made him consider changing the way he had always lived. Made him rethink a lot of things. Made him want to stay in Denver and keep their fling alive. Together they would figure something out when he had to take off. They should discuss shit like that. Lately, though, their time spent together was either working or…not talking, that's for sure. Probably why they were getting along better than ever.

He came out of the bedroom and tucked his phone into the pocket of his jeans. No shirt, since Velma had stolen the faded blue Dimefront tee he'd tossed on that morning.

She glanced up from some slick magazine she was reading while sitting on a stool at the kitchen counter. "Hey."

"Hey." Brek tugged the magazine from her grip. Some chick magazine about losing inches while still eating the things you love.

She snatched it back and smoothed the pages. "I was reading that."

His bare toes sunk into one of her foam mats as he opened the refrigerator, absently searching for a post-sex snack. He glanced to her.

She ran a fingertip over the glossy cover of the magazine.

He grabbed the half-full jug of milk and a tall cup because he didn't particularly want to piss off Velma.

She smiled at something on the page, and it hit him in the gut.

Brek stared at her nipples poking against the front of his tee. It wasn't particularly cold in the apartment. But you wouldn't know that with the headlights flashing toward hi—

"You want your shirt back?" she asked, interrupting him from gawking at her tits.

He took a gulp of the milk and set it on the counter. "Nope. Looks better on you."

"That's debatable." She flipped open the magazine again and skimmed a page.

He came behind her to wrap his arms around her shoulders. She had pinned her hair up into a mess on top of her head. Little pieces fell down against her back. She leaned into him as he ran his hands down her sides to the hem of his tee.

"There's some stuff I've been meanin' to talk to you about." He traced the collar of the tee with his fingertip.

"Yeah? What's up?" She set the magazine down, her fingertips digging slightly into his forearms where he hugged her.

"You're not wearin' panties," he muttered to her hair.

"So?" She craned her neck to meet his stare.

"So, how do you feel about counter sex?" He turned her and was already pulling up the soft fabric covering her chest, his hand grazing her belly button.

"Already?" She scrunched her nose. With a teasing glint in her eye, she glanced pointedly to his fly. The button on his jeans wasn't fastened, and the bulge her presence created made itself apparent.

"I'm gonna need that shirt back after all." He raised an eyebrow before kissing her until she squeaked.

"Counter sex sounds messy. Back to the bedroom sex instead?" she asked, eyes wide. "Maybe even sofa sex?"

"Aren't you even the least bit curious?" He nuzzled her neck, right next to the red hickey he had placed there days ago, and stepped between her parted legs. "Cool countertop, bare ass. My coc—"

"Don't call it that." She cupped her palm against the stubble of his jaw.

"What? My coc—"

"Bit's o' glory." She placed an index finger to silence him.

Fuck. She was adorable. "Bit's o' glory?"

"Or dangly bits. Just not the c-word." She nodded.

He dropped his hands to his hips but didn't step back. "You are not calling my dick *dangly bits*. He takes offense."

She pursed her lips, clearly biting back a grin. "Your...*it*...can't take offense. It's not sentient."

"See? Now you've done it. *He* is out to prove you wrong about that." A smile tugged at Brek's lips. He hooked his thumbs at his waistband and dropped his pants to the hardwood.

Her eyes sparkled as he pinned her on the stool, leaning over, an arm on each side of her shoulders. A laugh escaped her throat as he lifted her gently onto the hard slab of granite counter and crawled up after her. He shoved aside her not-so-subtle pamphlets about individual retirement accounts and grabbed the magazine. He rolled it into a tube, tapping it against his palm.

"You're going to break my kitchen." She scooted backward, her hands searching behind her as she went.

He pulled her legs open and tugged her back to him, kneeling there. "Nah. It's solid. I break it? I buy it. And, V? I'd have a damn good amount of fun breaking your counter."

She gulped and laid back, her legs spread, her perky rack practically staring him in the face. He ran the rolled-up magazine over her parted lips, down over the valley between her breasts, stopping just under her navel. She raised her eyebrows at him. He smiled his best attempt at a menacing grin, but she giggled. He tossed the glossy paper aside and did a push-up over the top of her, holding there until she squirmed. Lack of contact did that to her. He had noticed that.

"Am I going to like this lesson?" She covered her eyes with her hand, peeking out between two fingers.

"Oh. You're gonna like it. Then you're gonna owe him an

apology." He glanced down to where his bits o' glory stood at attention, ready to fight the good fight for honor and bravery.

She giggled, gripping the edge of the counter above her head so her belly arched to touch his. "Is that right?"

"Mm-hmm." His mouth found hers again as he lowered his body over her.

He'd talk to her later…about something important. At the moment, he couldn't think straight about anything other than the little noises she made when he moved inside her.

VELMA HAD GROWN to admire the way Brek plowed through life without hesitation or apology. Worry tugged at her, though, that his luck wouldn't last. He would plow too far, go too fast. She preferred safety…security. And, presently, scarves to cover the hickey Brek had left on her neck.

She toyed with a ballpoint pen and the yellow legal pad she'd brought along to Aspen's office at Montgomery Events near Cherry Creek.

"We should meet in the conference room," Velma suggested, changing the subject.

"Works for me." Brek followed her down the hall.

Aspen had decked out the meeting space in everything bridal—from the long white conference table with matching chairs and the fuzzy peach carpet, to the faux flower arrangements decorating one wall next to thick catalogs hawking everything from wedding stationary to veils. She had added wickless candles scented with essential lavender and vanilla oils, so the place smelled like a fancy spa.

"Sophie really didn't say what she wanted?" Velma straightened the chairs. Neither of them had heard a word from Sophie or Troy following the disastrous almost-wedding, until she'd called Brek yesterday to ask for a meeting.

He'd asked Velma to come along.

"Nope." Brek sat and leaned his chair back so the top of it touched the wall, his fingers linked behind his scalp, elbows wide. He was so going to crack his head and need stitches.

Velma dropped the pen on the notepad. Her stomach turned at the thought of how Sophie and Troy's wedding had gone sour. She couldn't help but feel guilty for her part in it. She hadn't been vindictive, but she also hadn't thought about the effect her words would have on a skittish bride on her wedding day.

"Is everything ready for the *Rosette* photo shoot?" Velma asked.

"Yup." A full day of scruff peppered his face since he hadn't taken time to shave before they'd left the apartment. Scruffy-sexy suited him.

His phone buzzed. He glanced to it, frowned, and tapped out a message.

"Everything okay?" Velma asked.

"Ma's having a rough day. It's the anniversary of my dad's car accident. Doesn't get easier for her."

The knots in Velma's stomach multiplied. "What happened?"

"I was seven. Aspen was three. Dad had a heart attack driving me to baseball practice. He swerved. The other car didn't. Aspen and I made it. He..." He shook his head.

Velma suspected something had happened to his father, but it had never been her place to ask. Men ran off all the time. She figured that was what had happened. Death had never crossed her mind. "I'm sorry about your dad."

"Me, too." Muscles in Brek's jaw skipped; his teeth ground together.

She crossed her legs toward him, her heart breaking for the boy he had been. A kid whose life had changed on the way to a baseball game. "Were you guys okay?"

"I was." He dropped his elbows to his thighs. "Aspen shattered her pelvis and broke her leg." His words held a raw edge she had never heard from him before. "This day always brings up stuff that shouldn't be brought up."

"By stuff, you mean feelings?"

He grunted.

"Is that why you run?" She figured a guy didn't run from a family he loved as much as Brek cared for his unless something had spooked him.

"I don't run," he huffed.

He totally ran. "I'll rephrase. Is that why you avoid Denver?"

"Is this the part where you turn into a shrink?" he muttered.

The jingle of the front door signaled the start of their meeting.

He wiped a hand down his face. "Showtime." He stood.

"Why am I so nervous about this?" Velma's voice shook.

"'Cause last time we saw 'em, you were wearin' my shirt as a dress," he replied, heading for the reception area.

Velma rose and smoothed her pink wool skirt, adjusting the high waistband where she had tucked a cream blouse. Brek, ever the creature of habit, wore his uniform of ripped jeans and a worn T-shirt that showcased his biceps and stretched across his pecs.

She hurried after him to find Sophie *and* Troy. They held hands. Hope that they could salvage their relationship bloomed in Velma's chest.

Sophie immediately dropped Troy's grasp. She moved quickly to Velma, enfolding her in a hug. Velma awkwardly hugged her, patting her on the back, because what else was she supposed to do with a runaway bride?

"I'm so glad you're here," Sophie whispered, pulling away. Tears welled in her eyes.

Brek raised an eyebrow at Velma. She shrugged. What the hell-o was she being blamed for now?

"Thank you for what you did," Sophie continued.

"What, exactly, did I do?" Velma asked cautiously.

"You gave Troy my note." Sophie stepped back to Troy, and now the tears streamed freely down her cheeks. He smiled at her like she held the meaning to all that was real and good.

A jealous twinge in the vicinity of her heart stopped Velma's breath. What would she give to have a man look at her that way? The way Brek looked at her like she was dinner and he was starving was nice, but it wasn't the same.

"We've spent some time figuring things out. Thanks to the note, I knew she still loved me." Troy's gaze never left Sophie. "Things just got away from us with the wedding plans. That's, uh, actually why we're here. We'd like you to help us plan a new wedding. A better one."

"Shall we move to the conference room?" Velma asked, herding them along.

"We can meet here. Troy? Sophie?" Brek gestured to the tight love seat and pulled up a chair from the reception desk for Velma. He grabbed one for himself from along the wall and straddled it.

Um. No. They had agreed to meet in the conference room. Velma had even turned on the scented-candle things. That's where she left her notepad. Brek didn't even have a writing utensil out here.

"Are you sure? We're uh…all set up in the other room." Velma tried to telepathically encourage Brek to follow her lead. He wasn't having it.

"We're good. I'm good. You good?" he asked the couple on the couch.

They nodded. Fudge. Velma reluctantly sat in the chair Brek offered. She leaned over to him. "My notepad is in the other room," she whispered.

He grinned at her. "You can go get it if you want. We won't need notes, though."

What event planner didn't need notes?

"Okay, then," Velma started. "What were you thinking for this wedding?"

"Simple," Sophie replied. "But special."

Simple was good. Simple wasn't tens of thousands of dollars on exotic orchids shipped in from the tropics.

"How'd you two meet?" Brek asked, his arms dangling over the top of his chair like a hooligan. A really hot hooligan, but still.

"At the Reach the Peak Marathon. Sophie handed out water bottles at the end of the course. I took one look as I ran by and knew she was the one for me. Corner of Broadway and Fourteenth Street, my life changed forever." Troy visibly squeezed Sophie's hand and pulled it to his knee.

"He was thirsty, that's all." Sophie bumped her shoulder against his and then cuddled closer. They were really sweet together, now that she wasn't so caught up in the whole bride-on-a-rampage thing.

Troy looked at Sophie with intensity. Velma and Brek should probably excuse themselves. "Asked her out on the spot," Troy continued.

Except. "I thought you worked for her father?" Velma asked.

Brek shot her a look. Crud. She had interrupted their moment.

"That was after we'd been dating for a while." Sophie glanced to Velma, breaking Troy's spell. "And Daddy was going to make him partner anyway, even if we didn't get married. I didn't know that. Troy wanted it to be a surprise."

"What budget are we looking at?" Brek asked, still entirely too relaxed. They were supposed to be planning a wedding, for goodness' sake. Weddings were serious.

"About a quarter of the previous." Troy looked sheepishly at Sophie. "We'll be paying for this one on our own."

"We were hoping that you two might come up with something. We can just show up and get married." Sophie gestured her French-manicured fingernails between Velma and Brek.

Velma squinted at Sophie. "You want us to pick it *all*?"

"We just want it to be memorable." Sophie smiled enthusiastically.

If it went anything like the previous version, it would definitely be memorable.

Brek glanced to Velma and raised his eyebrows. "How many guests?"

"No guests. No bridal party, either. Something special for just us." Troy wrapped his arm around Sophie.

"Do you have a date in mind?" Brek's phone buzzed, and he reached to his back pocket to silence it.

"We were thinking the middle of next week. Troy's got some time off, and we don't need it to be on the weekend since it's just us."

Whoa. Whoa. Whoa. Less than a week to plan a wedding. Impossible. Brek had to tell them it wasn't possible.

"Got it. Do you need a dress?" Brek asked, *not* telling them it was impossible.

"I still have my dress. It just needs to be cleaned. From the, ah…tree house," Sophie replied.

"We'll have it picked up. Troy, you good with your tux? We can send it for cleaning with the dress." Brek could not be serious. So, they had a dress and a tux. They still needed flowers, and a minister, and a freaking location.

"Perfect," Sophie replied.

"Great." Brek clapped his hands together. "I'll let you know where to be and when."

Velma sat still, lips parted in shock. How could they plan a wedding with just that? They needed ideas for flowers and location. With less than a week, there wouldn't be many options.

"I'm going to run and get my notepad." Velma hopped up, scooted down the hallway, snatched her stuff, and turned on her heel to hurry back to the reception area, wobbling only slightly on her heels.

No one was there. She glanced out the window.

Sophie and Troy were already at their car in the parking lot, chatting it up with Brek. He leaned against the passenger door of a black sedan, arms folded across his chest, a huge smile on his face.

Velma let out a long breath. She hugged the notepad to her chest and stepped out into Denver's latest heat wave. Beads of sweat immediately formed along her tense neck. The scent of French fries from a fast-food place nearby permeated the air. A delivery truck on the street blared its horn when the car in front of it slowed to turn into the pay-by-the-hour parking garage across the street.

"See you next week, Velma," Sophie hollered as she climbed into the black Lincoln sedan.

Velma gave a small, shocked wave. Brek shook Troy's hand before heading in Velma's direction. He tipped his sunglasses and smiled at her. He had no right to be that attractive when she was annoyed with him. Troy turned on the car and pulled out of the lot.

"How are you going to plan a wedding without any information?" Velma looked up to Brek, who towered over her even when she wore heels.

"Got an idea," he replied, holding the door.

The phone in his back pocket rang again. This time, he answered, leaning against the handle of the glass door as she passed through to the air-conditioned building.

"Eli, just the one I needed to talk to. I've got a wedding with a tight timetable. Thinkin' we'll do it like that time on Colfax... Nothing yet... About a week... Gonna need a bread truck, some of those orange cones you use in your parking lot, and...right...hold on." He covered the phone with his hand and glanced to Velma. "You think you can get your grandpa to perform the ceremony without any of that counseling bullshit?"

Pops was a retired minister, and he was thrilled to perform Claire's wedding. He probably wouldn't like premarital counseling referred to in that way. But he loved performing weddings, so he would probably do it. "I can ask. I'm sure he will, but, Brek—"

"Got the minister, dress. Will talk to Jase about flowers. Still gotta figure out the photographer. We'll need to be fast. In and out. You'll handle the transportation? Yup. No police. I really don't think anyone's gonna call them this time."

He paused, his forehead scrunched at whatever Eli said.

"Veal and tea cakes with the cucumber shit," Brek replied and shoved his thumb against the off button.

"Planning a wedding takes time. You can't do it in less than a week." Velma slumped to the love seat and fell back against the cushions, knees together, ankles wide.

"Eh. We'll make it happen." He sat down next to her, squishing her against the armrest. Remarkably unconcerned. "Dang. We'll need a cake. I'll have to figure that out."

If he wasn't careful, he would end up making it worse. What if the whole thing blew up in his face? Shooting from the hip at this point was a horrible idea. Calculated effort. Careful preplanning. Those were needed now, not gut feelings.

"I set up the conference room for a reason. Why couldn't we have met there?" She angled herself away from him.

"Velma," he said calmly. Too calmly.

She ignored him.

He turned her face toward him with a fingertip on her chin. "Did you see how close Troy and Sophie were? If you buy into that love language stuff, Sophie was absolutely into his touch. Makin' 'em sit on the sofa here meant he had to keep touchin' her. Moving to the conference table meant space. They didn't need space. They needed touch. Which, by the way, for the record, my love language is fuc—"

"What do you know about love languages?" she asked, ignoring the fact that he had a point about Sophie and where they should've held their appointment.

"I know your love language is acts of service. Which, if you'd just relax a bit, I'd service you. Here. On this couch." He pressed on the cushions, bouncing them in illustration.

"We'd have to close the blinds." She tried really hard not to smile at him. She failed. Perhaps she had a dirty love language, too.

"Good thing I brought the remote." He clicked something and the shades on the front windows slid down.

He kissed her shoulder, working his way along her neck.

"Is what you're planning for Sophie and Troy even legal?"

He smiled a devilish half grin. "Nope."

Chapter Seventeen

Brek shifted the phone against his ear, signed the credit card slip, and grabbed the pink garment box from the counter at the bridal salon. "Really need to lock in that contract. Anything I can do?"

"Can we meet up in Kansas City when I stop there? Hash out the details?" Hans asked.

"Right. Can't do that. I'll be stuck in Denver for a few more weeks."

"Let me check with the boys, see if anyone wants to swing by Denver." Hans hollered something to one of the band members spending the week with him. "Maybe play a club. Remind the boys why they play."

"That'd be great. See what you can come up with."

"Will do. We'll catch up later."

"Sounds good." Brek ended the call, let out a breath, and frowned at the counter.

He had done his best to keep Aspen's business alive, but his was suffering. One of his boys had checked out of rehab two days ago, which meant Brek needed to be on damage control, not schmoozing editors for a bridal blog. Presently, he couldn't leave town. Not until Dean and Claire's wedding was over.

"Thanks again," he said to the woman behind the counter.

"Hope she likes it," she replied.

So did he. Damn, he hoped Velma liked it.

Brek expected Velma would be home from work by the time he got there, but the apartment was empty. He dropped the box on the counter and was midtext to find her when the door opened. Velma came through with two oversized Macy's bags on her arm.

"I have news." Her cheeks flushed as she tossed the bags and her purse onto the couch and entered the kitchen.

When she buried her head against his chest and squeezed him, he smiled and held her close.

She planted a kiss on his cheek and filled a glass at the sink.

"I got you something." He picked up the box with the red lettering and slid it across the granite countertop.

"You didn't have to do that." She set down her cup to untie the satin ribbon.

He shifted and shoved his hands in his pockets, worried that she wouldn't like his effort. That she might misunderstand. Blame him.

She removed the lid, rooted through the white tissue paper, and paused. Eyes wide, she stood entirely too still. "Oh." Her fingertips traced the fabric.

He'd seen the way her smile had fallen when Claire had talked about the dress. And the way she'd picked it right back up and played along, as though nothing were wrong.

"I noticed you looked a little sad when Claire talked about the changes she made. Figured the dress meant something to you."

With Dean's help, he had tracked down the lace from her grandmother's dress and had it prepared so Velma could turn it into something later. He figured she might want to use it as a veil or whatever for her wedding.

Velma stayed still. Her expression unreadable.

And he'd fucked up.

Of course, she wouldn't want chopped-up lace for her wedding dress. His heart clenched uncomfortably.

Her wedding. To a groom. A groom that would be a man. And, holy crap, the apartment started to spin because, fucking hell, he couldn't let her wear her grandmother's lace to marry a man who wasn't him. Which meant…he was fucked.

Might as well hand her the wire strippers to attack his nuts now. Get it over with.

Her gaze never left the package. "Grammy's lace," she murmured, lifting the fabric and holding it against her chest.

His throat bobbed against emotions that seemed to mirror hers. He was turning into a total pansy. One with feelings and shit.

"Figured it's important to you. Thought you could do something with it if you wanted, when you…you know… church bells and an aisle and all that."

Had the room gotten hotter? He ran a finger along the collar of his tee. He couldn't even bring himself to say the word "married" in her presence. It wasn't like he was dropping on one knee right here, right now, asking her to be with him forever. Except he did want to be with her forever. But marriage? He never figured he would get married. He'd just get laid. A lot. Then he'd die a happy, happy man.

She nodded, still admiring the fabric, not meeting his eyes. He should probably go to her now. That was what a guy did when he realized he was in love with a woman. A woman holdin' her fuckin' wedding lace. The "Wedding March" seemed to play on repeat in his head. He yanked his hands from his jeans and tapped his thumbs on the counter.

He couldn't go over there. Couldn't make this a bigger deal. Not until he figured out what the hell to do about himself. And her. And them. Shit just got deep because he'd tracked down some old lace and let his guard down.

She carefully folded the fabric back into the box, tucked the tissue across it, and returned the lid. Still, she didn't glance up.

The air in the room went thick. He should have opened his mouth. Said something. But he waited with a hope that she would speak first. Whatever came out of her mouth would probably made a fuck of a lot more sense than what would come out of his. At this point, if he started talking, he'd probably end up reciting some sonnet about love or other bullshit.

She hiccupped and held the back of her hand to her lips. Then her shoulders started to shake, and fuck him, she was crying. Two strides and he was on her side of the counter, wrapping her in his arms, letting her tears soak into his T-shirt. There were a lot of tears.

"I shouldn't have done that. I'm sorry. I thought you'd want it." He'd really fucked the toaster on this one—presenting her grandmother's wedding dress massacre all wrapped up in tissue and ribbon. *Yeah, Brek. Great thinking.*

She hiccupped, rubbing her nose against his shirt in the process. "It's p-p-p-perfect."

Okay. Clearly, he'd misread something. He sifted his hand through her hair, stopping at the base of her neck and stroking the soft skin there.

"I can't b-b-believe you did this for me."

So, she was happy? He scooped her up and walked to the sofa, shoving the white sacks with the red stars to the side. On his lap, she cuddled closer, and his dick, always the traitor, responded against her ass.

"Happy tears, then?" he asked against her forehead.

She leaned back and studied his face for a moment.

"The happiest." She kissed him hard on the lips, using her tongue as she straddled his lap. Her lips were everywhere, the salt from her tears a contrast to the grapefruit lip balm she loved to wear.

His dick was so confused. Then again, so was he.

Her mouth stopped by his earlobe. "Thank you," she murmured.

Salty tears and grapefruit on his lips, the scent of strawberries in the air, and Velma rubbing against his jeans—he was a lucky son of a bitch.

She sat back so they were nose to nose. "Jase wants me to do a proposal to take over the 401(k) management of all their employees at The Flower Pot. I have to meet his family, convince them to move their accounts to me. It could be a huge account."

"That's fantastic." He framed her face with his hands. "Let's celebrate. I'll take you to dinner."

Brek couldn't look away from the hope reflected in her eyes. "Let's go have dinner. Then we'll go for a ride," he suggested.

She adjusted herself on his thighs and smiled against his mouth. "That sounds perfect."

"IT'S BEAUTIFUL." Velma nudged Brek and scooted closer to him where they lounged on the boulder. He slipped his arm around her.

She probably should've changed out of her skirt and twinset, but he'd insisted they celebrate immediately. He'd been weird ever since he'd given her the lace, mumbling something about his band. After dinner, they'd taken the long road up to Red Rocks on his bike. There wasn't a concert tonight, so the roads were pretty much empty. He'd driven past the amphitheater to one of the dirt parking lots overlooking the lights of the city.

"I saw my first concert up here." He nodded to where the amphitheater sat beyond the road and the canopy of trees.

"When you were a kid?"

He squeezed her tighter against his side. "Yeah, it lit the fire. I wasn't good enough to go pro, but knew I wanted to be involved in music."

"I like it when you play." He'd play for her at night, before they went to sleep. It was her favorite part of the day.

"You're biased." He didn't give himself enough credit, she thought.

"I never went to concerts. Claire did. I was too busy with school and debate club." Of course she hadn't gone to concerts. She'd been a good girl all through high school. She'd behaved. Done everything asked of her, and more. "I guess that makes me kind of boring, huh?"

"V, one thing you are not is boring."

That's not what her ex, Tommy Jordan, had said the night they broke up.

"It's okay, you know." She shifted a little away from him. "I can't really change who I am."

His arm tightened around her waist. Apparently, he wasn't about to let her scoot away. "Who said you're boring? I'm gonna kick her ass."

"Not 'her.'" It's not like Tommy had lied. What he had said was true. "'Him.'"

Brek raised an eyebrow. "Amended. I'm gonna crush his skull."

She rolled her eyes toward the stars. "Your readiness to defend my honor is duly noted."

"This guy really got in your head, didn't he?" Brek shifted her so she had to meet his gaze.

He had. His words had embedded themselves in her psyche all this time. Brek made her believe she might be different. Maybe she wasn't the boring financial planner with the choppy bangs and the turtleneck sweaters anymore. Heck, she was practically a biker chick these days. "Brek?"

"Yeah, V?" He snuggled his nose against the hairline at her temple.

She traced a finger along a rip in his jeans. "We're all alone here."

"Yup."

"And your bike's over there."

"What're you gettin' at?" His warm breath against her forehead sent little pops of fire through her bloodstream.

"Maybe we could…ah…you know. That thing we started the one time, at…" Fudge, she couldn't exactly say "at your mom's house" when she was propositioning him.

He pulled away and frowned. "You wanna hook up on my bike?"

She made a noise in the back of her throat. This was a bad idea then and a horrible idea now. "I shouldn't have said anything."

He stood and offered her a hand to help her up.

She took it.

"You only have to ask once." His words rumbled against her earlobe while his hands smoothed the fabric over her bottom, pausing at a very intimate spot.

"You're going to make me ask?"

He gave her a look that indicated he was, indeed, going to make her ask. Oh, for goodness' sake.

"Brek?" She tilted her head to the side.

"Yeah, V?"

"Will you have sex with me on your motorcycle?"

His grin practically split his face in two. "I thought you'd never ask."

He let go of her hand and turned on his heel to swing his leg over the seat—which was great and all, but what the heck was she supposed to do? She crossed her arms around herself.

There was no way this could work. Sex on a bike was physically impossible.

He turned over the engine and stepped off the bike. "Take off your panties."

They could always try, though. Drawing on the small bit of courage she still had, she hiked her skirt up, hooked her fingers over the edge of her lace underwear, and pulled them to her ankles. She wasn't exactly the picture of grace, but she managed to tug them over her pumps.

"Hand 'em over." Brek held out his hand and snapped his fingers.

What on earth did he want with her panties? Cautious, she placed the lace in his palm. He gripped the scrap of fabric and her hand to pull her into his arms.

He leaned his lips to her ear and ran his hand along the small of her back to the edge of her skirt. He lifted it to run his hand between her thighs. She parted her legs at the familiarity of his touch, and a shiver of carnal desire coursed through her.

"Shoes stay on." His voice was rough, his fingertips sliding against her already wet core.

She leaned against him, relaxing into the movement of his hand.

"I let go, you swing your leg over the bike. Like you're gonna ride her," he continued.

"Her?" Velma's own voice turned throaty.

"Don't worry. She'll treat you nice." Brek chuckled, his firm erection obvious through his jeans against her hip. "You two are about to become very good friends."

He circled her sweet spot with his thumb.

A moan escaped from between her lips.

"Just climb on. That's all?" Thoughts weren't coherent at the moment. She glanced up to him.

"To start." He did not look at all like he found her boring.

He withdrew his hand, and she nearly begged him to put

it back. But, no, she was being brave and trying new not-boring bedroom activities—activities that now involved his motorcycle.

Hopeful the dark night would continue to provide cover for what she was about to do, she stepped to the bike. The red gravel crunched under her pumps. Unsure, she tossed her leg over the seat.

Oh. Well, hello there. Brek was correct. She and his motorcycle were going to be good friends. Exceptionally good friends. The motor purred right where her lace thong had been. Her eyes seemed to close involuntarily as she placed her hands on the tank in front of her. Somewhere in the dark, the clink of Brek's belt echoed, but she didn't care because, at the present moment, his bike was teaching her how wonderful vibrations in a gravel parking lot could really be.

He slipped behind her on the bike and, sweet starlit heavens, the man wasn't wearing his jeans. He lifted her skirt, and his erection settled against her back. Only for a moment, because before she could say, *Hey, that feels nice*, he'd tilted her pelvis and, holy God, the stars in the sky blurred as her sweet spot slid into contact with the vibrating seat. His erection settled between her thighs, not entering her…just stopping by to join the party.

"Holy crap." She gripped the tank harder.

"Shit, V." He bunched her skirt around her waist. "I'm not even in you, and I'm about to—"

"Remedy that," she demanded, squirming against the erection near her entrance. "The inside part."

He chuckled low, his hand passing over her leg to pat the side of the motorcycle. "I see you two have gotten to know each other."

"I like her a lot." She pressed her bottom to his abdomen.

"Just wait." He rubbed the length of himself against her, his thickness throbbing between the leather of the seat and…well…*her*.

He ran his fingertips over her, spreading her open and, with one amazing thrust, joining with her. Immediately, he withdrew.

She nearly sobbed his name.

His breathing stilted as he seated his erection in her once more, a ripple of pleasure pulsing through her. Clearly, he was done with the cat-and-mouse portion of the evening, because he took her with everything she'd ever known him to have.

She gripped the tank as he delivered all he'd promised. Brek moving in and out of her with delicious force, she spiraled as the knot inside tightened—begging for release.

One hand around her stomach, holding her so she didn't fall, he reached the other to her fingertips and peeled them from the chrome. His hand entangled with hers as he moved it to the handgrip, turning something so the motor between her thighs revved in unison with his thrusts.

The knot inside her released, and while she'd never been a screamer, she was pretty sure an extremely unladylike sound came from her that was anything but a squeak. Her internal muscles clamped around him. His body stilled, the way it always did right before he finished.

Her body had effectively turned to mush.

With rough breaths, he cradled her against the heat of his body—pulling her up to him. He pressed his lips to the crown of her head. "Fuckin' beautiful."

Suddenly aware that he was in possession of her panties and his pants had been tossed on the gravel, Velma pulled herself together and started to move from the bike.

His arms tightened their grip. "Nope. Not yet. You need to hear what I'm about to say."

She paused.

"Turn around."

It took some maneuvering, but she managed to turn so they faced each other, her legs around his middle.

He stroked her cheek, his touch light. "You are a lot of things, Velma Johnson. You're high-strung. You're organized as all fuck."

She opened her mouth to defend herself, but his fingertip over her lips stopped her.

"Don't get on me about cussing right now, because what I'm sayin' is important. You take your living room art too seriously, and you care too much when my socks don't hit the hamper. But don't let anyone ever tell you you're less because of it. Or make you feel like you're boring because you like things the way you like 'em. Even me. You care deeply about the people in your life. If they can't see that, fuck 'em."

She glanced to the exhaust pipe, unable to meet his gaze as a tear slid out of the corner of her right eye.

He ran a fingertip under her chin and lifted her gaze to meet his. "If people can't appreciate all you bring to the table, they don't deserve to be in your life."

In that moment, for the first time in a long time, the stars aligned and the world righted itself. She believed him. Freedom-loving Brek, who would soon ride out of her life as easily as he'd ridden in. The thought caught in her throat, burning her back to reality. What on earth was she supposed to do with herself when he left?

Chapter Eighteen

COUNTDOWN TO CLAIRE & DEAN'S
WEDDING: 16 DAYS

Velma doodled a sketch of a poorly drawn motorcycle on her yellow legal pad. Annuity sales meetings were tedious. Her mind drifted from the conference room to her adventures on Brek's bike the night before.

"Velma."

She glanced up. Crud. How long had her boss been standing over her? "Sorry, yes?"

"There's a man in your office here to see you."

Velma's pulse dropped at the way Tim, her boss, said "a man."

"Um…" She glanced from where her boss stood at the door to her colleagues situated around the polished mahogany conference table.

"Perhaps you should take care of this…Brek?" Tim's eyebrows puckered, making the lines more prominent than usual.

"Yes, of course. Excuse me." She snatched her leather portfolio with the company logo embossed in gold on the cover and shuffled past him.

"Velma." Tim's voice commanded her attention.

She paused and turned toward him. "Yes?"

He strutted toward where she'd stopped in the hallway. "I trust this won't be a common occurrence? Guests are strongly discouraged while you're working."

She read between his lines easily enough—long-haired, leather-clad bikers were strongly discouraged. The sour feeling in her stomach doubled at the way Tim's pinched expression broadcast precisely what he meant.

"I understand." Velma's fingertips went cold. Portfolio pressed against her chest, she beelined for her office.

Brek stood there holding a marble paperweight from her bookshelf, turning it over in his hands.

Oh, no. No. No. Brek had his tattoos on display today with a short-sleeved black tee and one of his excessively ripped pairs of jeans. This pair was missing both knees and a decent amount of thigh material. The tee sported screen-printed lips with a giant tongue. Holy crap, her boss must've burst a blood vessel when he saw Brek waiting in the plush lobby next to their two-o'clock clients.

"Hi," she said.

"Hey." He dropped the marble paperweight back on the ledge with a *thump*. "Tried to call."

"Sorry. They've had me in meetings all day. What's up?" She skirted around the edge of the desk, dropping her notepad next to the phone.

He shoved his fingertips into his pockets. The bags under his eyes and the frustration etched in his expression were unusual for him. "Meeting Dean and Claire at the courthouse in thirty. Can't find where you put their stuff."

"Sorry, I have it in their file. I double-checked on the country club and the photo booth place over lunch."

"Everything set?"

"Yes." She grabbed her briefcase and pulled their file. "I thought you guys were doing this next week?"

"Change of plans. Dean's mom's coming to town, and

they're goin' up to Vail for a few days. Has to happen today." Brek's gaze raked over her. "You look pretty."

Her pulse skipped at his perusal. "Thank you."

She had picked the most professional power suit she owned that morning and twisted her hair in a French roll. So far it had only given her a headache.

He stepped close behind and ran a hand over her shoulder. Her stomach clenched. What would Tim think if he walked in right now?

"Not here, Brek," she said, her voice low. Not where her boss could see them.

His hand immediately dropped. "You have the papers?"

"Everything for the marriage license is on this side." She opened the brown file folder and pointed to the correct tab.

Brek slid an envelope across the desk with one finger. "We need this, too."

Velma ripped open the envelope and laid the papers in the pile, smoothing the creases. The wedding was two weeks away. Family members had booked nonrefundable airline tickets. Velma was absolutely fine with all of it. Excited, even. The weight against her chest when Claire and Dean announced their engagement had lessened to nothing, and there could only be one reason. Brek.

He was scowling at his phone. Again.

"What's going on?" She dropped the pages in the folder and flipped the file closed.

He ran a hand over the long hair she'd grown rather fond of. A lump lodged in her rib cage near her heart at the defeated look on his face.

She scooted across the office and pushed the heavy wooden door closed. Brek watched her without a word.

Screw Tim and his ideas of who could visit her at work. She stepped to Brek and ran a palm over the planes of his back, up to his shoulders. He leaned into her hands, a too-deep breath escaping his lungs. His back had been in knots lately. More than once in the past week, she had given him a massage before bed. The massages always led to other things. Whatever bothered him, he never said.

"Want to talk?" she asked.

"Nothing to talk about." He stared straight ahead. Clearly, there was a load to talk about.

"Liar." She leaned her head against his shoulder. "Maybe I can help."

"Not unless you can get my guys to behave. We're already knee-deep in promotion and ticket sales, and if they don't get their shit together, we'll have to cancel."

Well, seeing as the entirety of her music connections stood next to her, she probably wasn't any help in that department. "Has this ever happened before?"

"Normally, I'm out in the thick of things. Not a big deal. It's all about being present and keeping the connection." The exasperated tone in his words ached.

"If you weren't in Denver helping Aspen, what would you do?" She wished like heck there was more she could do for him than rub his arm.

He lifted a shoulder. "What I always do. Hop on my bike. Make shit happen."

She remained silent. He'd be able to do just that soon. After Sophie and Troy finally made it down the aisle—or whatever they would be walking down—and Claire and Dean said "I do," Brek would be free to do what he needed to do for the sake of rock 'n' roll.

Velma swallowed the heavy feeling rising in her throat.

Brek would be gone, dealing with his band. He was temporary. He wasn't about happily ever after. Soon she'd be alone, and this time the emptiness would be permanent. She would have to go back to her spreadsheet.

"I need a miracle." He dropped to the chair in front of her desk. "Things've been tight. More than tight. Sophie's mom caused a shit storm when the wedding didn't happen. This *Rosette* thing has to work or Aspen's gonna be out."

Velma's stomach turned upside down. "Out?"

"Of business." He let out a broken breath. "Did you have your meeting with Jase about their account?"

"I'm supposed to have dinner with the entire family." She was a little nervous. Their account would be huge. "Jase said they're loud."

"Maybe you should bring a hot date with you. A guy who knows a thing or two about being loud. A guy who also grew up close to the Dvornakovs. I'll come to dinner. Drink some vodka. Eat Russian food—which is the shit. I'll get a front-row seat when they agree with my assessment that they are totally fucked without you."

"You'd do that for me?"

He chuckled. "Yeah, V. I'll go hang out with my friend's family if it'll help my girlfriend feel more comfortable."

Her whole body tingled.

"Am I your girlfriend?" she asked.

He stared at her a beat. "You banging other guys?"

"No." Of course she wasn't.

"I'm not banging other chicks. So, yeah, that makes you my girlfriend."

Girlfriend. The word sounded sticky to her ears. Temporary girlfriend, maybe. Fling, even.

He stood to press a quick kiss to her forehead. "I gotta go."

He swung open the door. Her boss was loitering in the hallway right outside her office. A pointed glance her way made it clear she hadn't disposed of Brek quickly enough.

Brek caught the look and glanced from Tim to Velma. Not an idiot, Brek clearly got what was going on here. Namely, her boss could be a jerk.

"See you at home." With that, he left—without even a glance toward Tim.

Chapter Nineteen

COUNTDOWN TO CLAIRE & DEAN'S
WEDDING: 15 DAYS

Brek had two jobs: ensure Sophie got married and prevent anyone from getting arrested. He did a quick head count. Bride and groom. Check. Minister. Check. Photographer. Check. He and Velma would stand as witnesses. Check. Check. He held the walkie-talkie to his mouth. They could've used Aspen's Bluetooth setup, but the two-way radios were way more A-Team. "Ready to go, Eli. You copy, Dean? Jase?"

"In position," Jase replied. "Traffic cones going up now."

"What he said," Dean's voice crackled over the radio.

"In position," Eli parroted.

"Let's roll," Brek replied into the handset. He dropped the radio beside him on the wooden bench inside the back of the bread delivery van and settled Buttercup on his lap. The dog wasn't happy about wearing a mini tux again.

They had borrowed the box truck from one of Eli's suppliers after the owner finished his morning deliveries. Eli covered the bakery logos with new ones for the fictional Cal's Famous Pizzeria while Brek swept out the crumbs and installed the benches. They even added fake license plates so it couldn't be traced.

Velma squeezed in next to him.

His hand found hers. When she was nearby, it seemed he couldn't help but touch her.

"I'm suddenly craving some French bread with a side of extra carbs. This is torture." Her stomach rumbled in agreement.

"Didn't you eat before you came?"

"No time. Busy at work, then I had to grab supplies for Claire's shower and find a dress for tomorrow's dinner with Jase's family."

"They're gonna love you. I'll make sure of it."

She had been stressed about making a good impression. Jase's family could be intense, but Brek would be there as her buffer.

"I hope so. I really do. By the way, he told me how lilies are your go-to flower to pick up women. I'd be grumpy, but I really like lilies." Her eyes danced with laughter.

"You're the only woman I've ever picked up with flowers." Truth. Usually, he didn't need to buy flowers to get a woman to drop her panties. "And Jase needs to keep his trap shut. What else has he told you?"

"Things I'll never say." Velma raised her eyebrows and mimed zipping her mouth shut.

He needed to have a talk with his buddy about shit Jase should keep to himself.

The photographer shifted next to Velma, camera in hand. Velma's grandfather-slash-minister, Pops (he'd insisted Brek call him that), was perched on the bench across from them, along with the happy couple. Pops had a goofy grin etched on his face. Brek had caved, telling him the plan so he'd agree to get in the back of a bread truck. As soon as Pops heard what they were up to, he had been ecstatic.

"All aboard," Eli said before pulling down the rolling door and locking it in place. Everything inside went dark. Velma sucked in a breath. She gripped Brek's forearm, her fingernails biting into his skin. Not in the good way they'd done that morning.

Only a sliver of sunshine crept under the door. He probably should've brought something for light. Hindsight and all that.

Velma dug through the oversized duffle bag she'd placed at her feet, sliding a little as the van lurched forward. Brek caught her waist before she took a header onto the floor. She sat up and clicked on multiple flashlights. Well, huh. She'd come prepared. Of course she had. She was Velma—cell phone flashlights wouldn't cut it.

She handed one to him and another to Pops. The eerie glow of the flashlights gave this wedding a distinctly creepy feel. Buttercup yapped in apparent agreement.

They hit a bump and everyone bounced. Velma hit her head against the metal side of the van. Brek raised his fingers to rub her hair where she had bonked.

"That feels nice, but it'd be better if you told me what's happening," Velma whispered to him. He turned the flashlight beam to her.

"Sophie and Troy are getting married," he replied, breathing in the unique scent of everything Velma. He glanced to the duffle bag she'd filled with things. Flashlights, apparently. Who knew what else she'd packed into her bag of tricks. "You didn't need to bring umbrellas."

"You'll thank me when it rains." She pressed her shoulders back and raised her eyebrows at him.

He shook his head and nudged her knee with his. "Thanks for bringing flashlights."

"You're welcome."

"I want to take that dress off you later," he whispered in her ear.

"Brek," she whispered back, giving the side-eye to her oblivious grandfather. "Behave."

"It's gonna happen," he replied.

He couldn't help it. She wore one of her fancy business dresses that turned him on like a teenager at a Katy Perry concert. He'd also dressed up for the occasion in black jeans and another a starched, collared white shirt. Velma had already shown her appreciation for his effort by promptly undressing him that morning. Dean was making him wear a fucking tuxedo for his wedding. Brek held high hopes for Velma's reaction to him in a tux.

The radio propped against his hip cracked to life. "Dean to Brek."

He pressed the button on the side and raised the mic speaker to his lips. "Brek here."

"Cones are set. I've got traffic diverted. Where are you at?" Dean's voice muffled toward the end.

"Two minutes out," Eli replied for him.

"Okay." Brek dropped the radio to his lap and rubbed his hands together. "Boys and girls, this is how it's gonna go. We've gotta be in and out before the cops show up. I'm thinking we've got about five minutes before anyone realizes we have no business being where we're about to be."

"Cops?" Sophie asked, her voice higher than usual.

He swung the light from the flashlight her way, so shadows danced across her face.

"Don't worry, we'll be gone before they arrive. We've got all the traffic stopped at the intersection of Broadway and Fourteenth Street. Pops, you're out first. Then the photographer, then Velma, then me, then Troy, then Sophie."

Everyone seemed to be following. Although, Velma didn't seem to be breathing. "Breathe, V. No one's getting arrested."

She gulped a lungful of air.

"We're getting married where we met?" Sophie asked, her tone dreamy.

"It's almost perfect." Troy's voice was husky.

"Almost?" Sophie asked.

Troy slipped her the wooden case holding the family heirloom pearls. It took some effort, but Brek had gotten the regurgitated pearls restrung.

"Totally romantic." Sophie wore a chcek-to-cheek grin. Regurgitated pearls apparently did that to a chick.

Troy helped Sophie latch the necklace at the back of her neck. "I can't believe we never thought of getting married where we met."

Yeah, well, her previous wedding endeavor had been about keeping up with the Joneses. This one was all about *them*. About their story. Who they were and who they would become as a couple. Brek couldn't hold back a smile. Totally perfect.

"We've got a problem," Jase's voice came through the radio. "God's spitting on us."

Velma, apparently back on her game, pursed her lips and gave him a solid I-told-you-so look. "I think he means it's raining."

Brek held the radio to his mouth and smirked. "We've got umbrellas."

Velma was already on it, pulling out the umbrellas and handing one to Pops and one to Brek. "I'll hold for Sophie; you get Troy. Pops can hold his, and Dean can hold for the photographer."

"Dean is on traffic duty." Brek checked the latch on his umbrella to be sure it'd pop open.

"I'm good. I've got a waterproof case on this. Figured it might rain today," the photography guy, Alan, said.

Velma gave Brek another look. This time she shook her head.

"Coming up," Eli said through the radio.

"Ready," Brek replied.

The van lurched to a stop. Several cars outside honked in apparent disagreement with their decision to park in the middle of the street. The door slid open and the plan went into action. A thundercloud rolled in the distance. Brek popped his umbrella open and hopped out of the van. He immediately helped Velma down. She tripped over the lip of the edge, right into his arms.

He caught her. "Eyes on me. Don't look down."

Her expression went soft. "Thanks."

Troy came next, then helped Sophie down. She glanced at the impromptu space at the edge of the intersection, right where the finish line had once been. Brek had checked the location and confirmed this was where she had handed Troy his water bottle.

"This is perfect." She stepped beside Troy and took Buttercup's leash. Buttercup tore at the collar of his mini tux with his teeth.

Velma popped open her umbrella and held it over Sophie. Brek did the same for Troy. The rain was light, but thank fuck Velma had thought to bring the damn things.

Dean and Jase, decked out in orange reflective vests, directed traffic around them, but many of the cars stopped. The drivers openly gawked. This led to honking, but Sophie and Troy didn't seem to mind. Pops had already started the vows. Sophie slipped a plain gold band on Troy's finger. Her fingers shook, but her words were strong as she repeated after Pops.

The photographer snapped photos. Brek glanced to Velma. She'd been totally caught up in the ceremony, but when he glanced her way, she turned her head to him and a slight smile tipped her lips. He couldn't pull his gaze from her.

She gestured toward the ceremony and mouthed something about paying attention. He should probably listen, but he literally couldn't take his eyes off her. Not when she'd managed to grab his heart and hang on tight without even realizing what she had done. His entire body tensed. She'd become everything to him. When the hell had that happened? He shook away the feeling.

A siren wailed in the distance. Brek gave the signal to Pops to wrap it up. Jase and Dean blocked the traffic completely so Eli could collect the cones. This resulted in quite a lot of honking and some jackoff calling Dean a multitude of names.

Pops got the message to get things done and pronounced the happy couple man and wife. They kissed. Brek switched into panic mode to get everyone back in the truck. The sound of sirens moved closer. He had about thirty seconds before everything fell apart.

Jase peeled the decals off the side of the van. Brek's heart skipped as he helped Sophie inside. Troy followed with the dog, and they took their seats. Brek didn't stop to let Velma climb up. He just lifted her at the waist and climbed in. Pops scrambled in behind them and Eli slammed the door shut.

"Everybody sit." He adjusted the small train of Sophie's dress. "Where's Alan?"

He glanced around; his heart skipped uncontrollably. Alan hadn't gotten in, and they'd already left. They couldn't circle back for him or they'd get caught up with the police.

He held up the radio and pushed the button. "Dean, we're down a photographer."

The excruciating pause that came after had his heart thundering against his ribs.

"Got him," Dean finally replied. "We were mid-evacuation when you radioed. He wanted to get some parting shots of the van driving away. We're headed your direction now. Will meet up at Walgreens."

Brek's shoulders sagged. Thank. Fuck.

"That was crazy." Velma settled on the bench beside him. "And super romantic."

He caught her gaze in the dim, lit-by-flashlights glow. "Thanks again for the umbrellas."

She gave him a wry smile. "No problem."

"We make a good team," he said.

If they weren't being bounced around in the back of a bread van with her grandfather across the aisle, he would lay a kiss on her. Hell, if they were alone in the back of a bread van he would do a hell of a lot more than that. Instead, he squeezed her arm and relaxed against the metal siding.

Aspen would be over the moon that they'd gotten Sophie and Troy hitched. Next up, Claire and Dean, a big spread in *Rosette*, and then he'd never have to plan another wedding again. His gaze slid back to Velma, and visions of blue garters and honeymoon lingerie swam in his vision.

Fuck it. *If* they got that far with things, she'd have to deal with the wedding bullshit. He'd be in charge of showing up on time and the consummation afterward. Hopefully, directly after the ceremony—like in the limo on the way to the airport. But that wouldn't happen. He had to get a grip and stop thinking about forever. He didn't stay in one place long enough for forever.

A stretch limousine was waiting in the parking lot when they returned. He'd arranged for it to meet them at Walgreens and whisk Troy and Sophie off for their two-day honeymoon in the mountains.

"Brek?" Sophie asked.

He turned from where he'd started taking out the benches.

"Thank you. For today. I'll talk to my mother. Troy and I both will. We'll see what we can do to get her to halt her vendetta."

He nodded. Maybe Sophie wasn't so bad after all. "Appreciated."

The happy newlyweds left, Velma and Dean went back to work, and Eli set to pulling off the rest of the vinyl pizzeria decals while Brek disassembled the benches he had added inside the van that morning. He rolled up his sleeves and wiped sweat from his forehead.

"I suppose now would be a good time to ask what your intentions are with my granddaughter." Pops climbed into the back.

Brek's heart dipped. Words wouldn't come. What the hell *were* his intentions with Velma? They were sure as fuck not to let someone else bang her every night for the rest of their lives. He understood that much.

Pops grabbed a screwdriver and helped with one of the seats. He'd taken off his robes, revealing tan slacks and a blue polo shirt. "Saw the way you watched her during the ceremony. Reminds me of someone I used to know."

Brek dropped a handful of bolts into a waiting zip-top bag. "Yeah?"

"Me, son. Reminds me of when I was young and a different Velma caught *my* eye." He chuckled. "She looked a lot like your Velvet. Prettiest girl I ever saw."

"She meant a lot to Velma. She talks about her." Brek used the wrench on a particularly tight bolt, finally loosening it.

Pops held open the bag. "Back then, I was a traveling minister. Loved the life. Never thought I'd settle down until I met her. Best decision I ever made."

Brek paused, his gut twisting. He wanted Velma. He also wanted freedom. The two wouldn't mesh well. But he wasn't willing to give up either one. There had to be a third solution. Except, he couldn't figure it out. "I'm sorry for your loss."

Pops sighed. "Spent forty years together. My Velma could wind herself up tight about anything. In the end, before she passed, she wasn't worried about what would happen to her. Said she'd figure it out when she got there." He paused, a whisper of a smile on his lips. "She fretted over what would happen to me. Who'd make me oatmeal in the mornings? Make sure my robes got ironed? That's what she bothered herself with those last days. It all worked out, though. There's a diner up the road from our house that makes me breakfast, and I learned to use the iron."

Brek stood to stretch his back. He grabbed a bottle of water and handed another to Pops.

"Who's gonna make your breakfast?" Pops asked, tightening the cap on his bottle and setting it beside the bench.

Brek ran a hand over his face. "What?"

"Things you've gotta think about now, while you're young. Diner food is nice, but I'm grateful I didn't have to spend forty years eating it."

"Velma makes good breakfast." Brek gripped the water bottle in his hand, the plastic crunching under his grip. "I… uh…I know you're a minster, and she's your granddaughter. I don't mean to imply—"

"Things are different with kids these days." Pops opened his worn leather briefcase and reached inside. "My Velma, she had a few requests before she passed. Wanted Velvet to have this." He handed a small box to Brek. "Told me to hang on to it until the right time. I understand Velvet was upset about the wedding dress, so I figured I'd give her this today. But watching you two, my gut says to go ahead and give it to you instead."

Brek lifted the top, and his lungs spasmed against his rib cage. Inside was a thin gold wedding band with leaves carved into the metal. Not extravagant, but beautiful and clearly vintage. He'd been contemplating a life with Velma, but he hadn't expected to be holding a ring so quickly.

"Claire got the dress. Velvet gets the ring." Pops nodded toward the box. "Go ahead. There's an inscription. Paid extra for it. Jeweler charged by the letter, so I kept it short."

Brek lifted the gold band and squinted. The inscription had rubbed down with time, but he could still make out the words. "*To Velma, Forever,*" he read aloud.

"Short and to the point." The edges of Pops' lips dropped slightly.

"I can't take this." Brek tucked the ring into the silk lining and handed it back to the old man.

Pops shook his head. "Hang on to it. Might come in handy."

Yes, exactly. That was what scared the shit out of Brek. "No, really. I *can't* take this. I'm leaving Denver soon. Velma's staying."

"Keep it for now. You can give it back later. Consider it a favor to an old man." Pops' eyes sparkled with mischief. He snapped his briefcase shut and gave a little nod. "Well done today. Haven't had this much fun in ages."

The ring box weighed heavy in Brek's palm. "How'd you know? That your Velma was the one?"

"Didn't. Not at first." Pops glanced to the box and shrugged. "But knew I loved her and couldn't imagine a day without her, so I figured it was as good a place to start as any. Thought we'd travel together for a few years, but the babies came quicker than either of us planned. So, I found myself a flock, and we put down roots."

"Do you miss it? The traveling?"

"No." Pops caught Brek's gaze and held it. "Not for a second."

Brek swallowed against his thick throat. "Thanks for handling the ceremony today."

"Happy to do it." Pops nodded. "It'd mean a lot if I could officiate your nuptials...again, when the time comes. No rush, but, ah...keep in mind her mother may never forgive you if you two get married in the middle of an intersection."

A smile twitched at the corners of Brek's mouth. "Noted."

Pops stepped down from the van. "Forgive me if I'm over-stepping, but I've married a lot of people and trust my experi-ence—a man doesn't look at a woman the way you looked at Velvet today unless he already knows."

"Hey, I think I lost my earring..." Velma's out-of-breath voice trailed close.

Brek sucked in a breath. "V, I thought you left."

"Unless he already knows what?" Velma asked, climbing up into the bread-mobile.

Chapter Twenty

"Scripture," Pops said. "Unless he already knows the…scripture. Brek here's a real theologian."

Brek? No way. Then again, Pops could convert anyone.

"Scripture?" she asked, confirming she'd heard him right.

"Yeah, you know, Bible shi—tuff." Brek shoved his hands into his pockets. "What are you looking for?"

Somewhere between when they'd originally left and when they'd returned, one of Velma's favorite pearl earrings had disappeared.

"My earring. I barely got out of the parking lot before I realized one of the pearls was gone." She gave Pops a quick hug and grinned at Brek. "Have you seen it?"

"Seen what?" Brek asked, rubbing his forehead.

Velma raised her eyebrows. Was he serious? "My earring, silly."

"Oh. Uh…no." Brek shifted like he'd gotten caught with his fist in her candy jar of suckers. What was that all about?

"You're acting weird." She looked between Pops and Brek. "Is everything okay?"

"Oh fine, just fine." Pops had a mischievous glint to his expression.

"What he said," Brek muttered and knelt to run a hand along the floor.

She followed suit. "I swear if I dropped it in the street, I'm going to lose my mind."

"Dropped what?" Brek asked, glancing up.

"My earring." She scrunched her forehead.

"Earring. Yeah." He glanced back under the bench.

Velma looked to Pops. What the heck was going on here?

He raised a shoulder. "Long day for everyone."

"Uh-huh…" She stretched to feel along the edge. Something sharp poked her fingertip. "Got it!" She held up the small white bauble. "Thank goodness."

She caught Brek's blank stare. He was pale and being super weird.

"Are you feeling okay?" She lifted the back of her hand to his forehead. No fever.

"Long day, that's all." He kissed her palm and tangled his fingers with hers.

Pops cleared his throat. "Earring found. Crisis averted. I'll be going."

"Are we having brunch on Sunday?" Velma dropped Brek's hand to slip the pearl into the side pocket of her purse.

"Of course." Pops helped her climb down to the concrete parking lot. "No one makes pancakes like you." He winked at Brek.

They were both being so odd.

She glanced back up to where Brek stood at the mouth of the van. "Great. I think Brek can come, too."

"Yeah. I'll be there." Arms crossed, he had that funny look on his face again. "Can't miss breakfast."

"Sure you're okay?" She cocked her head to the side.

"Leave the boy alone, Velvet." Pops pushed his hand to her back, propelling her toward her Prius.

She glanced over her shoulder to Brek. "See you at home?"

"Yeah," he replied. "Home. Breakfast. All that."

Velma finished up at work and hit Nordstrom before she hurried back to the apartment. Her big plans for the evening involved candles, massage oil, and Brek naked.

She tossed the brown take-out bag with dinner on the table, along with a bouquet of hyacinths.

Brek lounged on the couch with his guitar, picking out the notes to one of her favorite country music songs.

She paused when he got to the chorus, her mouth dropping open. The music flowed through the room, and he caught her gaze and sang the rest to her.

Her whole being warmed. "Was that for me?"

"They all are, V." He set the guitar aside and eyed her plastic dress bag warily. "Another dress for the big dinner?"

"The other one bunched. I don't want to give the impression I don't care about my appearance." She let out a weighted sigh and draped the new outfit carefully over a chair. "And Jase said not to dress too formally, so I found a casual dress that doesn't bunch." She fiddled with the plastic film covering her new dress.

"V, seriously, you're gonna do great. You could wear a paper sack, and they'd still love you. Or you could go without a shirt. That's how I prefer you." His eyes were soft. "You didn't have to buy me flowers," he said, his voice light.

"I believe they're a you-were-right-and-I-was-wrong bouquet.'" She shook off all thoughts of tomorrow, plopped next to him on the sofa to peel off her red pumps, and stretched her toes against the rug.

"Wrong about what?"

"The wedding today. You were exceptionally romantic about everything, and I was wrong. You pulled it off." She twisted to plant a quick kiss on his cheek. "Out of curiosity, when did you become such a romantic?"

"About eighth grade, when I realized chicks pay more

attention to guys who do all that crap." His eyebrows bunched as he moved a pencil over some paper.

"Exactly what kind of romantic 'crap' can an eighth-grade boy do?"

"Flowers and chocolates and paying attention to the shit girls say."

He glanced at her then, and her insides melted. He didn't need to do any of that when he could get a girl hot with just a look.

She shifted for a better glimpse of the sketch pad beside him. "What's this?"

"Thinkin' about a new tattoo." He held up the drawing, and, holy goodness, it was really good—a charcoal sketch of a compass against an old-style map.

"That's fantastic." She ran a fingertip along the edge of the white linen paper. "Where will you put it?"

He tapped his right shoulder. "Thinkin' here, next to the dragon. Bleed the two images together."

"What does it mean? The compass?" He had cataloged his other tattoos for her one night after she'd asked. Each of them held special meaning. She hadn't realized he did the artwork himself. There was so much they still had to learn about each other.

"Nothing, just an idea. We'll see what happens with it. I drew you one, too." He flipped the page, revealing a gorgeous pencil drawing of a lily.

"For me to get a tattoo?" He couldn't be serious.

He studied the sketch. "Yeah, figured… maybe…eventually."

"It's really *big*. Don't you think? Where would I put it?" She lay alongside him to rest her head against his arm.

"Upper back, I think. That's what I had in mind while I drew it." He squinted at the pad. "It'll fit."

She narrowed her eyes. "Don't tattoos hurt? A lot?"

"The pain's temporary." He closed the book and reached

over her to place it on the coffee table with the charcoal pencil.

"You want me to get a tattoo of Jase's favorite hookup flower?"

He grinned and flexed his arms around her. "Nah, I want you to get a tat of *my* hookup flower."

She chuckled and snuggled into him. "Mr. Montgomery, you get an A-plus for avoiding my original question. What does the compass mean?"

"Told you, it doesn't mean anything." He tapped the tip of her nose with his fingertip.

He was such a bad liar.

"You mean you'd get ink that doesn't have special meaning?"

He flinched. "Would you believe me if I told you I have a sudden interest in cartography?"

"No," she replied, shifting on top of him. "But maybe if I loosen you up, you might talk."

"Maybe." He pulled at the collar of her V-neck blouse, glancing down her cleavage. "Depends on what you want to do."

"Well…" She walked her fingertips along his arm. "I read an article."

"Fuck." He knifed up, sitting her across his lap and pinning her against his chest. "Don't tell me you're taking away coffee *and* sex."

She laughed and shoved at his arms. "No. Actually, it's the opposite. Take off your shirt and your pants."

"See? Now, that's the kind of article I could get on board with." He yanked his T-shirt over his head and tossed it aside.

Velma climbed off him and stood, pointing to his crotch. "Pants off before I get back."

"Aye, Captain." The gleam in his eye said he enjoyed her commands.

She hustled to the bedroom to grab the edible massage

stuff she'd bought especially for tonight. Succulent Strawberry. Brek said he loved strawberries…guess she would find out if he meant it. He also said he preferred her without a top, so she tossed her cardigan to the chair and unbuttoned her blouse to pull it off. Ugh. *Be brave, Velma. Try new things.* Letting out a careful breath, she unclasped her bra and tossed it with her blouse. No lingerie tonight. She'd just go without a shirt, like he preferred. Her stomach dipped a bit with a combination of lust and uncertainty.

Point one. The sex therapist who wrote the article suggested women should be brazen. Bold. *Try new things that make you uncomfortable.*

Well, walking all over the house without a top on definitely qualified as making her uncomfortable. For good measure, she peeled off her panties but left her skirt on. That was from point number four. *Let him help with some of the undressing.*

She squeezed color into her cheeks, checked the mirror, and arranged her hair so it had a messy, sexy vibe. Then, with all of the confidence she could muster, she gripped the bottle and marched back to the living room.

Brek waited, sprawled naked on the couch. Holy crud, he had an amazing body. Thank goodness he had closed the curtains. The semidarkened room gave her a boost of confidence. Also, the neighbors in the building across the street wouldn't be getting a show.

Velma paused. She'd forgotten the candles. Darn it.

Well, too late for that.

Brek snapped to attention when she did her best attempt at a saunter. Sheesh, she was such a dope. No way could she pull this off.

His eyes went wide, probably at the sight of her traipsing about with no bra. She channeled all the brazen she could find and straddled his thighs, flicking her hair over her shoulder, totally exposing her breasts.

"What articles are you reading? Because I will buy you a lifetime subscription to that magazine." He lifted his hands to her nipples, stroking them with the rough pads of his thumbs. She glanced to his erection.

Point five. *Put your mouth there. Yes, there.*

He'd gone down on her more than once, but she'd never had the courage to do it for him. She had kissed his… uh…*penis* a few times, but self-conscious fear always snuck in before she took it further.

Her pulse kicked against her throat. She swallowed down her panic as her shins pressed into the leather of the couch. "I'm going to give you a blow job. But you have to swear you won't laugh if I mess up."

Brek's expression went blank. Like, totally blank. Nothing. Nada.

Shoot.

He didn't want her to do this. Of course he didn't. He had loads of experience with women who actually knew what to do. They didn't get tips from articles and muck it up. The room got too hot, and her breath caught in her lungs. Embarrassment sizzled up her spine.

"Never mind. I'm such an idiot." She rose to run away. Probably to Alaska. She'd heard there was a fantastic ice museum in Kodiak.

"You want to suck me off?" Confusion seeped into the words. "I thought you didn't like that."

"No. I just…I don't…I didn't want to mess it up. I'm a disaster. I'm sorry." Her shoulders sagged.

"You are most definitely not a disaster." He took her hand and wrapped it around the base of his shaft. "The article told you what to do? Or you want my pointers?"

His erection twitched under her fingers. Her throat went dry. She should get a drink. Water was definitely needed right now.

"V. The article? Told you what to do?"

"Yes." She mentally reviewed the main points: watch the teeth, focus on the rim, hand action at the base, and don't deep throat unless your gag reflex can handle it. She didn't trust hers enough to give that a go quite yet. She'd keep to the hand stimulation for now.

"By all means, then. I look forward to being your test subject." He leaned back against a pillow propped on the armrest, his fingers laced behind his head.

Velma glanced down as the erection in her grip throbbed. She clicked open the plastic top of the bottle of clear strawberry-flavored liquid and dribbled a bit in her hand. She rubbed it over the base of his shaft, massaging down to his bits o' glory as the article suggested. He groaned, and she looked up to his face. He bit his bottom lip and his eyelids drooped. Okay, so maybe she was off to a good start.

Carefully, she dropped her mouth to him and traced her tongue along the edges, focusing on the soft crevice at the front. Succulent Strawberry was really very yummy. He thrust his hips up, his thickness sliding in her hand. She caught the rhythm and slipped her hand along the slick skin, working him with her tongue and fist like the article suggested.

He groaned again.

She smiled inside like a bare-chested goddess. Giving head was actually…fun. She worked her mouth over the tip, and Brek made noises she'd never heard before. Good noises. Sexy ones. Her nipples peaked and her breasts went heavy, need pooling intimately at her core. Brek gripped the armrest above his head, pressing his thigh up between her legs.

Oh, glorious heavens. She was *such* a wanton. What. Ever. If this was bad, she didn't have any desire to be a good girl ever again. Not when the way he rubbed her with his thigh spurred her to push him harder with her mouth.

She lost her focus when he tangled his hands in the back of her hair. "Don't know what your plans are, but I'm close." His voice was ragged.

Okay. Good. He'd given her warning. She had three choices: *Swallow.* Ew. No, thank you. *Spit.* Also kind of gross. Or…*get creative.*

Still moving her tongue over him, she glanced about and looked at her chest. That would be creative. She reached for the strawberry stuff and squirted a stream between her breasts. She leaned forward, pressing her breasts together so they cradled his erection.

His eyes popped open. "I think I'm living my favorite wet dream right now."

"I'm doing okay?" Her hand slid upward, rubbing over the places where she'd used her mouth.

He dropped his head back and grunted a reply that sounded like a cuss word followed by "yeah."

The article was definitely a keeper. He met her rhythm and let out a moan as he finished.

"Fair warning, I had an unhealthy fascination with your tits before, but now my obsession with them is gonna be off the charts." Brek's hands went under her armpits, dragging her up his body. She leaned up on her forearms and he grabbed his T-shirt and wiped off her chest. He didn't seem to mind, but she totally owed him a new shirt.

His arms crushed her, holding her against him. One hand stilled at the base of her neck, squishing her against the ink on his pecs. Broken breaths filled the air, and she felt his heart beat erratically.

"The compass is so I can find my way back to you," he announced.

Her pulse skipped. What? Holy crap. She had to be misunderstanding him.

"Brek?" She tried to raise her head. He held her tighter.

"Also, I think my dick's in love with you." His voice strained with emotion.

"Your"—she made a noise in the back of her throat; she'd

just had it in her mouth, but she wasn't ready to say the word—"is in love with me?"

He paused. Her pulse hammered loud behind her ears. Neither of them spoke.

He rubbed her neck with his fingertips, finally allowing her to lift her head and meet his gaze.

"It happened shortly after *I* fell in love with you." He'd gone pale again, and the vein in his throat pounded visibly.

Her world slammed to a stop, spinning her right off into the black unknown. He loved her? A simple thank-you was all she'd expected for her efforts. Not this…

"Brek—"

"You don't have to say anything. I know we agreed we wouldn't do this. We were supposed to be temporary."

She swallowed the pressure in her throat, her lungs grasping for oxygen but only finding that the weight of the world had settled in her chest.

"I guess that's what happens, though. That's what Pops told me. That you just know."

He'd talked to her grandfather about this? That must've been the religious experience they'd discussed earlier. He searched her face, looking for something. What? She had no idea.

"Brek…" She glanced away, silent because, at that moment, she didn't know anything. Words didn't feel right. Not "I love you," not "thank you," not "let's order takeout for dinner."

She hadn't signed up to fall in love with someone so far removed from her carefully crafted plans. Someone temporary. Someone like him.

Then again, she wouldn't do what she'd just done to any of the guys who fit on her list. He sucked in a breath and held her tighter. All the words in the world aside, his embrace pulled her out of the black void and back into their reality.

He flipped her on her back, rested her head on the couch

pillow, and raised himself over the top of her, braced on his arms. "I like living here. You like me living here?"

She glanced up to the ridiculous pigeon painting he had added above the mantel. The thing had grown on her.

"Uh…yeah." She couldn't move, her body rigid. Where was he going with all of this?

"You think you can handle being with a guy who rides a motorcycle?"

"Your bike and I have become good friends." She smiled in an attempt to release the tension inside.

"Maybe you and I should look at that disability insurance bullshit… And I've gotta get a haircut."

"Brek, you don't need to cut your hair."

He shrugged. "Don't mind."

She raised her calf and rubbed it over the hair on the back of his leg. The pressure in her chest diffused a little once they were in the safe zone of conversation that had nothing to do with the three-word bomb he'd just dropped.

"And I've still got my band and shi—stuff. The boys agreed to play a club in Denver next week, but I'll get them settled and then I'll be at your dinner. Being a band manager means I've gotta leave sometimes. But my job's steady." His expression was stone. "Steady income. Steady work. And I'll have your compass to show me the way home."

He was coming back. He'd leave, like they'd planned, but he would return. Warmth spread through her. She ran her hands over the blank space on his shoulder where he said he would put the new tattoo.

"Now I'm gonna go down on you. You good with that?" he asked.

Time began moving again, towing her along for the ride. Her pulse still beat, Brek was still there, the three words hadn't changed anything.

Just everything.

Chapter Twenty-One

COUNTDOWN TO CLAIRE & DEAN'S
WEDDING: 8 DAYS

Velma reached for the platter as Jase's brother Zak passed yet another cake—this one chocolate with mousse filling and berries. She took a slice for herself, knowing she wouldn't be able to eat any. Nerves were getting the better of her tonight.

Velma glanced around the overflowing dining room table at the Dvornakovs's house. The family was extremely loud and daunting. Meeting Jase's family was…she drew a deep breath and let it out…yeah. The interview/dinner was really more of a Russian family free-for-all with everyone talking over each other while the fancy-schmancy imported vodka flowed.

Brek still hadn't shown up.

"You're doing great," Jase whispered in her ear.

"Do you think Brek's okay?" Velma glanced to the slice of strawberry crumb cake on her dessert plate.

"Sometimes his job gets so crazy he can't keep a schedule. It's always been this way. What time was his meeting?" Jase raised his voice over his siblings who were arguing about something in Russian. Velma really hoped they weren't fighting about hiring her.

"He was supposed to be done three hours ago." The

Dimefront guys agreed to play tonight in Denver at one of the clubs. Brek said it'd remind them why they do the gigs, keep themselves clean. It was a huge breakthrough for Brek.

Before the set, they were getting together for drinks and then he swore on his...manhood...that he'd meet Velma at the Dvornakovs' as soon as he got them settled. She'd been a nervous wreck preparing for the evening.

Velma lined up her dessert fork with the plate. "I'm starting to worry."

"Tellin' ya, relax. He's fine. Have some vodka." He topped off the glass she had barely touched. "Takes all the worries away."

She pushed the drink toward him. "Can't. I'm driving."

"Velma, relax. We don't bite," Anna hollered over the mayhem. Of the four Dvornakov children, Anna was the eldest—in charge of the Colorado Springs shops and extremely enthusiastic to have Velma managing their finances.

Of course, relax, relax, relax. Velma drew in a deep breath and let it out.

"She lies. Anna bites. I have the scars to prove it," Zak, the youngest brother, chimed in. He leaned his arms across the width of the table, tapping at a small scar.

Jase grabbed the forearm and studied the puckered mark. "Pretty sure he got that at a brothel in Belgium."

Velma shifted in her seat. Brek would know what to say to something like that. Her? Well, nothing came to mind. She glanced at the clock on the wall and back to the empty chair next to her—an exclamation point to the evening, since they were already at the dessert course.

She dismissed her disappointment and shoved up the long sleeves of her striped dress, pointing to a small crescent-shaped scar on her elbow. "My twin sister bit me when I was ten. Three stitches."

"Sisters are the worst," Zak agreed, tossing a smirk to Anna.

"Badass. I hope you bit her back." Jase raised his hand to give Velma a high five.

She lightly tapped her palm to his.

Her fingers itched to check her phone again, but that would be rude. She had looked at it ten minutes ago when she'd slipped off to the bathroom—for the third time in an hour. Brek hadn't reached out, and he wasn't answering her calls and texts.

"Can I just point out how much I love that Jase got a financial planner who shows her scars at dinner?" Anna raised her glass in a toast. "To Velma. I think it's fair to say we're all on board for working with you."

"Velma, ven is the vedding?" Babushka rasped in her thick accent. She sat across the table as she spooned strawberry sauce onto her plate.

"Sorry?" Velma asked, scooting in so she could hear the old woman better.

"You and our Jason, you vill be married soon, yes?" Babushka raised a bushy eyebrow.

Velma frowned. She must have misheard.

"And then the grandchildren vill come." Babushka clapped her hands and stood, raising her glass. She tapped a spoon against the side. The rowdy table went silent.

"A toast, to my future granddaughter. May she and Jason be happy forever and have many babies." She smiled a toothy grin and beamed at Velma.

Jase choked on a bit of cake and grabbed Velma's vodka, downing it in three gulps and banging on his chest. Velma glanced around the table at the shocked faces.

"You're a couple?" Jase's father asked, confusion marking his expression.

"Velma's not my girlfriend," Jase said on a wheeze.

"We're not together." Velma shook her head against the

sudden urge to climb under the tablecloth and hide. "I'm seeing Brek."

"She's Brek's girl, Babushka." Anna laid a hand on the elderly woman's shoulder.

"No," Babushka replied, pointing a crooked finger at Velma and giving her a good once-over. "You are not girl for Brek." She gestured to Jase. "She is girl for you."

Jase scrubbed a hand over his face. "Babushka—"

"She's not exactly Brek's type." Anna wiped her lips with her napkin.

Velma's heart sank. Of course she knew this. She didn't need it rubbed in.

"Too much sophisticated for him." Babushka shoved a forkful of cake in her mouth.

"I've seen some of Brek's hookups. They're nothing like you," Anna assured.

"They're hella fun to look at, though," Zak replied. "There was this one time he came to the shop with—"

"Shut up, idiot." Jase reached across the table to smack Zak across the head.

Velma caught her breath. She so didn't want to think about Brek's *type* or the girls he used to sleep with.

"You're not one of his hookups. It's a good thing. Have more dessert." Anna scooted the strawberry cake toward Velma.

"This girl, she does not deny. Jason, you will buy her kol'tso and make children for me to spoil." Babushka nodded.

"I'm not buying her a ring." Jase dropped his forehead to his hand. "She's not my girlfriend."

"Mama, leave the kids alone. This is a business dinner," Jase's father boomed.

Babushka snorted in reply and went back to stabbing at her cake.

Velma poked at a berry on her plate with a fork, her chest heavy. Brek said he loved her, so the words from a confused old woman and Jase's sister shouldn't have had any impact.

Only they struck close to home because these people knew Brek way better than Velma did. She probably was strung too tight for someone like him. That didn't matter, though. They were figuring things out. Maybe. If he would just show up, already.

"If you'd bring a girl home more often, you wouldn't confuse her," Anna stage-whispered across the table to Jase, scrunching her forehead.

"If he brought girls home more often, he'd just confuse her more," Zak replied, slicing another piece of cake. "We'd have a wedding every week."

"The vedding is next veek?" Babuska asked Jase. "This is fast. Fast is best."

"Yup, next week. Why wait when you've met the perfect girl?" Jase nodded to Velma and poured more vodka.

Velma's jaw dropped to her toenails. "Stop," she muttered and snatched the bottle, setting it beside Brek's unused plate.

"Where did you propose?" Babushka's eyes lit with joy.

"At the shop, yesterday. We're all very excited," Jase said, deadpan.

Velma stomped on his foot under the table. "Stop."

"Jason," his mother said in what had to be her best listen-to-your-mother tone.

"What?" He shoved another bite into his mouth. "She thinks we're together. Might as well play along. Right, Sugar Lips?"

Velma stared at him, unable to close her mouth.

"She'll forget tomorrow, anyway." He shrugged. "Toss me more vodka so I can forget, too."

"No more alcohol for you. And, seriously, 'Sugar Lips'?" Velma pinched her not-sugary lips together.

"Tastes just like strawberries." He winked at her.

She blinked, her cheeks burning. "What?"

Brek wouldn't have told anyone what she'd done on the couch.

"Strawberries. Sugar Lips. Tell me I'm not the only one who gets that?" He held up his fork with a strawberry stabbed in the tines.

Velma opened her mouth and closed it again. Her phone vibrated in her purse. Thank goodness… It had to be Brek.

"Would you excuse me?" She grabbed her bag and pushed out her chair.

"Not a problem, Sweet Potato." Jase grinned up at her as she stood.

She pulled out her phone and clicked it on without checking the screen as she headed toward the sitting room. "Hello?"

"Velma? It's Pam."

Velma's heart stopped. She gripped the back of the sofa. Had something happened to Brek?

"Is Brek okay?" she asked, gripping the upholstery harder.

"I was hoping you could tell me," his mother said, exasperated. "I've been trying to reach him for hours. Aspen's water broke. We're at the hospital. They say it shouldn't be long now, and I figured he'd want to meet his nephew."

Velma's breaths went shallow. Brek had said a couple of days ago it was still too early. "Is she okay? Is the baby okay?"

"Everyone's fine. Baby's got the all clear to come. I thought Brek was with you?"

Velma shifted her phone to the other ear. "No, he had a meeting tonight. But I'll go find him and make sure he gets there. Are you at St. Luke's?"

"Yes. Hang on." Pam mumbled something in the background before returning. "Let me know when he's on his way?"

"Of course. I'll be in touch." Muscles in Velma's neck cinched tight.

"Thanks, dear." Pam disconnected.

He'd mentioned offhand the name of the club—what was it?

Velma clicked off her phone and tried Brek. He didn't answer. She shoved a hand through her hair as she waited for his voice mail. "Brek, it's me. Aspen's at St. Luke's. Baby's coming. I'm on my way to find you...call me."

Velma tossed her phone in her bag and hurried back to Jase. "Aspen's having the baby. I need to get to Brek to tell him. Can you help me find him?"

She'd already brought up the search engine on her phone to check social media for the club name.

Jase dabbed his napkin against his lips. "By all means, let's go clubbing. Thanks for dinner, Mom. I've got to take my fiancée to find her boyfriend."

"Nice to meet you. We'll talk next week?" Anna rose and squeezed Velma in a hug. The Dvornakovs were loud, and they were huggers. Velma would have to get used to both.

"Perfect." Velma turned to go, but Babushka waited behind her, arms wide. Velma leaned down to squeeze her.

"Grandbabies come soon, yes?" the old woman asked.

Velma glanced up to Jase and glared.

"Nah, we want to wait and get to know each other better." Jase tugged Velma's sleeve. "C'mon, Baby Cakes. You're driving."

"Because...vodka?"

"Yup," he replied, heading toward the front door. "Whisk me away in your chariot."

They ended up parking over four blocks away from the club. Apparently, word had spread quickly of Dimefront's impromptu gig. Dozens of paparazzi hung out on the sidewalk in front of the expansive nightclub. The corded line to get inside wrapped all the way around the building.

People spilled into the alley and lounged on curbs while police lights flashed nearby. Velma's stomach twisted itself into knots. How would she ever find Brek in this mess?

"Well, this is a cluster." Jase zipped up his windbreaker jacket with The Flower Pot's company logo across the back.

"We could try reasoning with the bouncer." Velma nodded toward the hulky guy with the buzz cut standing guard at the entrance.

Jase squinted at the crowd that grew by the second. "Or you could flash your tits. That might work better."

Velma's cheeks burned. She refused to look at Jase. "This isn't Mardi Gras."

"Ahh…but it could be. See? I wouldn't even peek at yours, because they belong to my buddy and that would be wrong." He gave her a look like he was teaching a really important first-grade lesson. "The key is, you'll start a trend. It'll be like a wave at a stadium, but way better."

"I can see why you and Brek are friends." She refused to acknowledge his suggestion with anything more. Instead, she squared her shoulders and took a deep breath. "I'm going in."

"Right behind you," Jase said, gesturing ahead of them.

Before her nerves took over, she looked both ways and hustled across the street. She stepped onto the curb and headed straight for the door, marching right up to the muscled bouncer, chin held high.

"Sorry, miss," the deep baritone of the huge guy's voice washed over her. "Line's the other way."

"Hi." She nodded at him. *Be brave.*

"Hi," he replied, his face a stone mask.

She raised her hands in front of her. "You probably think I'm here trying to meet that band."

"Probably." His expression didn't change.

Ugh. He didn't get it.

"I'm not. I assure you that I don't even like their music. Seriously, it's all overly loud nonsense and cussing."

That cracked the mask. Bouncer dude squinted toward her.

"No, I'm looking for my boyfriend," she continued. "He manages Dimefront. Brek? You probably know him. His sister's having a baby, and he needs to go meet his nephew. So, I'm just going to sneak in, find him, tell him, and leave." She nodded and moved to get past, reaching for the handle of the door.

"You're Brek's girlfriend?" He shifted to step in front of her.

"Yes."

He looked her over top to bottom. "Not how this works. Nice story, though."

"Hey, bitch? Get in line like the rest of us," a teased-up groupie shouted from behind the velvet rope.

Velma ignored her and tried once more. "Please."

"Please?" he asked. "So polite. Hang on. Hey, Jack?"

Another even hulkier guy ducked out from a stool near the doorway. Velma moved her head up, up, and up to meet his eyes.

"Seems this lady needs to find Brek because he needs to go meet his nephew. She said 'please.' You want to handle this for me?" Mr. Bouncer said.

Was she mistaken or did he flex his arm muscles? Whether he did or he didn't, they rippled under his formfitting black Henley.

"His sister's having the baby right now," Velma added to drive her point home.

"That right?" Jack lifted his chin, his squint matching the other man's.

Velma gripped her purse and adjusted the strap on her shoulder. "Yes."

Thank goodness, they were finally getting somewhere. The burly dude *could* be reasonable. She tossed an I-told-you-so look to Jase.

"Follow me." Jack jerked his chin toward the edge of the building.

"Thank you so much. You have no idea how important this is for him. His sister went into labor early. It was a whole thing. Everyone's been so worried." Velma dodged a wad of gum on the sidewalk as she scurried along after him. "Is this the way to the back entrance?"

Jack didn't reply. They came up to a group of people and he stopped, pointing to a crack on the concrete. "Wait here."

Gah, no.

"This is the end of the line." Velma gestured to the group that wrapped around the building. There had to be over five hundred people standing in front of her.

"Sure your boyfriend won't mind waiting to meet his nephew when he's watching Dimefront play their set." The way he said "boyfriend"…he didn't believe her.

She deflated.

"Tell him I said congrats." Jack moseyed back to the stool by the entrance. Velma glanced up at the never-ending mass of bodies. Her heart sank.

"Told you, you should have lifted up your shirt. If I had jugs, I'd do that all the time." Jase stepped up beside her, his hands in his pockets. "I'd get the best parking spots, never have to wait in line…it'd be awesome."

"Where were you?" she asked, her tone deep, her face hot.

"Right behind you." Jase gestured to where the bouncers huddled.

"You didn't even think to help?" She dug for her phone in the hope that Brek might have called.

Jase lifted a shoulder. "Figured you had it covered. You were on a roll. That part where you said you didn't even like Dimefront? Epic. Everybody likes them."

"I don't," she muttered. After tonight's outing, she liked them even less.

Velma glanced through the large windows of the club, searching for Brek. She stepped out of the line and mashed her palms to the cold glass, scanning the overflowing club. "Oh my gosh. There he is."

He leaned against the side of a table, near the back of the room. A huge smile covered his face, and he tossed his head back because something was apparently hysterical in his bubble of life. Interesting, Velma wasn't finding much funny out there on the chilly sidewalk.

Brek gestured wide with his hands, a beer dangling between his fingers. The woman next to him in a tight skirt, displaying an abundance of cleavage, burst into laughter. She gripped his biceps with her perfect red fingernails.

She squeezed.

Brek's bicep.

Over his ever-present T-shirt. Velma didn't need him to take it off to know the woman had squeezed right where the dragon's tail blended into the tribal ink.

Velma actually felt her blood get hot and her eyes go wide.

He glanced to the tight-skirt lady. She went onto her tiptoes and whispered something into his ear.

Velma's stomach turned, and her throat got thick. It didn't take a degree in body language to know what the woman wanted.

"That's not good," Jase mumbled from behind Velma. "Danger, bud. Danger."

Brek glanced to the man next to him and nodded, disentangling the woman's fingertips gripping his arm. He said something to her, and she pouted her ridiculously overpainted lips. Then she tucked something into his hand.

Oh heck no. The hairs on the back of Velma's neck prickled. That woman had no business passing her phone number to Brek.

"Toss the number," Jase said under his breath. "C'mon. You've got an audience."

Velma held her breath. He couldn't. He wouldn't. He was her Brek.

"Don't worry. You're way prettier than she is. She's only pretty in the obvious way." Jase crushed her to the glass as a group pushed past them. "Shit. They need some crowd control out here."

"The obvious way?" Her body still scrunched up against the window, her gaze focused on the slip of paper Brek held with the bottle of Coors.

Velma couldn't pull her gaze from Brek's fingers…the note…the bottle. Would this be her life? Always unable to get ahold of him? Even his family couldn't reach him. And how much of a chance would she ever have with the band groupies surrounding him all the time?

"You know it doesn't mean anything if he keeps the number. Nothing. Means nothing," Jase said with absolutely no conviction.

Brek laughed again and dropped both the bottle and the note on a random table as he followed the guy, skirting behind the back of a booth.

Jase fist-pumped and moved backward as the crowd shifted. "Told you. Never doubted him."

Velma turned, poking Jase in the chest. "What do you mean? The obvious way?"

"You know, like…she's got all the fake…you know, I think I'm going to shut up now." Jase raised his hands in surrender.

Velma shuffled toward the end of the line and slouched against the big blue mailbox. They had already lost their place, and the line had grown another twenty people deep. "There's no way we're going to get to him."

"C'mon, think positive. We could always climb on the roof and break into the club." Jase stared at the top of the building. "I could hop on that Dumpster, climb up and grab the edge of the window, slide to the side and see if any of them are open. It'll work."

"And you could break your neck in the process, which means Brek will lose his best friend and Babushka will hate me. Do you have any money?" She reached for her wallet. She only had a twenty. Darn.

He raised his eyebrows at her. "Uh…yeah. Why?"

"Like, cash? We could slip a hundred dollars to the bouncer and see if that helps our case." She pulled a handful of change from the depths of her bag. No dollars. Crud.

He shook his head. "Already tried that."

"When?"

"About the time you were going off on how much you dislike the band. Didn't work. Do you always carry that many pennies with you?"

"No." Velma dropped the money back into her purse as a charge went through the air. She glanced back to the windows. The guys from Dimefront took the stage and the crowd outside screamed in response. Velma craned her neck but couldn't see Brek anymore.

Muscles in her chest tightened. The throng surrounding them shoved each other to get a better view of the band. People pushed all around them…well, her… Where the heck had Jase gone? She glanced back and forth, searching for him.

More bodies pressed her farther from the building, toward the street. She waved her hands over her head and shouted, "Jase?"

She needed to get out of here. The vibe had gone from annoyed-but-waiting to get-the-heck-out-of-my-way danger-ous. Holding her purse tight to her side, she headed to cross the street just as a police cruiser bleated a siren. She'd made it to the curb when a rowdy group heaved by her.

Tottering on her heels, she fell hard against one of the cars parked along the street. Crud. That hurt. She rubbed at her hip.

"Velvet?"

Thank goodness.

She closed her eyes, squashed away the sour ache in her chest, and glanced up to Wayne. She flashed back to when they were seven, and she had biffed it on her bike. He'd come to her rescue then, as well.

His arm holding her waist, he helped her across the street to a concrete flower planter in front of an all-night convenience store.

"You okay?" He dusted some nonexistent dirt from her shoulders, holding her a little too close and lingering a teensy bit too long.

She slumped to the edge of the planter, taking care not to crush the azaleas. "I'm fine. I'm just…I'm trying to get to my boyfriend to get him a message."

"Ah." He frowned, stepping in front of her. Wayne was generally soft spoken, but he had to raise his voice to be heard over the crowd. His radio crackled on his shoulder. He said something in return.

"You should probably get back to work." She nodded to another group of people headed up the sidewalk toward the club.

"Backup just got here. I'll see you to your car first." He held his palm out to her.

She shook her head and waved at the building. "I have to get in there. Brek's sister…she's having her baby and he's going to be an uncle and he's not answering his phone."

"Velma." Jase jogged to her, out of breath. "Holy shit, it's a mosh pit."

"She fell," Wayne said, rubbing her shoulder.

Fine, so she had taken a small tumble. It hardly counted.

"I saw. That car totally came out of nowhere. Way to nail the landing, though." Jase raised his eyebrows at Wayne's hand resting on her shoulder. "Who are you?"

"Wayne. Friend of Velvet's," he replied. Velma absolutely

noticed that he didn't offer his hand to Jase. Nope. It stayed right on her shoulder. She subtly shifted to try to knock it free.

Didn't work.

"We grew up together." Velma checked her phone. Still nothing.

She shook off Wayne's hand, *still* on her shoulder. This time he let it fall.

The radio on Wayne's shoulder crackled to life.

Velma couldn't make out what they said on the other end. "What's happening?"

"Crowd's too big. Fire marshal's clearing the sidewalk." Gosh, why did Wayne's eyes always have to be so freaking kind?

"There's no way in, Jase. How are we going to get in ther—"

Jase put a finger up to her lips. "No more blah-blah. Go home and put some ice on your ass. Let me do this my way."

Gah. His way involved climbing on a Dumpster. With a side of breaking and entering.

She batted his fingertip away. *Enough already with all the craziness of this night.*

"Fine." Velma stood, but crud her hip really hurt. She winced and sat back down. Ice sounded really good right about now.

Jase raised his I-told-you-so eyebrows.

"If you want to try to catch Brek, that's great. I'll call his mom with an update and head...home." She looked to Wayne. "I can walk myself to my car."

"Nope." Wayne glanced to the unruly crowd. "I'll see you get out of here in one piece." He held his hand to her once more. This time, reluctantly, she took it.

Chapter Twenty-Two

The deep bass of Dimefront's signature chorus pulsated through the building as the band rocked the stage. Brek felt those chords down to his marrow, but he pulled the contract closer. Tonight, he had business.

Hans shouted across the small table, but hearing was impossible. Even this far away from the speakers, the music filled every molecule of air.

Brek stilled his tapping foot. He used to crave the sensation—the music, the lights, the endless string of women and booze.

Tonight, he only craved Velma.

Hans whisked the pen along on the dotted line. Brek let out a breath of relief. He folded the papers and smacked them against his hand, the tempting pull of the exit a siren's song. He needed to get to Velma. Explain to her everything that had happened. Or…almost everything.

"Looking forward to the future." Hans stuck out his hand.

Brek shook it. "Me, too."

Brek and Hans had not only come to an agreement with the band that they'd stay together through the scheduled tour, but Hans would act as full manager when Brek needed to be home. If everything went as they'd discussed, Brek wouldn't have to travel as much in the future, and he could focus his attention on all that he now had in Denver.

The whole thing was hush-hush for now until a firm agreement could be hashed out. But soon he'd be able to tell Velma.

Then he'd find a comfortable bar he could buy and renovate, and he would use his connections to bring the best bands to Denver.

"Sorry about your phone." Hans winced.

Brek shifted where he stood. "Shit happens."

Shit *had* happened. Shortly after he'd arrived, Brek had excused himself to call Velma and let her know his plans had to change. As it generally happened, one woman had leeched onto him. She had shamelessly flirted. He'd ignored her. Then she'd snatched his phone and with a coy, "Oops," dropped it in a pitcher of Budweiser. Pouting her Botox-filled lips, she said something about needing his full attention. He couldn't hear her exact words due to the blood rushing through his ears at the time.

Needless to say, the phone was fried, and he couldn't reach Velma. He'd had Botox Barbie removed from the club. That went about as well as you'd expect. She spit and hissed the whole way to the exit. The bouncer had the fingernail scratches to prove it.

Then the next groupie took her place at Brek's side. And when he shook her off, another, and another.

At one point in his life—hell, a few months ago—he'd loved that part of the business. Now? He had Velma. She may not have been ready to declare her feelings for him, but they were there. He hoped like fuck they were there. They had to be there.

"Brek!" a guy called over the music.

He turned to the direction of his name, scanning the packed room.

Jase shoved through a mass of VIPs and Brek's chest went tight. What the heck was Jase doing there?

Brek hurried toward Jase, leaning to yell in his ear. "How fucked am I?"

No doubt Velma had handled the dinner perfectly, but he felt like shit for standing her up. Hopefully, all he'd worked for that night would make amends for his screwup.

"Aspen's in labor," Jase hollered back.

Brek's pulse skipped and a headache formed at his temple. "How long?"

"No idea. Velma tried to get in here to tell you, but she got hurt when the crowd went crazy outside. Don't worry, the car had nothing on her."

"Car? What? Is she okay?" Brek's breath hitched.

"Should be home by now. I left her with a cop who was *way* too handsy for my liking. She said they know each other, and he promised to help Velma to her car." Jase started toward the nearest exit.

Sweat formed along Brek's neck, and not from the heat of hundreds of bodies shaking their asses on the nearby dance floor. God, Velma had to be all right. "I've gotta get to her."

Jase caught his shoulder before he could leave. "Yeah. You should know she saw that chick give you her number. Velma wasn't thrilled. But A-plus for ditching it fast."

"Fuck." Brek muscled his way through the crowd.

Which of the multitude of *chicks* had Velma seen?

He threw open the thick black exit door. Cool Colorado air provided a soothing balm against the bullshit of the night. The group outside parted only slightly. Brek and Jase had to elbow their way through the crowd. A drunk chick with over-teased hair bumped into Brek and caught his arm. She flashed a fake grin. "What's the hurry?"

He shook her off.

Shit. There were literally people everywhere. *This is insane.*

Jase headed toward the street. "The fuck happened tonight?"

Brek matched his stride. "Phone died."

"You should've seen Velma at dinner. She kept looking at the door and checked her cell about a bazillion times."

"Long story," Brek muttered.

Jase smacked his shoulder. "Hope it's a good one."

"How'd you get in the club, anyway?" Brek asked as they moved around the edge of the crowd.

"There are certain things no one needs to know." Jase smirked as they moved through a cloud of cigarette smoke. "Call your mom, check on Aspen."

Brek took the phone Jase handed him and dialed.

"Ma, how's Aspen?" He stopped walking and held a hand up against his other ear so he could hear.

"Things slowed way down. She's resting. They're not thinking anything's going to happen until morning." Ma sounded wiped.

"You need anything? I can come wait with you." Brek dropped his head.

"Go on home. I'll call you when things change."

"I want to be there for you. When you need me." Soon he'd be an uncle. He blinked against the emotion in his throat.

"There's nothing anyone can do right now. Get some rest tonight. Love you, Brek."

"Back at you." He swiped at the screen to end the call.

"Everything okay?" Jase asked.

"Yeah. Gonna be awhile." Brek started dialing Velma's number.

"Are you Brek?"

Brek glanced up as a cop strutted over to them. Full uniform. Full jackass. Brek trusted him about as far as he trusted gas station sushi.

"Yeah?" Brek asked, only stopping because the guy blocked them from continuing down the sidewalk.

"You're the guy with Velma?" the cop guy asked.

"Look, man. Now's not a good time." Brek held up a palm and tried to move forward.

The idiot stepped closer, right into Brek's space.

"Wayne." He stretched his hand to shake Brek's.

"Brek." Brek shook it.

Wayne had balls. Brek gave him that. He also had a uniform and a gun, so Brek elected to behave.

"She's home." Wayne glanced from Brek to Jase and back. "She deserves better than to be left on the curb like that."

"Trust me, Officer. You do not want to do this tonight." Jase stepped into position at Brek's right.

Wayne held up his hands in mock resignation. "Not doing anything. Just making sure she's being taken care of."

Wayne crossed his arms but clearly made sure his badge stayed visible. Yeah. Brek got the message.

"You're gonna break her heart. And when you do, I'll be there to put it back together."

Jase moved in closer and jerked his chin toward Fuckwit. "She's only warming one bed tonight, and it's not this jackass's."

Wayne smirked like a fuckin' candy-ass. "For tonight. We'll see what happens tomorrow."

Brek leaned through the few inches Wayne had left between them. "Leave her. The fuck. Alone."

"Or what?" Wayne narrowed his eyelids, sizing him up.

"Not stupid enough to threaten a cop, asshole. You sure you want to play this game? Because you'll lose." Brek's fingertips itched to strangle the son of a bitch.

Jase grabbed Brek's arm.

"I'm not thinking that's gonna happen. Which of us would make her the happiest? Pretty sure you know that's not you." Wayne moved to the side. "Have a good night, gentlemen."

Wayne strode away.

Brek clenched his back teeth so hard they should have cracked.

Jase rocked back on his heels. "We both know he's wrong."

"Yeah." Brek stared down at the phone in his palm. He punched in Velma's number. Her cell rang several times before her voice mail picked up: "Hi, you've reached Velma, please—"

He hung up and handed it back to Jase.

Jase pinched his lips closed. "Probably better you talk to her in person."

Brek jogged toward his bike. An acrid twinge pinched in his chest. He would never outrun the truth of Wayne's words.

VELMA LIMPED to her bedroom with her laptop under her arm and an ice pack against her backside. She propped a pillow under her hip, grimacing at the ache.

Her ringtone came from her phone in the other room. Ugh. She'd left it on the counter. She slipped her legs over the edge of the bed and hobbled to the kitchen.

"Hello?" she said into the phone, dropping her elbows to the counter.

Double ugh. She'd missed the call from Jase. She dialed him back. Voice mail.

Claire had asked her to do a slide show for the reception, and all that was left was the background music. Velma had hoped Brek might help her choose the songs, but it looked like she would be on her own. She moved back to the bedroom.

Frustration from the night bubbled in her veins. She shook it off and lifted the screen on her laptop. Instead of clicking the video maker, she clicked open her spreadsheet program. Her cheeks flushed when she stared at her long-neglected dating file.

She tapped the arrow keys, scrolling the file to the bottom. She fell back against the pillows and added Wayne's name. No surprise, he got a nine. But Wayne had never once made her toes curl or her blood pressure rise—in the best way. He'd never challenged her or made her try new things. Not the way Brek had.

Brek's encounter with the groupie at the club. His absence at dinner. They replayed in her mind as she stared vacantly at the cells. She smacked her laptop lid closed and placed it aside.

"Velma?" Brek shouted from the kitchen. The clank of his keys against the counter and his boots against the wood floor were a relief she hadn't expected.

"I'm in here." Her voice cracked. She pushed herself up.

He burst in, dropped next to her on the bed, and wrapped her in his arms. It had only been one evening, but it felt like forever.

"Thank God," he said against her forehead. "Jase said you got hurt."

He held her away from him, his gaze settling on the pillow she'd propped against her backside. His hand went to her waist, just above the bruise. "How bad is it?"

"I'm fine. Really. It's nothing." Their breaths mingled as he pulled her to him once more. "Aspen's in labor. Did Jase tell you?"

"Called Ma. No baby yet. She'll call your phone when I need to head that way." He let out a long sigh, not releasing her. "I fucked up and I'm sorry. Shit happened tonight at the club, and my phone's no longer capable of making or receiving calls. What happened was a fluke. I don't want to miss anything."

"You seemed to be having a good time when I saw you there," she said against his throat.

He shifted on the bedspread, laying her back into the cocoon of pillows she had settled into earlier. His heavy boots clunked to the carpet. He stretched out beside her, resting his hand on the ice pack. "Things took longer than expected."

"Did it go okay? The meeting?"

Something funny passed over his face. "Yeah."

"That's good." Just because it was good didn't make it okay that he'd missed being where he'd promised.

"Sometimes my job gets in the way. Your job gets in the way. That's how it goes," he pointed out.

"My job doesn't have groupies." She traced one of the flowers on her comforter with her fingertip.

He frowned, his expression hard. "Maybe not, but you've got an asshole cop friend."

Whoa. What the heck?

"Don't talk about Wayne like that. He hardly compares to the girl feeling up your muscles." Velma glanced to the balcony, ignoring the pang of hurt in her heart.

Brek tugged her chin back so she faced him. He squared his jaw. "I'll avoid the groupies. You avoid him. He made it clear tonight he wants to move in on what's mine. I'm not puttin' up with that."

Velma gasped. "What?"

"Didn't stutter. Wayne's a giant dick with a little prick. It's bad enough he's got a badge. I'll keep the groupies at a distance, you keep that asshole away."

She didn't particularly care about Wayne, but he was a friend and Brek did not get to barge in and tell her whom she could and couldn't see. She met his stare in a silent standoff.

Her phone rang again. She reached for it.

Pam.

"It's your mom." Her words sounded scratchy as she held up the screen.

He didn't answer it, instead holding it until it stopped buzzing. "I'll call her back after we sort this out."

Velma crossed her arms under her breasts and met his stare. "You're being totally ridiculous about everything. Wayne's a family friend. I'm not banning him from seeing me."

"He's a *family friend* who wants you for himself." Brek tossed his legs over the side of the bed and stood.

"That's really unfair," Velma said, the words soft.

Brek headed toward the bedroom door. He paused. "I don't trust him. Guys like that weasel their way into your life and screw everything up."

"Why are you acting like this?" she asked, leaning on her elbow. "Jealousy? You've got to be kidding. It's not like that with him."

Brek dropped his hands to his waist. "Not asking for a lot, just that you respect what we have enough to send him packing."

He dipped his head and the muscle in his jaw ticked.

"Brek…" she started to say, but he was already heading for the door, her phone pressed against his ear.

Chapter Twenty-Three

THE NIGHT BEFORE CLAIRE & DEAN'S WEDDING

They'd placed bets on how long it would take to get tossed out of Hank's Bar during Claire and Dean's coed bachelor-slash-bachelorette party. "They" being Jase, Eli, Heather, and the bride and groom. In other words, everyone was in on the bet but Brek and Velma.

Brek took a pull of his Coors. Eli lounged on the other side of the booth. Dean and Claire wouldn't get off the damn dance floor—they slow danced even to the fast songs. And Heather and Velma had taken up residence on a pair of stools along the bar top to gab.

When Brek had asked Dean what he wanted to do for his bachelor party, this was not what he'd had in mind.

Then again, nothing in his life lately was what he'd had in mind.

"You know what we should do next?" Jase asked.

"I bet you're gonna tell me."

"We should knit lace doilies and then go to one of those paint-by-number places where they serve wine."

"I'm in." Eli jerked his chin in their direction. "It's either that or we head back to your apartment and play drunk Pictionary."

Brek grunted in reply. He flagged the waitress for another round.

"Why are Velma and her friend over at the bar?" Dean slid into the booth across from Brek. He grabbed his beer and took a slug.

"'Cause Velma and Brek are having a tiff." Jase leaned forward, apparently ready to dish.

"What're you two fighting over that's making the boys and girls separate like a middle school dance?" Dean wore the *Buy Me a Shot, I'm Tying the Knot* T-shirt Velma had bought for him.

Claire had a matching pink version of the tee, along with a rhinestone tiara and black sash that read *Bachelorette*.

Velma hadn't stopped there—the rest of them got sashes that read "*I Do*" *Crew*. They'd all actually worn the damn sashes, too. Jase, 'cause he was Jase. Brek, 'cause he didn't want to hurt V's feelings. And Eli, 'cause everyone else was.

"Oh. My turn to tell." Jase waved for everyone to lean in closer.

This ought to be good. Brek scooted forward.

"See, Brek missed an important dinner." He was right so far. "Then Velma fell on her ass and got hit on by a cop." Still accurate. "Then Brek's sister had her baby." Also correct.

Well, that was the drunk CliffsNotes version of events.

Velma had been tense since he'd asked that she stay away from Wayne. He got that she didn't want to be told what to do. What he did *not* get was why this Wayne idiot remained so important to her. The dude was a first-class, grade-A prick.

"I'm going to go dance with the pretty bridesmaid talking to Velma." Jase scooted out of the booth and headed for Velma's friend Heather.

"Seriously, what's going on with you two?" Dean squinted at Brek.

Dean had been busy with all the wedding stuff, and given he'd be Velma's new brother-in-law soon, Brek was keeping his lips zipped when it came to their relationship until he figured out what he was going to do about everything.

"I'm in love with her." There. He'd said it out loud to someone who wasn't Velma. She knew. The rest of the world might as well know, too.

Brek should've had his camera ready to capture Dean's shocked expression.

Dean paused. "I don't think that means what you think it means."

"I know what it means, jerkwad." Brek replied.

"She love you?" Eli asked.

He'd bet money she did, but she hadn't said it. Here he was working on a plan to stick around Denver, and she hadn't even said the words. "Pretty sure she's getting there."

"Then I'm happy for you two." Dean clinked his beer bottle against Brek's. "Here's to the Johnson women."

"What're you going to do about the tour?" Eli asked.

That was the shit of it, wasn't it? Brek had to leave soon.

"I've gotta go. But I'm working on plans so I can make Denver my base. Travel less. Stay with Velma."

"Does she know?" Dean jerked his chin toward where Velma and Claire stood together by the jukebox.

He hadn't told her. Not yet. "I've been waiting until I get everything sorted before I bring it up."

"My advice? Don't wait too long." Dean stood. "I'm going to go dance with Claire."

"His advice is good." Eli followed Dean out of the booth. "Communication is a good thing."

What the hell did the single guy know about communication?

"Hey." Velma approached the table.

His pulse did a nosedive before picking up again. He'd gotten used to her presence doing that to him.

"Hey." He held his arm out so she could slide beside him. "You wanna dance?"

She grabbed his hand to pull him out of the booth. "I thought you'd never ask."

Hands on her hips, he pulled her close and nuzzled Velma's neck. "Thought we might call a truce."

"I like that idea." Her arms around his neck, she met his gaze. "Claire said we have to be out of here by midnight. She wants everyone to get sleep."

"Then we've got approximately thirty more minutes to figure out a way to get kicked out of this bar." He twirled her in a circle.

"What do you have in mind, Mr. Montgomery?"

He pulled her palm to his mouth and pressed his lips against it, then kissed each of her fingertips. "I'm going to start a bar fight."

"Claire will literally kill you if you show up tomorrow with a black eye and ruin her pictures."

He grinned. "Then I guess I'll just make out with my girlfriend."

And he did.

Chapter Twenty-Four

CLAIRE & DEAN'S WEDDING DAY

Velma dropped her laptop onto the cart holding the video projector. She'd been running around all day getting things ready for the wedding. All that was left was to set up the slide show for the reception and then watch her sister get married.

Claire would actually be Dean's wife by the end of the day. The wedding video Velma compiled had come out fantastic—if she did say so herself. She tapped a finger against the top of her computer. Now she had to figure out how to set the darn thing up.

The ballroom was perfect. The "Purple Rain" theme had been a challenge. But Brek and Jase had hung lights strategically from the ceiling of the country club, so it appeared to be drizzling. They added various water fountains staged meticulously around the dance floor, and the tulips hung from the ceiling in the entryway. The place would've made Aspen proud. The editor from *Rosette* was already losing his mind over the photos they were getting.

Velma and Brek continued with their cautious truce. He hadn't been around much since their argument, between preparing for the wedding and spending time with his sister and his nephew. Brek had clearly fallen in love with being an uncle.

Could Velma ever really make a relationship work with him? She opened her laptop and stared at the screen. He would always be Brek, and no matter how much she changed, she'd always be Velma.

She slid the curser over the video program but skipped it to click on her spreadsheet file instead. With a few keystrokes, she added Brek's name and filled in the accompanying cells. The algorithm she had worked so hard on gave him a…four.

Her heart cramped.

"Except…" She brought her face closer to the screen and jolted.

Finger on the mouse, she clicked through the columns. "Oh my gosh."

He had been so odd the day he'd told her he loved her, asking her random questions and making crazy declarations about haircuts and disability insurance. He'd asked all those silly questions because he'd been checking off columns of her spreadsheet. She pinched her eyes closed, hope rising in her belly. This is what he had meant? He had been worried he wouldn't be enough. That *he* needed to change.

Her breaths came quickly.

He loved her.

And, holy goodness…she loved him. She. Loved. Him.

Her heart stumbled over itself. They would be okay. They loved each other.

The spreadsheet could never account for how Brek made her feel. Like she mattered. Like he genuinely cared about her. Trying to ward off a heart attack with this new discovery, she dug her knuckles against the pressure forming in her chest. He wanted to be the man she needed. She wanted nothing more than to let him.

BREK JOGGED up the stairs of the country club, trying to find Velma. Claire had insisted the entire bridal party get ready at the club before heading to the church. Some shit about pictures on the lawn and champagne in the lounge.

He glanced to his watch. T-minus two hours before Claire and Dean said their vows and then embarked on their European honeymoon. The church was finally ready. Brek wrapped things up and headed back to the country club to confirm everything there was a go and to connect with Velma.

Brek checked in with the hairstylist downstairs, but Velma wasn't there.

Meanwhile, his tuxedo was irritating as all hell. He still itched from the too-short haircut he had gotten earlier that morning. When Dean's barber had brought out the electric buzzer, Brek knew he was screwed.

He missed his jeans. And his hair.

Seriously, where the hell had Velma gone?

He reached the top of the steps and turned toward the ballroom.

Aspen and baby Bronson were headed the same direction.

"What are you doing here?" He hurried toward them, reaching for his nephew. The tyke had quickly become one of Brek's favorite people.

Aspen handed the baby over. "We needed out of the house. I figured we'd stop by and see how everything's going."

"Did you hear that, Bronson? Your mommy came to check up on Uncle Brek." He snuggled the kid against his cheek.

"Well, there is that." She wiggled her fingers toward the baby. "Uncle Brek is finally getting haircuts like a grown-up."

Brek rolled his eyes. "I did it at the request of the bride. Jacob know you're here?"

She laughed. "Uh. No. Don't mention our little outing to him."

"C'mon in and take a look how everything turned out." Brek led the way to the ballroom.

She followed. He grinned as he entered...both from the view of Velma in her short tube dress bending over the projector and how his team had transformed everything in the room purple—literally, everything—from the tablecloths to the plates.

"What're you doing?" he asked Velma.

She jumped and yanked at the hem riding up against her thigh. "Trying to get the projector to work. The audio is all fuzzy."

Two cords hung limp in her palm.

God, she was beautiful. He liked the way she looked all decked out. Today they actually looked like they belonged together.

"Velma, that dress is fantastic." Aspen took Bronson back. He fussed during the transfer. Of course he did, he loved his uncle.

Aspen did a sway-bounce combo to settle him.

Velma looked up at his sister. Her eyes got bright. "Oh my gosh, you brought the baby! Hi, Bronson."

"Let me take a peek at the cables." Brek shoved his hands in his pockets so he wouldn't reach out to run a fingertip along the edge of her dress on the way by. With Velma around, he would have to keep reminding himself he had a job to do today.

She glanced to him and the smile froze on her lips. She sucked in a breath. "I'm going to murder whoever did that to your hair."

"I think you're making an impression on him. He's getting big-boy haircuts and everything now." Aspen was in full-on little sister mode.

He refrained from sticking his tongue out at her.

"You don't like it?" He ran a hand over his trimmed hair. It hadn't been this short since high school.

Velma's lips parted, and she paused for slightly too long. That didn't bode well.

"V?"

"It's just not what I'm used to." The fabric of her skirt rode up again as she draped the cords over her laptop.

That dress was the fuckin' best.

She straightened. He pulled her to him. Her fingertips smoothed the lapel of his suit coat. "I'll get used to the hair. Do *you* like it?"

"Fuck no." Why people did this regularly, he'd never understand. "Figured it was more your thing."

Her lips tilted at the edges. "Tastes change, I guess."

He leaned to kiss her, which wasn't as far down as usual, given her three-inch stiletto heels.

"Diggin' the shoes," he said.

Velma turned her head to the side, so he missed and kissed her cheek.

He kissed the tip of her nose instead.

"Ahem." Aspen cleared her throat.

Brek looked over his shoulder to the sister he'd forgotten was standing there. She was grinning wider than he'd ever seen. "Mom's gonna get such a kick out of you two."

"Don't you dare bring our mother into my relationship," he grumbled.

"I won't have to. She's Mom. She'll find a way in."

"Aspen stopped in to check up on me," he said to Velma.

"Well, the last wedding didn't exactly go as expected." Velma scratched the little dimple at the tip of her nose.

"Actually, I wanted to tell you both thank you, for everything you've done for me." Aspen shifted the baby in her arms. "And I was also checking up on you."

"Told you." Brek reached toward Bronson, letting the kid wrap his hand around Brek's index finger.

"Anyhoo, since everything is under control, and I have a newborn, I should check in with *Rosette* and get Bronson home. I'll leave you to it." She cooed to Bronson as Brek disentangled his finger.

She left, and Brek's heart about burst with happiness for what his sister had.

A sigh escaped Velma's lips and her expression turned soft. "It's impossible to be annoyed at you when you look at your family like that."

"Then I guess now's the time to make my move." He kissed her with the urgency of a man who had to keep looking at her in that dress and do nothing about it. They were both breathing heavy when he finished.

The grip she had on his jacket lessened. "I need help with the audio."

"Audio later. This now." There had to be a closet or something around here they could utilize. Anywhere private, as long as she wore those damn shoes. His fingertips toyed with the slider on the zipper of her dress.

"Audio now. *This* later." She giggled and pointed to the rolling cart with the projector.

He sighed dramatically and followed her. Even with the wires adjusted, the audio wasn't playing right.

She slipped off her shoes and tossed them on one of the banquet folding chairs with the fabric covers. "I'm going to break my neck in those heels."

"Nah, you start to fall, I'll catch you. Those shoes are the shit." He adjusted an adapter, but it still didn't work. "I'm gonna grab Dean. He's good with this stuff."

His phone buzzed in his pocket. He glanced at his cell.

"Check it out. Pictures of the little beefcake." The screen held the latest snapshot of his nephew. Aspen sent new photos regularly. His little nephew already had Brek wrapped around his finger. When the kid turned eighteen, Uncle Brek had big plans to buy him his very own motorcycle. Of course he didn't mention this to Aspen—she'd lose her mind.

"Oh my gosh. Look at his chubby cheeks." Velma's own forehead relaxed, her eyes bright, expression soft.

The look suited her. Fuck, he loved her.

"Brek?" Jase stuck his head in the room. "Got a flower situation. Need your approval."

Velma tilted her head to the side with a coy smile. "Rain check on the…uh…other thing?"

"Unfortunately. But it's gonna happen later." He pinched her chin and gave her a solid once-over. He'd have to be careful not to wreck her hair once he got her alone and that skirt hiked around her waist. He jerked his thumb toward her discarded heels. "Wear the shoes."

"Are we working here? Or is this high school prom?" Jase huffed before he walked out.

Brek practically dragged his feet, but he followed. Turned out the tulips they'd ordered arrived in periwinkle instead of royal purple. Whatever the hell that meant. Purple was purple. Brek signed off on the change before he checked in on a sweaty, pacing Dean.

The guy was strung way too tight today.

"Get him an amaretto sour from the bar," Brek said to Eli.

Eli's eyes glittered with agreement. "On it."

"Just one drink." Brek held up his index finger. The last thing he needed was a sloshed groom at the church. Pops wouldn't appreciate that, and neither would Claire. *Keep the bride happy.* "And Velma's having audio issues. Can you check it out, Dean?"

"Sure thing," Dean said and headed for Velma.

Eli headed off to the bar.

Brek pulled out his recently replaced phone and checked with the assistant he had hired for the event. She verified the families were all in place, the *Rosette* editor was happy, the minister was ready, and the guests would arrive shortly. Brek called to confirm the limousine was on the way to pick up

Claire and her bridal party at the country club once they were finished getting ready.

Dean would ride to the church with Jase and Eli.

Brek would take his bike so he could get back and forth without waiting for a limo.

Everything was a go.

He glanced at his watch. He had approximately fifteen minutes to show Velma just how much he appreciated her.

With the one-track mind of a nineteen-year-old boy, he took the stairs two at a time. Emerging at the top of the staircase, he thanked the God of Getting Laid when Velma nearly smacked right into him. He caught her around her waist and yanked her to him.

She let out a surprised "eeep."

Give him ten minutes. He would have her making more noise than that.

"We're workin' a deadline, no time to stop." He laid a kiss on her that relayed the depths of his dedication to this hookup and hoped she wouldn't pull any bullshit about responsibility.

Both of them were breathing heavy when he let her go. She swayed a little and a tentative smile touched her lips. "Where are we doing this?"

Responsible Velma had left the building. His dick did a fist pump.

He snagged her wrist and pulled her toward the coat closet he had scoped out earlier. The door locked from the inside, which led him to believe they wouldn't be the first couple to use the small space. Country clubs were classy like that.

Velma's fuck-me-please shoes tapped along behind him on the polished marble tiles.

He tossed open the door, slipped inside with Velma, and kicked it closed—making sure the lock clicked into place.

The softness of her body contrasted with his as he pressed her against the wall. His mouth met hers.

A little moan escaped from her throat.

Today, her hair didn't smell like strawberries. No, today it was flowers and peaches and whatever the hell goop held it in place.

Strawberries were better. He missed them. Along with the ability to touch her hair without worrying he'd fuck it up.

"Anyone tell you how pretty you are today?" he asked, nuzzling her neck.

She cleared her throat. "Not yet."

Screw the wedding. He'd spend the day in the dark closet worshipping at the altar of Velma. On that thought, he dropped to his knees and ran a hand along the backs of her calves and up the exposed skin of her thighs to shove her skirt up.

"Totally unacceptable, your boyfriend is lying down on the job." His fingertips grazed the silky skin between her legs.

Her breath caught and she parted her thighs. "Is he? I should talk to him about that."

Amen and hallelujah, she was ready for him.

"You really should. You deserve sonnets 'n' shit." Hooking a finger along the elastic of her panties, he pulled them aside and peppered kisses along the edge of the fabric, right to her sweet spot.

"I don't think my boyfriend knows any…uh…sonnets."

Fuck, if he were any more turned on, he'd split right out of his pants. Not good, since they were rented.

"I'm going to call this one, Ode to Velma's Pu—"

"You should stop talking now." Her entire body squirmed under his touch, kneading the toes of those killer shoes into the carpet. "Timeline. No time for poetry." She grabbed at his head when he ran his tongue along her crease.

"Fuck, I could do this all day," he said against the heat of her. That was about the only poem he could think of right now, and it didn't even rhyme. His eighth-grade English teacher would be so disappointed in him. Wouldn't be the first time.

Unbuckling his fly as he stood up, he sprung himself free. His dick would never forgive him if he didn't get to play, too.

Velma reached her fingers around the base of his shaft and squeezed right in the spot where it drove him crazy.

Droplets dripped from the tip. Her thumb massaged them, and he nearly blew right there.

Rented pants. Not good. Keep it together.

Goose bumps trailed along her skin as he gripped the back of her leg and hitched it around his waist. He centered himself and drove home, bracing her against the wall.

His fucking phone rang.

He ignored it. Two minutes. He needed two more minutes.

Someone banged on the door. Neither of them responded.

"Seriously, Brek. Know you're busy, but Dean can't get the audio to work, either," Jase shouted.

Brek paused midthrust.

Well, that ruined the mood.

He glanced to Velma; her eyes were wide and her mouth slack. With the reluctance of a martyr, he withdrew and accepted the fact that he'd be walking around all day with a shiny new set of blue balls.

More banging. "C'mon, man. I hate to cock block, but you've got to get out here."

"Comin'," he shouted back.

There was a long pause. "Out here or in there?"

"Shut up, asshole. I'm on my way." Brek kissed Velma quickly and dropped her to her feet, waiting to be sure she wouldn't tip over.

She adjusted her dress, and he ran a hand over his no-longer-there hair.

This day sucked balls.

Jase gave him a decent side-eye but kept his trap shut as he led them to the ballroom. Velma clicked behind them on her heels.

"Hey, man, the cable's jacked. I think we need a new one," Dean said when they got to the ballroom. "I can try one other thing, but Velma's laptop timed out. I need her password."

Velma slipped around to the front of the computer and typed in her password. The glow of the projector filled the room.

Brek's gaze shifted to Velma. She'd gone stiff. Her cheeks abnormally pale. Frantic, she started typing keys, but her fingers kept slipping.

He glanced up to the screen and…motherfucking cock-sucker…Velma's spreadsheet in all its projected glory lit up the giant screen behind the dance floor. The thing was so long that all of it didn't fit on the screen, but she'd highlighted three rows. Dean's. Wayne's. And his.

"No," Velma said, her breath shallow. She turned her now-pleading eyes to him. The room seemed to spin as Brek read his name on the last line. Beside it was the number four. The time stamp said she had entered Brek's name that day.

Numbness took over. Everything sounded like it was in a vacuum. Brek stretched his hands, but he couldn't feel them. Not with the world around him crashing.

The four stung, no doubt. But what burned? Wayne's name above his with a bullshit nine in the next column. And Dean with his ten above that.

Fuck.

"Is that your dating spreadsheet Claire was talking about?" Dean asked, focused on the screen. "Why am I on it…?" His words trailed off at the end.

Sour betrayal pooled in Brek's gut as he carefully unclenched his hands. "Same question. Why am I on it?"

She said she'd given up the spreadsheet. So, this is what it felt like to have your heart broken. No wonder he'd never taken the plunge before.

"Brek…" Velma started toward him, but he raised a hand in defense of his heart.

"Not the time," he said quietly. Damn if his voice didn't crack.

Velma's chest heaved with big breaths. She pushed past him and yanked the cords from the back of her computer. The room dimmed with the loss of the light from the projector.

He couldn't deal with this at the moment. Focus on the gig at hand—this was his job.

OH GOD. The way Brek's face had twisted with pain when he saw the score her algorithm had given him.

Velma glanced away from him and swallowed past the regret of her idiocy. She should never have added him to her spreadsheet. Of course she had figured that out right after she'd done it. But he didn't know that. Judging by the way the muscle in his jaw twitched and the light in his eyes burnt out, she had crushed him.

"Velma, seriously, why am I on the list?" Dean's expression was blank.

The room spun, and it seemed someone had pressed the pause button on her lungs.

"I…um…" She should just tell him. Get it out there. "I used to have a little thing for you before you started dating my sister. Totally benign. I'm over it, and I'm so happy for you and Claire."

I love Brek now.

All she had to do was tell him.

"Is that why you did that thing you used to do in the

office?" He frowned. "The one where you wouldn't look me in the eye? I thought you didn't like me. Huh. It makes sense now."

Brek hadn't moved since the spreadsheet was on the screen. Hadn't hardly breathed.

She sucked in as much air as she could. "Can we go outside?" She reached for Brek's arm.

"I've got work to do." He didn't even look at her. "We need to get a new audio cable. I'll send Amy to grab one. Leave your password so she can get it working."

Okay. That's fine. She lowered her hand. He wasn't ready to let her apologize. He had work to do. She understood that. But he still loved her. She knew it in the depths of her damaged soul.

Dean glanced to Brek, then Velma, then back to Brek. "Velma, you should go find Claire. Make sure she's good."

She grabbed a sticky note from the projector cart and wrote her password on it, *BrekenridgeMontgomery*, and handed it to Dean.

She shrugged the strap of the duffle bag, full of her emergency wedding supplies, over her shoulder. With as much dignity as she could muster in her too-tight maid-of-honor dress, Velma went to find her sister.

Onward. Forward. Except…Brek.

Sometimes the hard thing isn't to run. It's to stay.

Velma stopped midstride and gripped the gaudy purple fabric on one of the chairs—she had to fix things with him. No matter what, she couldn't run away.

With all the effort she had, she laid her bag on the nearest table and pressed her fingertips against her eyes.

She glanced to Brek, but he wore a strange look on his face and wouldn't meet her gaze. His expression remained solid. The sting of the situation covered her like a thick serum of bull crap.

"Brek?"

His eyes flared. He shook his head before walking out with Dean right behind him. Dean gave her a sympathetic look and shook his head lightly.

Velma had never felt more incompetent in her entire life.

Someone cleared their throat. Velma looked behind her.

"Well…" Pops shoved his hand through what was left of his hair and grimaced. Claire and Heather stood beside him, their expressions unreadable.

Tears that had threatened before started to leak from the corners of Velma's eyes. She brushed them aside with her knuckles. "I've messed everything up with him."

Pops smelled of the spicy cologne he always wore as he rubbed her back in that awkward way of his.

"How much did you see?" She collapsed onto a chair and dropped her elbows to her knees.

"Enough." He sat beside her and leaned forward, his hands folded in his lap.

"Pretty much everything." Heather's words were soft. Sympathetic.

"I thought you stopped using the spreadsheets?" Claire pulled out a chair and sat.

Heather followed suit. "Why'd you rank Brek? And at a four?"

"And Dean? Why did you put him there?" Claire asked.

Velma wiped away more tears and threw up her hands. "I don't even know where to start."

"Let's start at the beginning, then," Pops said with the patience of a man who had conducted countless counseling sessions over the years.

She told them everything. Including her old crush on Dean. Minus the part about the things Brek had done to her on the back of a motorcycle.

Pops sat silent for a few beats.

"You never said anything about liking Dean." Claire's

words were delicate. "I never would've dated him if I'd known."

"That's one of the reasons I'm glad I didn't tell you. You two are perfect for each other. But I still don't know how to fix things with Brek." The spreadsheet was wrong. Like always. Numbers would never account for feelings.

"You see things in black and white, but you've got to change that. The rainbow has a multitude of colors. Just because Brek doesn't measure up to a silly standard you created doesn't mean he's wrong for you." Pops's eyebrows drew together thoughtfully. "Doesn't mean he's right for you, either. But the only way to see that for sure is to open *your* eyes. They've been closed awhile now."

Pops was wrong. Brek had opened her eyes. She'd just pinched them shut again when things got hard.

"I've ruined everything." Her shoulders drooped further.

"He's still here. There's time to fix things." Claire grabbed her hand and squeezed.

Doubtful. Her life had imploded all around her. "I need a new plan. A better one."

"Maybe you don't need one at all. Go where it feels right and stop making the easy things hard. Use your intuition." Heather took Velma's other hand.

She had her friends. They hadn't given up on her.

"Velvet, dear. Keep your eyes open." Pops smiled wistfully.

She nodded and set out to make things right with Brek.

With her shoes in hand, she took the stairs with as much speed as her dress allowed.

She finally found him on his phone, relaying messages to the staff at the church.

"Brek," she said when he hung up.

He tossed her a distant look and the muscles in her chest tightened.

"I messed up. I'm sorry." That summed it up, right? She stepped closer.

He shoved his phone in the pocket of his suit pants and studied the ceiling, the cords of his neck pulsing against his obvious frustration. "I thought you were past all of this."

"Past what?" Why wasn't he touching her? He always found ways to touch when they were close.

He dropped his gaze to the floor, hands on his hips. "Your head shoved up your ass."

Velma shifted on her bare feet. "That's not fair."

This time he did meet her eyes. Her breath caught at the devastated emotion mirrored back at her.

He brushed past her down the steps.

Her heart broke more than a little as she watched him go.

An aching distance separated them at the church. Brek threw himself into the coordination as soon as they arrived. Work couldn't wait, and Velma got that, but the way he blatantly dodged her attempts to communicate began to grate.

"Have you seen Brek?" Jase asked Velma as he sauntered into the Sunday school room they used as a staging area for Claire's bridal party.

"I don't know. Last I saw, he was talking to Pops near the rectory." Velma pushed away a nonexistent strand of hair from her cheek. "Jase, about what happened…"

The light in Jase's eyes dimmed. "He's my buddy. It's best if I don't get involved in this."

But she needed everyone to know that filling out the spreadsheet with his information was a mistake. "When I filled out the spreadsheet, I didn't understand him. I get it now, but he's blocking me out."

Jase scrubbed a hand over his military-grade haircut. "You gave him a four."

Velma tried to roll the tension from her shoulders. Technically, the algorithm gave him a four, but that didn't seem to be a good point to argue. The spreadsheet was wrong. Absolutely wrong.

"Jase, they need you at the chapel." Brek's chirpy assistant, Amy, clapped her hands to get everyone's attention.

Jase squeezed Velma's arm and left to take his place next to Dean…and Brek.

"Everyone ready? Anyone need anything? Water? Restroom? Now's the time," Amy continued.

Velma fluffed Claire's veil and forced herself to smile. "Ready?"

Claire nodded. A sprinkle of tears dusted her eyelids through the mass of tulle. Gram's repurposed now-sleeveless dress hugged her chest and waist tight, and the A-line silk skirt with the vintage lace overlay was perfection.

The *Rosette* photographer adored the history of the gown. They planned to post Claire's image next to the one of their grandmother.

Grams would've loved that.

They moved to the chapel, waiting at the closed doors. The flower girls and ring bearer lined up near the entrance, then Heather, Velma, and finally Claire with their father.

Velma took her place behind Heather, gripping her purple roses that Jase had wrapped tight with white ribbon. He had included a variety of shades of lavender, amethyst, periwinkle—there were practically fifty shades of purple roses.

They were gorgeous.

A string quartet started an instrumental version of the "Purple Rain" inspiration song in the chapel. Velma turned to Claire and gave her a thumbs-up.

Claire took their father's arm.

Velma took a huge breath.

"Wait." Claire stopped Amy just before the doors opened.

Oh no. Velma's heart nearly stopped beating. Claire couldn't run. Not like Sophie. Not with the blog photographer snapping photos. At that moment, he was on the other side of the doors waiting for them to open.

Claire disentangled her arm from their father's and handed him her oversized bouquet.

Velma couldn't move. Claire had to get married.

The quartet continued on in the chapel without the bridal party.

"What are you doing?" Velma whispered.

"Are we running? I can get a car?" Heather peeked from behind Velma.

"No." Claire threw her arms around Velma, "I'm not running. I just…"

Velma raised her eyebrows at their incredibly confused father. She patted Claire's back with her bouquet-free hand.

"I'm getting married." Claire held Velma tighter.

"Yes. That's what you should be doing right now." Velma glanced to Heather, who looked as confused as she felt.

"Like, literally, right now," Heather added.

Claire stepped back and did a deep-breath-arm-wave. "I'm getting married."

"Uh-huh." Velma took the bouquet from her father and pressed it into Claire's hands. "Let's go do that."

Claire nodded. Velma got Claire resituated.

Velma waited her turn, then stepped into the chapel. The purple rose petals along the red carpet smashed under her footsteps. She kept her focus on Brek.

He never looked in her direction. A chink formed in the armor around her heart.

The bridal chorus played, and still Brek didn't look her way.

All through the ceremony, he avoided eye contact. Claire kissed Dean, and they beamed at each other down the aisle. Brek took Heather's arm at the end, and Jase took Velma's.

"He'll come around," Jase commented as Mendelssohn's "Wedding March" played through the organ pipes.

She smiled tightly and nodded at her aunt Marlene, the whole time praying Jase was right.

The receiving line took forever. About halfway through, Velma realized she'd never eaten lunch. Her blood sugar crashing right along with her world, she finally arrived at the reception and took her place at the head table.

Claire and Dean had decided on a three-tiered, purple-tinted vanilla and coconut cake, but they went with what Maggie called naked frosting. To Maggie, that meant she used the barest amount of icing, leaving the purple cake tiers exposed. To Brek that meant...well, he'd illustrated for Velma exactly what he thought that meant. It didn't take much imagination.

There was no smashing of the cake in faces—just a playful attempt by Claire. Their mother wasn't amused.

"Velvet?"

Her cousin Lance stood behind her—a sweet still-sort-of-teenager who had passed the awkward preteen stage and was becoming a man. "Lance."

She stood to give him a hug. "I missed you at the receiving line. Pops said you brought a girlfriend with you?"

His cheeks turned red. "Everyone's talking about it, huh?"

"So far the verdict is that everyone likes her." Velma squeezed his shoulder.

"You're with the biker guy?" he asked.

"I am." She pinched a smile. Not that anyone would possibly know they were together, given he hadn't spoken to her. He'd disappeared when the band had started to play.

"I don't like him." Lance pulled a face.

Velma scowled at her cousin. "Why not?"

"Because you're sad and he hasn't done anything to fix that." Lance was sweet, she'd give him that.

"It's not his fault. He's busy with the wedding." She swallowed the thick lump of emotions that threatened to spill.

"Well, I came over here to see if you'll dance with me." He held his palm out to her. "What do you say?"

Getting her groove on wasn't in the cards while things were so messy with Brek. "I'm not feeling much like—"

A glass clinking over the loudspeaker drew her attention to the stage.

Brek stood under the floodlights in a patch of bright white among a sea of purple. A flute of champagne gripped in his hand, he raised it to where Claire and Dean stood on the dance floor.

Velma's breath dissolved in her lungs at the sight of Brek. Onstage. In his element.

She loved that man.

A waiter brought the bride and groom champagne. Brek kept his focus on them, not once glancing her way.

"I first met Dean in the hallway outside Mrs. Haulman's ninth-grade Greek literature class," he began. "Jase, Eli, and I were headed to learn about *The Odyssey*. Dean was about to get his ass kicked by a couple of football players." Brek scratched at his temple as the crowd laughed. Velma swallowed back an onslaught of tears, absorbing everything Brek. "I think it's fair to say that we never expected Dean to find a girl like Claire—not everyone is lucky enough to find their other half, but when you do, you hang on tight." He tossed a sincere smile to Dean and Claire. "Congrats, you two."

He raised his glass, and the room met his gesture… everyone except Velma, who couldn't seem to move.

"Velma?" Heather caught her arm. "We need to help Claire change out of her dress."

Velma shrugged at Lance. "Duty calls. Rain check?"

"Absolutely." He hugged her again. "Find your smile, Velvet."

By the time the bride and groom were ready to leave under handfuls of purple rose petals, Velma's eyelids seemed to have weights attached to them.

Dean stopped her at the exit where he and Claire waited for their cue. "Brek'll come around."

She gave a little nod, biting her lip. Of course he would, he was Brek. Her Brek.

Claire set her hands on Velma's shoulders and looked her square in the eye. "Are you okay?"

"I'm fine," Velma assured her, but the words sounded weak even to her own ears.

"Dean. She's not fine." Claire shuffled her feet, her face a mass of concern. "We can take a later flight. I'm not leaving for a week, when she's not okay."

Velma slipped Claire's hands from her shoulders and squeezed them. "I'm fine." She drew out the last word. "I can't exactly tell him I'm in love with him when you're hovering."

"But you'll call me?" Claire asked. "After you talk to him?"

At this rate, they were going to have to force her out of the country club and into the waiting car.

"She will call you. I will call you. Everyone will call you." Heather shooed Claire along as she silently mouthed to Dean, "We're not calling."

"Everyone ready?" Brek strode around the corner. "Your stuff is all loaded. Claire, your purse is in the back seat. I checked with the hotel and airline, everything's set."

Dean held out his hand to his best friend; they did a combo shake and bro hug that was more of a smack on the back. "Wedding was kickass. You did great."

Brek tossed him a lopsided grin. "You owe me."

The doors opened, and the family cheered and threw rose petals and birdseed as Claire and Dean ran to the waiting limousine.

Brek had found them a purple Hummer limousine. It was perfect.

Velma felt him behind her. His presence. He stood right

there. A step back and she could've leaned right into his embrace. Everything was going to be okay. He had her back. She had his. It's what they did.

Claire turned as she climbed into the back of the Hummer, her eyes meeting Velma's. They sparkled with happiness. She made a little phone with her thumb and pinky and held it to her ear.

Velma shook her head.

Dean scooted into the car after Claire, and they were off.

Her sister had found Mr. Right, and she'd wasted no time in marrying him. Velma was done messing around with ridiculous five-year plans and spreadsheets that told her absolutely nothing.

She turned to tell Brek she loved him. Right there at the wedding. He needed to know.

He wasn't there.

She found Amy in the country club kitchen. "Where's Brek?"

"He took off. Said he had business he needed to handle." She gave Velma a sympathetic look, but Velma had no energy left to figure it out.

So, he'd already left? That was okay. They could talk at home where it was quiet. It'd be better this way.

Still…a niggle of doubt tickled. The little chink in Velma's heart cracked further. She should have hurried home, but a twinge of avoidance had her turning left to take the long way, instead of right.

It didn't matter. Brek's parking space in the garage was empty when she pulled in next to it.

She held her computer bag tight and headed for the apartment, each step harder than the last. This was ridiculous. He wasn't there. That didn't mean there was anything to worry about. He'd made it clear that when you find the one you are meant to be with, you hang on tight.

She pushed the door open. Lights burned bright in the living room.

Brek never left the lights on. Something was wrong.

Really, really wrong.

Her pulse quickened, taunting her as her feet seemed to move on their own through the hallway to the bedroom. She flicked on the light.

His things were gone.

Not that he had a lot of them, but the motorcycle jacket he always tossed over her vanity was absent. Socks that never made it to the laundry bin had disappeared. The crack in her heart widened past a dull ache to full pain.

She tossed open the closet and the rucksack usually shoved on the top shelf wasn't there.

The fracture trenched deeper as she moved through the fog in her head to the bathroom. His razor was gone.

He'd actually left.

He'd left her.

The blood in her veins dipped like when an airplane was landing and there was that millisecond where the body was in free fall. Except the feeling didn't vanish. The landing gear wasn't going to save her, and Brek wasn't there to catch her.

A manila envelope propped on her pillow caught her eye.

No.

She crawled onto the bed she had made that morning. The one they had shared the night before.

The seal on the envelope slipped open, and she dumped the pages to the bedspread. A sob caught in her soul. She curled into a protective ball, but it wasn't enough. The pieces of her heart scattered to the wind.

He'd left the drawing of the lily he made for her…and his compass.

Chapter Twenty-Five

ONE WEEK AFTER CLAIRE & DEAN'S WEDDING

Velma crawled onto the bed, her phone against her ear, and waited for the tone to beep on Brek's voice mail. A week had passed, and he still refused to talk to her. She reached for the drawing of his compass and pressed it against her chest.

"Brek, hey, it's me." She tucked her bare feet under her thighs, running a hand into the hair at her temple.

"Jase asked me to say hi…you know, since you're not picking up his calls, either. Actually, he used a lot of cussing that I'm sure you'd appreciate, but I told him I wouldn't be repeating those words." She paused and pushed a pillow behind her head. It still smelled a little like Brek, so she couldn't bring herself to wash the pillowcase.

All week, she'd called him every night at seven and left a message. He had yet to respond.

"Your mom and Aspen are worried, too. I get that you're angry at me, but could you call them?" She squeezed her eyes shut against the reality of her new world.

"Aspen got your text, but she would really like to talk to you." He had only checked in once since his big disappearing act to assure his family he was alive. Everyone was still worried, though. Velma had explained to them why he'd left, expecting them to hate her.

They didn't, and she wasn't quite sure what to do with that, so she decided to embrace it. Aspen stopped by regularly with the baby, and Pam called all the time to check in. Claire made it a point to call from her honeymoon. Claire and Dean had been great about the whole thing, even going so far as trying to make Velma's spreadsheets a joke they could laugh about at future Thanksgiving dinners.

While Velma appreciated their support, what Dean thought didn't matter anymore. The only man who mattered had left.

"I went shopping with Aspen for a baby swing after work," she continued. "She's hoping it might help Bronson calm down a little easier. I offered to stop by tomorrow and watch him for a little while so she and Jacob can have a break. Work's going well. You know how it is."

These one-way conversations were mentally exhausting, but she wouldn't give up on him. On them.

"Oh, and Jase finally agreed to buy disability insurance." She laughed, but her heart wasn't in it. "He'll thank me someday, if he gets hurt and can't run the shop. I think I've also convinced him to do some commercial real estate investing while the market's still down." She paused, the weight of the oxygen in the room too heavy. "You probably stopped listening about two minutes ago…but, Brek, I miss you. Okay. I guess I'll call you tomorrow? Same time. Night."

Velma tossed her phone on the bedside table with his drawing and did what she had done every evening for the past week. She held tight to the black tee he'd forgotten in the hamper and inhaled her drug of choice—Brek's scent.

The tears started. She let them fall until they wouldn't come anymore.

Her eyes grew heavy, and she burrowed into the bedding, drifting until sleep took hold.

Her phone buzzed, jostling her from the honey-coated haze of fatigue. She fumbled through the darkness and slid her thumb across the screen to turn it on before she opened her eyes. "Hello?"

It sounded more like "'Lo." She cleared her throat and tried again. "Hello?"

Silence met her on the line. She peeled her eyes open and glanced at the screen.

"Brek?" She sat up abruptly, a spike of adrenaline hitting her core.

"Yeah," the word came out as a half grunt, half exhale. He sounded exhausted.

She glanced to her alarm. The clock read a little after midnight.

Her mouth open, she couldn't get her lips to move. All the unsaid words between them jammed against her tongue. She'd rehearsed this so many times, and now she couldn't remember what to say.

"Are you okay?" That was a good start.

He didn't answer. That was all right, though. Talking to herself had become second nature.

"I've been so worried. I just wanted to—" she started.

"You've got to stop calling." He had never sounded so tired.

She dropped back on the bed, her legs still tangled in the sheets, her breathing stalled. What had she expected him to say? Of course he wanted her to leave him alone.

"I checked in with Ma tonight," he continued. "I'll call Aspen tomorrow when she's awake. I won't call you again. It's time for both of us to move on."

No. That's not what you did when you loved someone; you *held tight*. Especially when they loved you, too.

"Where are you?" Velma clenched the top sheet toward her chest and curled into herself. "Just tell me where you are, and I'll come there and we'll sort this out. I know I messed up. It doesn't cha—"

"We've talked about this shit enough for a lifetime. Time to stop talking and move along."

"I don't accept that," she said, ignoring the fear curdling inside her.

His breaths were muffled against the speaker, like he was holding the phone too close to his lips. "You deserve better than a four."

A pinching sting settled in the center of her chest. Not a quick poke, either. This was the kind that stuck around to remind a person pain still exists, even in the midst of numbness.

"And I deserve to be with someone who doesn't think I'm a four," he continued.

Oh. Oh God. Her mind went blank, and her mouth wouldn't work to form words.

Not when he was right but also so wrong. Two plus two didn't really equal…well…*four* in this instance.

"Time to move on, Velma. It was fun. Go find your ten." He dealt the final blow, and the line went dead, mirroring her heartbeat for the briefest of seconds. His firm words pulsed like a living thing around her.

She stared at the blank screen on her cell, her blood pressure rising.

Oh. Heck. No.

"It was fun?" she said into the darkness, absolutely stunned.

Why would he say that? After everything they'd been through and all the promises?

He was trying to hurt her. That had to be it, so she would let him go and move on and find—who? Someone dull? Like freaking Wayne?

Brek had never been an idiot, but who had their eyes closed this time?

She kicked her feet over the side of the bed and traced her foot along the carpet until she found her slippers. Sliding them on, she clicked on the lamp and shuffled to the kitchen.

Strategy. She needed a solid plan to convince Brek to come back. Sure, she'd totally mucked everything up, but it couldn't be too late. She refused to even consider that as a possibility.

Frantic, she rifled through the drawers for paper. She needed to write out a new plan. She rummaged for her notepad, and Sophie's pink thank-you note with the gold embossing slipped through her fingertips. Velma lifted it from the drawer and skimmed the lines of cursive handwriting Sophie had sent after the middle-of-the-street wedding.

I gave up on love. Thank you for showing me I was wrong.

Velma paused and closed her eyes. She dropped the note, and it fluttered to the counter. Deep breaths. Everything would be fine, because she and Brek were meant to be together.

This time, she wouldn't write out a plan to get Brek back. No, she would follow her heart…and show him the way home.

Chapter Twenty-Six

TWO WEEKS AFTER CLAIRE & DEAN'S WEDDING

Velma sat at her desk and checked her cell phone. No voice mails. Despite Brek's cease-and-desist request, she continued calling him every night.

A week had passed, and he still didn't answer. A little twinge of pain hit every time she got his voice mail. The delete icon was likely his favorite button these days, and he probably didn't even listen to the messages.

Her gut said to keep calling, so she did.

"Velma?" The receptionist's voice came through her desk phone.

Velma pushed the talk button. "Yes?"

"Dean asked to meet you in the conference room."

"Oh. Okay," she replied.

They'd been working on a proposal for a new client this week. She headed to the conference room and pushed open the door. Claire sat beside him, with Aspen on a chair to her right, baby in her arms. Pam sat to his left, with Jase beside her.

Velma had been ambushed. Crud, she didn't have time for this.

"Pull up a chair." Dean pointed to the chair beside Aspen.

"What's up?" Velma asked, suspicion continuing to rise in her blood. Cautious, she sat and crossed her legs under her black pencil skirt.

"Here, would you hold him?" Aspen plopped the baby right into Velma's arms.

"What?" Velma glanced to the squishy bundle of snuggles. Oh, hello. She inhaled the scent of baby powder.

"Now she won't run," Aspen said, clearly proud of her ingenuity.

"Run from what?" Velma did the bounce thing that came naturally when holding a baby. "And why do you all look so guilty?"

"Well…here's the thing…" Jase grimaced.

Pam and Aspen didn't meet her gaze.

"Anyone going to tell me what's going on or should I just hang out with Bronson?" Velma asked, looking down to admire his teeny-tiny nose.

"We've decided it's time for you to stop sulking." Dean leaned forward, elbows on the desk.

She ran a fingertip across Bronson's chunky cheek. "I'm not sulking."

Sad, yes, but that's because she felt like her heart had been ripped out and put back in upside down.

"Claire says you don't eat." Pam slid a paper grocery sack across the table toward Velma.

"It's true," Claire chimed in. "I saw your fridge. And your cupboards. There's no food."

All right, well, she hadn't had much of an appetite since Brek took off.

"I eat. Is that why you came here, to tell me not to skip lunch?" Velma raised her eyebrows at the paper bag and glanced back to Pam.

"You've lost weight," Jase accused.

Well, yes. One of the byproducts of heartache was apparently dropping a pant size. All those years of dieting, and in reality, she only needed to get her heart crushed. "Is that a bad thing?"

"Brek's not here to take care of you, so that's our job. Mom brought you cupcakes, and I brought baby therapy." Aspen started digging through the sack and opened a bakery box.

"Claire?"

"Just be glad I didn't call Mom in on this meeting," Claire replied.

Their mother worried way more than she should. She'd have Velma's refrigerator filled with meals from the church ladies if she caught wind that Velma wasn't eating.

Velma shook her head slightly. "You came all the way down here to bring me cupcakes and have me babysit?"

Pam rubbed at her temples, her expression pained. "No, that's only a temporary fix. We came down here to convince you to go get Brek."

"His communication has gone to crap, and we know that, wherever he is, he's not eating, either," Aspen added.

Velma shifted the munchkin in her arms. "What makes you think Brek wants me to get him?"

"He probably doesn't know that he wants you to get him. Guys are dense like that." Dean absently rubbed Claire's back.

Velma cocked her head to the side. "He wants me to get him but doesn't know that he wants me to get him?"

"Such is love." Pam dug out a chocolate cupcake, dropped it on a paper plate, and slid it to Velma.

"First, we've got to find out where he's run off to," Aspen mused, gazing longingly at Velma's cupcake.

"Give me a second." Velma handed the baby back to his mother. She pushed the cupcake toward her, too. Without another word, Velma pulled the green file folder from her attaché case. She tucked her latest spreadsheet back inside the bag—Pam and Aspen didn't need to see that.

Velma dropped the file onto the table. "Brek is on the Western Slope. A little town called Collbran. He's been there since he left Denver."

"How the fuck'd you find that out?" Jase snatched the file and flipped through it.

"I called his band members." She glanced around the table. "You're not the only ones who care about him."

"Asshole's staying at a bed-and-breakfast while we're all sitting here worried? I'm gonna kick his ass." Jase scanned Velma's notes and came to the confirmation for Velma's airline tickets.

Her legs suddenly shaky, she leaned against the cool metal of the table.

She'd bought the tickets online as soon as she'd found out where he had gone. She hoped like heck Brek would still be there when she arrived on Friday night. Even more, she prayed he wouldn't immediately send her packing.

"You're going to Collbran?" Dean asked, holding up the paper.

"Let me see that." Jase reached for it.

Velma shrugged. She refused to think anything more about it until she was waiting for takeoff on the tarmac. "Well, he hasn't come back. So, I'm going there. Any idea why he'd be there?"

"Tucker McKay," Jase said offhand, still reading her flight itinerary.

"Who's Tucker McKay?" Velma asked.

"Shut up. You don't know who Tucker is?" Aspen gaped.

"Clearly not," Velma pointed out. "Seriously, who is he?"

"Five-time Grammy nominee, three-time winner. Used to be with the Skintight Bandits but went out on his own." Jase gave her the evil eye. "Seriously, you don't know him?"

Velma shook her head. "No."

Jase threw his hands up in the air. "He and Brek are buddies, but I wouldn't have suspected Brek would go visit him. Guess that's why he went."

Aspen shifted her son and laid a kind hand on Velma's shoulder. "Thank you for going to get Brek."

"Do you have a plan for when you get there?" Pam asked.

Velma let out a worried breath and shook her head. "No."

No plan. That was the plan.

It had to work.

Chapter Twenty-Seven

Bullets of sweat beaded along Brek's hairline. His big plans for the night included a beer, his guitar, and dinner. He paused on the concrete sidewalk outside the bar up the street from where he was staying and checked his phone again. No voice mail.

His hands shook, which was unacceptable. He had moved on. Velma was free to be happy. Free to live her life.

He shoved the phone into his pocket and reached for the door. Except, she called every night at seven. On the dot.

But not tonight.

His throat constricted like it had when he'd seen the score on Velma's spreadsheet. He should probably touch base with Jase to make sure Velma was okay.

A coat of regret covered his tongue. He swallowed and looked back to his bike. The thing had taken a beating in the elements over the past week, but it had held up. His mind worked to calculate the distance back to Denver.

Five hours. Way too long.

Maybe he could call Ma and have her go check on Velma? Nothing major, just a *Hello, I'm making sure you're not dead in a ditch or something* welfare visit.

His cell buzzed against his palm.

He practically jumped out of his fuckin' motorcycle boots. Velma's name and picture showed up on the caller ID. The pic he'd snapped when he brought her tacos for lunch the week before everything had gone to shit.

Thank God. Not that he was a praying man or anything, but he sent a silent salute to whoever the hell was in charge. Gratitude and all that. He itched to answer the phone. Hear her voice in real time.

Her smile lit up the screen, and his dick stirred with the hope he might actually call her back this time.

He couldn't. She deserved her ten, and it wasn't him. Acceptance would come eventually, and they'd both figure out their lives.

The stucco siding of the bar dug into his leather jacket when he slumped against the building. He would get dinner and head someplace quiet so he could listen to Velma's voice mail over and over again, like every other night since he'd left.

He had become a pussy-whipped pansy. Soon enough he would be doodling hearts with her name in the middle like a lovesick idiot.

Time for dinner and to figure out his next move.

Tucker was happy to entertain him, but Brek had taken enough of his time already. Tucker didn't need a moping jerk wrecking the little time he had with his family.

Brek headed inside and waited the few seconds it took for his eyes to adjust to the dark interior. Typical dive. The scent of grease hung heavy in the air. Low lighting slipped through a handful of small windows, slicing through the air where the dust motes swirled. A couple of pool tables sat on one side, and music blared on the jukebox—country, this time. Along the edge of the room was a long bar with the resident jackass trying to pick up a pretty blonde. Perfectly combed hair, a pink sweater and skirt, and matching Mary Janes. She had clearly wandered into the wrong place.

He couldn't make out her face because she was turned away from him, but he could've sworn she looked like Velma. Except Velma was tucked away in Denver. He shook his head in an attempt to dislodge the thick molasses that seemed to always be trapping his thoughts lately.

Everywhere he turned the past week, he could swear he caught Velma's scent or her image out of the corner of his eye. Once, he'd followed a woman into a gas station when he thought she was Velma, but the chick standing between the display of Bugles chips and the fountain drinks was brunette and definitely not Velma. He'd stomped out in a worse mood than when he had started the day. But that wasn't today. Wasn't now.

This woman wasn't Velma, either. His brain was mind-fucking him again.

Except…

She laughed, and a zing of awareness shot straight through him. He knew that laugh.

"Velma?" he asked, positive his brain was tripping.

The blonde turned on her barstool. Velma's gray eyes met his.

"Brek?" He did know that voice, and those eyes, that mouth, that body. Hell, he'd spent months tasting every inch of her. How had she found him?

Brek swallowed hard. He'd learned long ago that certain events burned themselves onto the retina to be taken out later and mulled over—the memories that never fade. No, they always stayed as crisp as the original memory. This was one of those times. The image of Velma sitting at a bar in the mountains with a small stream of sunlight playing across her face would stay with him forever.

He was fucked, and he didn't even care.

"You with him?" Jackass jerked his chin toward Brek.

"I'm not sure." Velma shifted and toyed with the white paper wrapper from her straw.

She looked smaller, her eyes haunted.

Jackass stepped back, and Brek got the full punch of Velma. Fuck, he missed her.

He was lost. No point in fighting it. He wouldn't be able to walk away again.

"Am I?" she asked.

"What?" he replied.

She tilted her head to the side. "With you?"

Brek briefly studied the dried mud caked on the toes of his boots.

"I need to talk to him," Velma told Jackass. "Alone."

Dude got the message, because he grunted in disgust at a conquest lost, grabbed his beer, and headed for the pool tables.

Brek strode to her, his boots stuck against the sticky floorboards from spilled drinks and God knew what else. He planted his ass on the stool next to her and inhaled her scent.

Strawberries and Velma.

"I just called you." She dropped the paper straw wrapper and angled her body his direction.

"I know." He rolled his shoulders, but he couldn't meet her eyes again. Not yet.

"Some things can't be said on a voice mail. I figured I'd come tell you in person." She placed her hand on his and linked their fingers together.

He let her.

The wall in front of him held a huge mirror and an assortment of whiskey to numb the type of pain he had experienced. Her thumb stroked his knuckles, and his heart stalled.

"I think I figured out when I fell in love with you," she said finally.

"Velma." He dragged his hand from hers and ran it through his hair. God, this hurt.

"It happened around the time you decked that guy for me."

He glanced to her. The light in her eyes caught in his heart. They couldn't do this. "Velma, don't know what you're here searchin' for, but it's pretty clear lookin' at your spreadsheet…you don't know a thing about me."

"You're Brek. We went up to Red Rocks together." She hauled a zipped canvas bag onto her lap, dug through it, pulled out a bound report with a clear cover, and handed it to him.

He glanced at the rows and columns…another fuckin' spreadsheet. Her spreadsheets didn't know jack shit. He pushed it away. "Not interested."

Clearly ignoring him, she continued on as though he hadn't spoken. "I printed it. Not really logical to lug my computer all this way." Carefully, she flipped through the pages and landed on the last one. "You're on this page. I highlighted your row."

She had added columns, including number of orgasms given, spontaneity, creativity, and about a dozen other things.

"I went back through and added everything I could think of that really matters. Then I updated the algorithm. You got a five thousand six hundred and ninety-two." She squinted at the number as she read and traced the tip of her finger over the number highlighted in yellow. "You lost a few points for taking off and not telling anyone where to find you."

His throat worked as he swallowed. He caught the bartender when he moved past and ordered a Jack on the rocks.

"Also, I talked to Wayne. Jase told me what he said to you. You'll be happy to know my algorithm gave him a negative ten thousand. I showed him the spreadsheet, so he could see he doesn't have a chance."

Brek blinked quickly and snagged the report. "You

showed the guy who wants in your pants a spreadsheet that details how many times I've made you come?"

Velma drew little circles on the bar with her fingertip, and a sly smile touched her lips. "I don't think he'll bother either of us anymore."

Holy shit, Brek would have loved to be a fly on the wall when that had gone down.

"Also, I got inked." Velma's cheeks flushed.

"What?" He took the glass the bartender slid his way. She got a tat?

"Your lily…" The sleeve of her pink sweater dropped, and holy hell, she was serious. The lily he drew for her stretched across the skin of her shoulder, up toward the back of her neck. The artist had even included Brek's signature.

She'd marked herself for him.

His blood heated, and his dick asked for permission to come out and play. Brek had never been more turned on by anything in his life. And given his experience with Velma's tits on the couch, that said a lot.

He reached out and ran a fingertip along one of the petals. She winced.

He jerked his hand back. Fresh ink stung.

She considered him, her expression soft. "You should know, I also figured we should get married."

He stilled. "Say again?"

"You know. Married. Like husband. Wife. Someday kids." She shrugged but wouldn't meet his gaze.

"Velma Johnson, are you proposing to me?" He couldn't help the grin playing on his mouth. Picture-perfect, little-miss-traditional proposing to him? In a bar?

"Well…yeah." She lifted a shoulder. The one with his ink.

Yeah, he would marry her. Right there in the middle of the bar if she'd have him.

"You're not on one knee," he pointed out.

She grimaced. "Have you seen the floor in here?"

"This proposal wasn't very well planned out."

"The best things never are," she said on a breath.

He cocked his head to the side. "Did you at least get me an engagement ring?"

She paled. "Um…no. I hadn't figured…"

Reaching into the pocket of his jacket, he grabbed the box with her grandmother's ring and set it in front of her. Pops had asked for it back if Brek didn't intend use it, but Brek couldn't bring himself to send it.

"Brek?" Her fingertips twitched as she weighed the box in her palm.

"Open it." He took another swig to calm the sudden case of nerves tromping around in his stomach.

She flipped the lid up and gasped. Tears misted her eyes. "This is Gramma Velma's."

He lifted the band from the box, his fingers clunky and big against the thin band. Standing, he pushed his barstool back with the bottom of his foot. Then he got down on one knee. In a bar. For Velma.

"Velma Johnson. Will you marry me?"

"Always." Velma held her left hand to him, and he slipped the ring over her knuckle.

It fit.

"There's an inscription, too." He squeezed her fingertips. "It's short, 'cause Pops was bein' cheap. But I'll add somethin' to it before the wedding." He paused. "You really love me?"

She nodded, reaching a hand to the stubble of his cheek as he stood. "Yes."

"I love you, too." With everything he had.

She gnawed at her lip like she did when she got nervous. "Can I kiss you?"

All innocence. All Velma. All his.

"Fuck yes." He leaned over her, catching her lips with his in an indecent kiss that involved liberal use of tongue. When he pulled away, they both were panting hard.

"I'm not wearin' a tux, and we're not having a big wedding. I'm thinking close family and friends. And chocolate cake with dark-chocolate frosting. I know white is supposed to mean purity, but I think we established in the coat closet of the country club that purity isn't exactly our thing." He ran his thumb over the apple of her cheek, his mouth close to hers.

"Are you going to be a total bridezilla?"

He thought for a long moment. "Fuck yeah. I think I've earned that right."

She grinned against his lips. "I can live with that."

Epilogue
SEVEN MONTHS AFTER CLAIRE & DEAN'S WEDDING

"Brek?" Velma called, panic settling in her belly because there wasn't a shoehorn in the world that would squeeze her swollen feet into the satin flats that matched her wedding gown. Her specially made, six-months-pregnant, maternity wedding gown.

She had been so upset when Brek had left, she'd forgot to take her birth control pills a few times. Whoops.

"What's wrong?" Brek took three strides into their bedroom, lickety-split. He was already dressed for the ceremony—black jeans and a white button-up shirt. He stood firm on the no-tuxedo ultimatum. The truth was, as long as he stood at the end of the aisle, she didn't care what he wore.

"My shoes won't fit." She fell backward onto their bed and rolled to her side. She could just stay here today and lounge in her bathrobe. No need for shoes or wedding gowns. "I knew we should've gotten married right away."

"Waiting was your idea." A half grin flashed across his lips. He smiled all the time, ever since the little line on the pregnancy test had turned into a plus sign in the stall of a Target bathroom.

Like she could have waited to get home to pee on the

darn stick. But he was right, pushing pause on the wedding until after his tour had been her idea. One she now regretted.

The baby remained absolutely perfect and on schedule. Aside from an intense craving for green apple suckers at three a.m. and ankles that swelled to the size of softballs, Velma was fine, too.

"I knew I shouldn't have eaten potato chips last night." Salt was not her friend anymore.

Brek knelt at the end of the bed and compared the shoe to her foot. She already knew the laws of physics weren't on her side today, because no way would she be wearing those darn things.

"Go barefoot. Your dress is long enough. No one will know." His hands began doing magnificent massage things to the ball of her right foot.

Velma moaned and smacked the comforter. "I cannot get married barefoot in a bar. I have standards."

Not as many as she used to have, but growth and all that nonsense.

Funny thing: Brek had bought Hank's Bar when they'd gotten back to Denver. The acquisition was part of his plan to stay put and not have to travel so much. Though she really didn't worry if he had to go on the road with his band. He'd already gotten his compass tattoo, and she never doubted he would find his way home.

"I'll call Aspen. She'll fix this." He snagged Velma's other foot and went to work on her toes. "She'll send Ma to the store or something."

Claire had agreed to stand up as witness for Velma today. Heather and Aspen, too. They'd spent loads of time together after Brek had returned to Denver. Velma had even helped a few times at events when Aspen was in a pinch. The *Rosette* article had done everything Aspen had hoped. She had a client waiting list three pages long.

Baby Montgomery took that moment to do a loop the

loop in Velma's belly. She pressed against her ribs, trying to extract the kid's foot from her lungs.

"Martin's practicing to be an acrobat." If his antics inside were any indication, when he said hello to the world, he would be off and running. The kiddo never stopped.

Brek put his lips to Velma's belly button. "Trixie, be nice to your mama."

They had decided to go for the surprise at birth. Brek insisted she carried a girl while she remained certain the baby was a boy. When Velma was a little girl, she had decided her son's name would be Martin—a nice, normal name that wouldn't invoke teasing from the other kids.

Brek wasn't on board at all. He said it was a sissy name, and he would use his veto power. This only prompted her to call the baby Martin more often. Whatever. Brek said if she was a girl, he wanted to call her Trixie. Velma had veto power, too, and she wasn't afraid to use it.

"He's not listening to you." Velma propped herself on her elbows.

Brek grinned his lopsided grin. "Just like her mama."

"Do you want to put on your dress here or there?" Brek climbed onto the bed beside her and kissed her forehead.

"There. You're not supposed to see the dress before the wedding." She leaned against him and tossed her arm over her forehead.

"Thought we established the rules don't apply to us?" He nibbled on her earlobe. Her breasts felt a little heavier with each nip. "What about just a quick roll in the sheets before we head over?"

He worked his hand lower down her thigh and lifted the corner of her robe.

"People will be there soon, we should go." With great effort, Velma rolled over and planted a kiss on her almost-husband.

"Waiting's gonna kill me." He took her hand and pulled

her up, stopping to hold her shoulders until she got her balance. "You good?"

She nodded. "I'll call Aspen and ask her about shoes."

Early on, Velma had asked Brek if he wanted a theme for their wedding. He said the only thing he wanted was her naked in the limo afterward.

She ran her hands over her swollen belly. Limo sex would be interesting at her size, that was for sure. "Are you going to tell me what your big surprise is?"

He kissed her nose. "No."

"When will I find out?" she asked.

"Soon. You get your things. I'll get the car." He headed for the garage, and Velma glanced down to the socks he had tossed to the hamper.

They hadn't quite made it in.

And it was wonderful.

HANK'S BAR had gone through a transformation after Brek had bought it a couple of months ago. Next week it would reopen as Brek's Bar. He had upgraded the space with a better kitchen, a stage, and a sound system. Eli had helped create the menu and agreed to consult as needed. Staying in Denver had become a priority, and who knew how long Dimefront would stick together, so Brek needed a plan. Hans had agreed to handle most of the on-the-road management. They had already hashed out the details.

Aspen had decked out the bar in sunflowers and candles for the wedding. She moved out the tables and arranged the chairs in a makeshift aisle. The guest list was small—close friends and family only. Brek didn't particularly care who attended, as long as he had Velma.

Jase nudged Brek in the ribs as Tucker McKay played the bridal chorus on his guitar and Claire sashayed toward them.

"Can't believe you got Tucker McKay to play at your wedding. Bad-fucking-ass," Jase said out of the corner of his mouth.

Pops cleared his throat and tossed Jase a look. He liked cussing about as much as Velma did.

"You have the ring, right?" Brek asked Jase. The guy had one job to do. Well, two: show up and have the ring ready.

Jase tapped his pocket. "Yup."

Brek had added to Pops's inscription. Now it read, *To Velma, Forever My Ten.*

"And, seriously, could you tell your mom to lay off on the matchmaking?" Jase spoke from the side of his mouth. "She's been parading women through the shop like they're walking a catwalk. It's distracting as fuck."

Pops cleared his throat louder.

"Now's a good time to shut it," Dean mumbled beside Jase as Velma emerged from the hallway on her dad's arm. Brek's breath caught at his collarbone. Her grandmother's lace covered her gown, and she held a simple bouquet of red roses. His almost-wife was beautiful every day, but today he couldn't peel his eyes from her.

Pregnancy seemed to agree with Velma. He'd never seen her happier than she had been over the past months.

She winked, and he felt warmth in his gut.

He forced his gaze to Tucker and nodded.

Tuck cleared his throat. "Brek, uh, asked me to sing something special for Velma. So, this is for her."

Velma narrowed her eyes slightly and raised a questioning brow. Tucker was a rocker, but he had a cowboy soul. Brek had convinced him to let it shine today.

Tuck dropped his voice low and sang directly to Velma—one of those sappy-ass country songs she loved. She smiled huge, stepping toward Brek and their future. The toes of her white satin slippers peeked from under her grandmother's lace—Aspen had come through on the shoes—and her face went soft, her eyes bright.

Everything in the world was right.

"I love you," she mouthed.

Three. Little. Words. Only three. And they meant everything.

Stay in Touch

There's more Brek and Velma!

A special bonus scene Christina created especially for newsletter subscribers!

Sign up for the bonus scene at:
ChristinaHovland.com/goingdown-bonus

Acknowledgments

Thank you to my husband, Steve, who supported, encouraged, and held my hand through this dream of mine to write books. My kids—all four of them—for being patient as I, "Just finished this chapter." Over and over and over.

My mom, Shirley, and my sister, Sereneti. You both are such a huge part of why I'm able to do what I do.

My best friend, Karie, who knows me better than I know myself and doesn't hesitate to come rescue me at midnight whenever I need it. (Which—let's be honest—recently, it's been a lot!)

Kiele, thank you for always keeping me grounded. You are my person.

Courtney, Dallas, Leeann, Lindsay, Sarah, Shasta, Stephanie for supporting me, always.

Courtney, thank you for being one of my first beta readers and my reading buddy.

Shasta, you are Queen of the Comma. Thank you for always being willing to answer my grammar questions.

Sarah, thank you for helping me unravel plot tangles and encouraging me.

Lindsay, I'm so blessed to have you as my cheerleader.

Thank you to D'Ann Lindun, A.Y. Chao, Cheryl Pitones Rider, Colette Dixon, Sara Dahmen, Wendi Sotis, and Shannon Patterson for your advice and notes.

Todd for answering random questions about the legal needs of fictional characters.

Beth for being the best author assistant ever.

L.A. Mitchell for making me believe this dream is possible.

My agent, Emily Sylvan Kim, who made this book happen on so many levels. Thank you! Thank you! You are, quite simply, amazing.

Kristi Yanta, for helping me make this story the best it can be—and for always being supportive and awesome.

Holly Ingraham for being my editor, mentor, and part-time counselor on this project. I am so grateful to you!

Michelle Hope for being the eagle eyes I needed on this manuscript. Thank you so much.

Laura for the care you always take with my manuscripts in the final stages. Making them shine is your superpower.

Diane Holiday for being my first line critique partner on this story and for always being available to help me.

C.R. Grissom for always being there for me with a ready ear and a shot of infused vodka.

Scarlett Peckham, Catherine Stuart, Susannah Erwin, Deb Smolha, LeAnne Bristow, Sarah Morgenthaler, Miguella T. Twosias, Laura Harris, and Anne Morgan for the critiques, beta reads, and friendship.

The amazing Rebelles. I am so blessed to be part of your group.

And, finally, thank you to the Romance Chicks: Dylann Crush, Jody Holford, and Renee Ann Miller.

Enjoyed the Story?

**Turn the page for chapter one of
Rock Hard Cowboy!
A prequel novella to Going Down on One Knee.**

A supercouple for Christmas.

Rock 'n' roll cowboy Tucker McKay's muse has left the building. Returning to his roots at his Colorado ranch might be the inspiration he needs, and he's done everything he can to ensure his reputation shines for his eventual return to the public eye, should his muse show up again. Ready to leave town, he's not prepared for the paparazzi frenzy after a starlet falls face down on his lap at L.A.'s trendiest new night club.

America's Sweetheart, Mackenzie Bennett's career is on the rocks after a few lackluster movies damaged her studio appeal. She needs something to change, and fast. What she does not need is the firestorm that ensues after an ill-fated spill is caught on camera. Spending Christmas in Colorado with the man she publicly embarrassed is her only option to turn around the bad press.

While a fake relationship might drum up the publicity needed to save both of their careers, a small-town family Christmas may be just what they both need to figure out what truly matters…

Rock Hard Cowboy

CHAPTER ONE

Two Weeks to Christmas

CHRISTMAS SUCKED.

Also, Tucker McKay had great hair. Amazing black hair. Not too long. Not too short. The perfect length for running a girl's fingers through. And that little bit of a beard? It worked.

He was tall, dark and…never ever, ever.

On that thought, Mackenzie Bennett nursed her tall glass of seltzer water with a twist of lime while making herself seen in the newest hoity toity, excessively expensive Los Angeles nightclub. The fizzy bubbles in her drink had disappeared over an hour ago.

Music pulsed around her, the strobe lights on the dance floor below making the revelers appear as disjointed puppets. Funny that. If there was a disjointed puppet on the premises, it was her. Always doing what she was told. Always standing where directed. Always being someone else.

She kept a smile plastered on her face and her expression light. That's what a good actress did. Never show how you really feel when you're on the job. Always let the character shine through. In that moment, the character was the version of herself the public got to see. The smoky-eyed, shiny-haired starlet who really, deep down, wanted to spend her evening bingeing on Netflix while eating a grilled cheese sandwich created with the most over-processed American cheese product she could find.

God, she missed food like that.

She held her gaze on rocker-legend-slash-cowboy Tucker. The way he was propped up in a corner booth in the VIP section. The way his head bopped ever so slightly to the thump of the blaring music. The way his muscled arm was slung along the edge of the booth and his laughter permeated the VIP lounge.

"You're not having any fun." Her best friend and business manager, Leah, waggled a tipsy red-painted fingertip in her direction. Half her nails were red, half green. Very festive and all that.

"We're worried about you." Their not-quite-drunk friend Abby squeezed Kenzie's arm. "Do I need to call Taylor? Get the whole gang together?"

"We should do a holiday cheer intervention," Leah suggested. "We'll drink eggnog and make her sing 'Jingle Bells.'"

Kenzie couldn't help the smile that played at the corners of her mouth.

These women made up Kenzie's entourage. The ones who got the messy reality alongside the Hollywood glam. The ones who knew Kenzie had a secret passion for 1:00 a.m. bubble baths and writing screenplays that would never be produced. The ones who, no matter how adept an actress Kenzie was, would know she was putting up a front.

They knew her better than she knew herself most times.

So she didn't lie.

"I'm just doing my time." Kenzie nodded toward a group of women a level down on the dance floor. That group of ladies had been watching her for a solid twenty minutes.

One of the women waved back tentatively, giggled, and huddled with her friends.

"Your holiday spirit is seriously lacking." Leah snagged a martini from the waiter circulating a tray loaded with the drink of the day. Something orange and red—and it probably tasted like pineapple, if Kenzie had to guess.

"I'll find my Christmas cheer once the offer comes through." Kenzie eyed the sunset-colored drink. She wanted one, sure, but she wouldn't have one. Not when she was in public. Not when she was on a job. Even if the job was stupid. She was being paid an absurd amount of money to be at the club tonight. A club she had absolutely no intention of ever visiting again.

That wasn't the point though. Once she was seen somewhere, patrons would show up again and again, hoping to catch a glimpse of her. And since her last two box office receipts had been lacking, she filled in her budget gaps with appearances. Until the next opportunity moseyed along. Which would, she prayed to Lady Luck, be soon. Soon-ish.

"Any day. They'll come around any day now," Abby assured.

That was easy for her to say. Her life wasn't publicly and personally entwined in her ability to stay on the big screen. Sure, Kenzie had been smart with her money. Saved it. Invested it. But with the way Hollywood worked, her savings could only take her so far. She needed to nab a new role.

"Don't look back. The future is ahead." Leah made a dramatic hand motion like a soldier heading into battle.

Negotiations on Kenzie's latest movie—a romantic comedy about a farm girl in the big city—had fallen apart weeks ago, after her latest film flopped at the box office. Someone from the studio had leaked that they were eyeing other actresses for her part. Kenzie felt like the trap door had dropped open, spilling a washed-up actress just shy of stage left. It was all very, very public.

Very, very humiliating.

"I'm not looking back." No, she was looking straight at Tucker.

Kenzie's gaze slid the length of him. He might be a rock 'n' roll legend, but he was also muscled, charming, and a total jerk.

A jerk she'd shared a moment with at her premier last month. It was like in one of her movies, where the heroine sees the hero from across the room. They trace each other with their eyes, up then down, both liking what they see. And then something more—a connection—forms. Love at first sight? No, that doesn't happen. But definitely more than lust.

They'd chatted about the business, his music, her movies. He'd told her about his family, his ranch. She'd shared about her dreams of time away from the world, where she wouldn't always be the focus. Her job was her passion, but sometimes she dreamed of a break. Those were the times she'd doodle out a scene or two of her own creation. She'd told him that bit, too. Only those closest to her knew about her writing.

He was entirely too easy to talk to.

For a glimmer of a second, she'd thought what she and Tucker had between them was real. Not even the Hollywood brand of real, but out-of-the-spotlight *real*.

When she'd searched him out later that night to make a move, he was gone.

Then he told the press she was a crappy actress.

Then her movie lost a shit ton of money at the box office.

So, yeah, she was a little raw about it all.

That treatment from nearly anyone else? She'd merely smile and move along. She'd been in the business long enough to understand everyone had an opinion. But, for some reason, Tucker's mattered. His criticism stung. Tonight, she would remedy that. As soon as she figured out what to say.

CHRISTINA HOVLAND

"You should dance." Leah slipped her arm through Kenzie's and tugged her toward the VIP dance floor.

Abby linked her other arm and helped Leah scoot her along.

Not nearly as packed as the one downstairs, this dance floor was created for visibility throughout the club. Kenzie was being paid to attend tonight, and it was expected she appear to have a fabulous time.

Her contract said so.

"In a sec. I'm gonna talk to Tucker first." Kenzie disentangled her arms, stood tall on her stiletto heels, and weaved through the crowd toward him.

"That's a bad idea…" Leah continued talking but Kenzie ignored her.

What she was going to say? She had no idea. But she was going to tell him…something. Find out why he'd said mean things about her, what she'd done to offend him. That kind of thing. She'd figure it out.

Maybe something about how he'd hurt her feelings and he should apologize.

Yes, that's what she'd say. And she'd say it with style, and class.

The nearly transparent dress her stylist had outfitted her in made hustling anywhere practically impossible. The heels didn't help. So she took her time sauntering across the VIP section. Her bodyguard shadowed her movements. He was behind her, but she knew he was there. He was always there when she did these appearances.

"Tucker?" she asked, approaching his table.

His gaze lifted to hers. It softened for a split second. "Hey."

"I came by to say hello." She fidgeted with her glass. Which was unacceptable. She set it on the table and nudged it from the edge with her finger.

"Have a seat." He gestured to the other side of the booth. The guy sitting there scooted over to make room for her.

She didn't sit.

"I was thinking we could chat alone, about some of the things you mentioned to a reporter about my movie."

"Oh. That." He ran a hand over his neck. The movement made the defined muscles of his triceps bunch.

Dammit. She wasn't over here to check out his arms.

"Have your people call his people," one of his people said.

Kenzie leaned toward Tucker, ignoring his entourage. "I'd really like a conversation."

"Look." His eyes were soft again. He gave a nearly imperceptible shake of his head. "Magazines print what magazines print."

She took a deep breath.

"I just think—" Someone—a bulky someone—bumped her from behind.

The stilettos wobbled, her balance precarious. She threw her arm wide to catch herself. It didn't work.

Her knees buckled.

Damn. This was going to hurt.

She fell forward.

"Shit." Tucker moved to grab her.

Too late. The momentum caught her.

And that's how, two weeks before Christmas, she found herself face-first in Tucker McKay's crotch.

Enjoyed the sample?
Rock Hard Cowboy is Available Now!

Also by Christina Hovland

The Mile High Matched Series

Rock Hard Cowboy, A Mile High Matched Novella
(October 1, 2018)

Blow Me Away, A Mile High Matched Novel, Book 2
(Coming 2019)

From Entangled Publishing
The Honeymoon Trap

About the Author

 Christina Hovland lives her own version of a fairy tale—an artisan chocolatier by day and romance writer by night. Born in Colorado, Christina received a degree in journalism from Colorado State University. Before opening her chocolate company, Christina's career spanned from the television newsroom to managing an award-winning public relations firm. She's a recovering over-achiever and perfectionist with a love of cupcakes and dinner she doesn't have to cook herself. A 2017 Golden Heart® finalist, she lives in Colorado with her first-boyfriend-turned-husband, four children, and the sweetest dog around.

ChristinaHovland.com

 facebook.com/HovlandWrites

 twitter.com/HovlandWrites

 instagram.com/HovlandWrites

91776708R00187

Made in the USA
Middletown, DE
02 October 2018